THE
SEASTONE

FRANCESCA TYER

Printed and bound in Great Britain by Clays Ltd, Elcograf S.p.A.

Authors Reach
www.authorsreach.co.uk

ISBN: 978-1-8382204-7-1

Dedication

For my family

Acknowledgements

I'd like to thank all those who have helped me bring *The Seastone* to life, particularly Rhodri and my mum for their edits and continual support along the way, my grandma and Sandra for their feedback and encouragement, Richard and Teresa for their additional comments, Maureen Vincent-Northam for her professional edits and Gina Dickerson for her stunning cover design and interior formatting. While I am not able to name everyone here, I am grateful to all those who have been a part of this journey.

Chapter 1

THE faint ticking could not be silenced, even by the sound of the train rushing over the rails. It was stubbornly persistent, like a fly that refuses to exit through an open window and continues to batter itself against the glass.

James Fynch closed his eyes, trying to shut out the sound. Ever since he'd boarded the train, the gold clock in his pocket had ticked with increasing insistence. The once comforting sound was starting to grate on his nerves and he almost couldn't bear it. Somehow, he couldn't shake off the feeling that it was trying to match his own sense of urgency, the sense which had driven him to board this train.

Slouched in a rather uncomfortable seat, his rucksack pressed against the window, James grimaced. A thin, grey-haired man occupied the space beside him, his long black coat flowing over the boundaries of his seat. The man's face was hidden behind a large copy of *The Times*, the front page of which was decorated with images of the cricket. James could hardly believe people read the paper anymore when it was much easier to flick through the news on a phone.

Struck by the urge to look at his own phone, he drew it from his pocket. The device was new and the smooth screen rested safely in a black case. His parents had bought it to replace his old one and had told him, rather distantly, that they'd continue to pay for the bills. While he was grateful for the gift, the device failed to hold the same power over him as it once had, in a time when he hadn't known about the existence of magic.

Slipping his phone away, James turned to look out of the window. The continuous ticking of the clock matched the monotony of the scenes flashing past and he sighed. Reaching into his pocket again, he took out the offending object which he almost always kept there. Cupping it in his palms, he watched as the clock's delicate hands ticked steadily on past noon.

'Going somewhere with that?'

James started and turned to find his neighbour staring at him. He folded his hands over the clock, shielding it from view.

'Nowhere important,' he mumbled.

The man nodded understandingly and folded up his newspaper. 'I used to have a clock just like it.' His voice crackled like a poor phone line, but his eyes flashed with youthful curiosity.

'You did?' James asked with forced politeness.

'I could never get mine to tick,' the man continued, 'but I see yours doesn't have that trouble. If it ever does, I know a place not far from here. Used to be a thriving workshop in its heyday, but not so much anymore.'

James glanced at the man suspiciously, wondering if he was referring to the same shop from which his own clock had been acquired almost a year ago. The same shop which was, in fact, his destination today. He opened his mouth to question the man further, but his companion stood up and moved out into the aisle.

'Must go and spend a penny, if you'll excuse me,' he crackled. 'Not long until we land.'

2

James watched as the man moved away down the carriage. He walked with a child-like bounce in his step, leading James to conclude that he must be senile or at least on the verge. Frowning to himself, he shrank back in his seat and turned the clock over in his hands. He had just settled down again when he was startled by the reappearance of his companion. The man paused in the aisle and leant on the closest seat, his eyes bright and staring.

'Count the Hours is the name, on Silver Street. If you ever do go there, send my greetings to the clockmaker.'

With that, he turned again and was gone. James stared after him, wondering if he'd heard correctly. He had the uncomfortable feeling that the stranger knew exactly where he was going.

Frowning, he looked down at the clock. The previous night, at ten to twelve, its regular ticking had changed to a slightly quicker beat. Unable to sleep due to its persistence, he'd stayed up all night and eventually convinced himself that he needed to find the clockmaker. He'd left for the station that morning, slipping from his house on Greenwood Avenue just after his parents had left for work.

Now, several hours later, the outskirts of London were just flashing into view beyond the grubby glass. The carriage display panels flashed up with London Victoria as the next stop, and seeing this, James slipped the clock away. As he reached to take his bag from the storage compartment above his seat, his gaze fell on the surrounding carriage. Almost every seat was occupied, despite it being a Wednesday lunchtime. Most people were glued to their phones and laptops but a few were engaged in private conversions. He was about to look away, when he noticed that he wasn't the only one staring. Two rows down, on the opposite side of the carriage, a man in a black

3

coat and hood sat watching him.

Dipping his head out of sight, James ran a nervous hand through his hair. He was sure the man hadn't been there a moment ago and the train hadn't stopped for a half hour. Raising his head again, he peered over the seat in front of him. For a moment, he couldn't see the man, but as his eyes focused, he let out a sharp breath of air. At first glance the man looked ordinary, but on closer observation his body appeared to be vaguely translucent. Looking at him, James was suddenly and horribly aware of how the man had appeared without him noticing. Fighting back his urge to run, he gathered up his things and slipped out into the aisle.

Step by step, he passed down the carriage and through the automatic doors at the end. He didn't look back until they had closed behind him, creating a barrier between himself and Carriage D. Behind him, the black coated man also stood up, but his path was temporarily blocked by the food trolley. The figure was undeniably faint in the daylight but none of the other passengers seemed to notice. To James' relief, the train began to slow and the tannoy system announced their imminent arrival. Feeling his phone buzz in his pocket, he pulled it out and hurriedly answered.

'Dad?'

'It's me, your mum,' a clear voice piped. 'My phone's out so Phillip let me borrow his.'

James sighed. His mum had a habit of referring to his dad as Phillip, even when it wasn't strictly necessary. In fact, he couldn't remember Louisa Fynch ever referring to him as 'your dad.'

'Is everything OK?' he asked.

'I got a message from you.'

'Really? What did it say?' He frowned. It was unusual for

4

him to send messages to his parents and it wasn't like them to worry unless there was an emergency, which there never was.

'It didn't say anything,' his mum returned. 'It was blank so we just thought we'd check up on you.' She paused. 'Are you on a train?'

'It was probably a pocket text,' James replied firmly. 'It happens all the time. I'm fine, really.'

'Well alright then,' she conceded. 'I'll see you later?'

'Yeah, see you later,' he muttered and hung up.

Glancing through the carriage doors, he saw to his discomfort that the man in black had disappeared. The gangway wobbled beneath him as the train drew to a halt and pressing the door button, he prepared to exit the train. He'd only been to London Victoria once before, with his cousin Clare after his flight to Valencia had been cancelled last summer. It looked exactly the same, busy and a little run down in places. Stepping onto the platform, he nervously checked the surrounding area for any sign of the black coated man, but he was nowhere to be seen.

Unsure of his route to the clock shop, he opened the maps on his phone and searched for Silver Street. Nothing showed up so he tried the hotel he and Clare had stayed at instead. Glancing up as the location loaded, he caught sight of the man who'd been sitting beside him on the train. He was standing on the edge of Platform 7, squinting at the digital signs. James took a step towards the stranger but stopped as another figure, dressed entirely in black, suddenly appeared on the platform. James' view was temporarily blocked by a large woman who stopped to pick up her scarf. When she finally moved, he saw that both men had disappeared.

Suddenly, someone screamed. James flinched but for some reason his legs wouldn't move. He stood frozen to the spot, watching with distant horror as chaos materialized before him. A young girl was standing on the platform, pointing at a body on the rails and screaming. People crowded around her, trying to calm her with their own panicked voices. At the front of the crowd, a young man broke from the arms of his girlfriend and lowered himself onto the tracks. His girlfriend started shouting, but her voice was drowned out by the sound of an approaching train.

The hands of many strangers reached down to pull the victim onto the platform. The young man was hauled up afterwards and the crowds packed closely around the pair. Although James couldn't see the victim, he knew that it was the man who'd been sitting next to him on the train. He shrank back as the incoming train screeched to a halt against the buffer and the driver jumped out to join the crowds. Amongst the incessant chattering and the sound of ambulance sirens, he heard a clear voice speaking.

'He will live.'

Startled, James looked around for the source. His eyes fell upon the black coated man standing at the edge of the gathering crowd.

'Who are you?' he asked inside his mind. 'Why are you here?'

'He will live,' the voice repeated. 'Give us what we want and he will live. The days of Arvad and the light are over and the reign of the Belladonna has begun.'

James shuddered and forced his eyes over to where the victim was being lifted onto a stretcher. As his gaze fell on the man's wrinkled features, a realisation dawned on him. At the time it had seemed odd that the man knew about the clock shop, but it now made perfect sense. The man wasn't such a stranger after all. He was the clockmaker.

Turning away from the chaotic scene, James knew with absolute certainty what he had to do. Spotting the sign for the loos, he secured his bag and began to run. He didn't care that people were staring and didn't slow down until he reached the steps which led down to the bathrooms. One or two people hurried past him as he descended, but he soon found himself completely alone. Pausing on the bottom step to find some change, he noticed that he was standing next to a metal gate. The lever latch was padlocked and a no entry sign was fixed above it.

Glancing around to make sure he was alone, he gave it a gentle push. To his surprise, the rusty padlock popped open and he slipped silently through. On the other side, a set of stone steps plunged into darkness and flicking on his phone torch, he began to descend.

He emerged onto what looked like an abandoned underground platform. The line was blocked on either end by plastic barriers and graffiti smeared the walls. Above his head, a low-hanging sign said, Danger: Flooded Rails, in bold letters. A sub-line below said: This line is temporarily closed. The deep rusting on the rail line suggested however that this was more of a permanent closure.

Slipping his phone away, James took out the gold clock and turned it over in his hands. Running his fingers over the cold dials, he carefully turned the larger of the two. Images of Arissel filled his mind and he didn't need to open his eyes to know that he had left the station.

Chapter 2

THE city was just as he remembered it, dull and grey, yet somehow splendid. Protected by its vast wall, it bore an impressive simplicity. It was quiet and fresh here, the air untainted by the roar of trains and the stinging scent of burning brakes. James breathed in deeply, his lungs tight after the brief and suffocating darkness that had carried him from Victoria station to Arissel. He was puzzled as to why he hadn't passed through No Man's Land and wished Albert was here to provide explanations.

Looking down the narrow street on which he stood, he noted how lifeless it was. No one else wandered through the streets and he was completely alone. The feeling was familiar but he realised he didn't mind. He was about to start walking when he felt a prickling sensation on the back of his neck. This feeling too was familiar and it made the hairs on his arms stand to attention. He paused mid-step and slowly turned around.

Hovering beside the city gates was a black cloaked figure. Although their body looked solid, James knew that it was the same man who had spoken to him at the station. He began to run, not quite knowing where he was going. The underground city sprang to mind, but he wasn't sure how to get there. The street he was currently stuck close to the city wall, running behind the low grey houses. Months ago, he'd run down a similar street with Will Aeton, on the night the city had been attacked. The buildings had been partially destroyed then but all had been restored as if nothing had ever happened.

Pausing to catch his breath, he cast a quick glance behind him. To his relief, the street was empty and slinging his rucksack from his shoulders, he delved inside. After a brief rummage, he pulled out a bundle of black cloth and shook it out to reveal a cloak. It was full of tears and stains, untouched since he'd last worn it. He'd thought about asking his mum to mend it, but she was hardly ever around. Donning the cloak, he picked up his bag and hurried onwards. Turning a sharp corner, he caught sight of a figure in the street just ahead of him. Wondering if they might know the way, he hurried to catch up.

'Hello?' His voice sounded dry in his throat and he came to a halt at the stranger's side.

He found himself looking at a boy who could only have been two or three years younger than himself. His youthful face was covered in smudges but his eyes were startlingly bright. The boy stared at James mutely, his gaze steady but expressionless.

'Erm, hello?' James tried again. 'D'you understand what I'm saying?' The boy shrugged and James sighed. 'D'you know the way to the underground city? I need to find a friend there. It's urgent.' He attempted to mime his words but the translation was difficult.

The boy continued to walk and James followed, unsure whether he'd been understood. They passed along three more streets before the boy stopped and pointed ahead. A few metres away, nestled in the corner of a sloping street, was the gate that led to the underground city.

'Thank you,' James said, pushing his palms together. The

boy mirrored this gesture before slipping away behind the houses.

Alone again, James walked towards the gate. He'd seen others open it before and pulling up his left sleeve, held his star spattered symbol up to the metal. A tingling sensation spread across his wrist and he rubbed at his skin. The feeling was both familiar and strange at the same time. Back in his world, he'd tried to create magic a number of times, but it had never really worked. Whether his abilities had temporarily vanished or he'd been too nervous, he didn't know. The city gate slowly opened and he slipped through. He was immediately swallowed by the tunnel on the other side and began his descent to the underground city. No one else accompanied him as he passed through the subsequent gates and entered the cave beyond.

The city was more impressive than he'd remembered, the vast cave patterned with glittering orbs. Voices echoed everywhere, loud but strangely weightless. As he stepped forward, a wave of rich smells hit him. These drifted across from market stalls which stood side by side to form narrow streets. Exotic spices mingled with roasting meat and perfume to create a sickening but intoxicating scent. Feeling a thrill pass through him, he dived forward into the colourful crowd.

'Mani cake?' A woman blocked his path and pressed a tray of small brown cakes against his chest. He shook his head but she refused to step aside. 'Fresh from the kitchen,' she insisted.

Giving in, James took a fifty pence coin from his pocket and handed it to her. She stared at it suspiciously but let him take a cake and move on. The snack was sickly sweet but he ate it in two bites as he pushed his way through the milling crowds. Other sellers tried to bombard him with wares, pushing books, food and animal skins against his hands. He ignored them all, letting his feet remember the way back to the city library where he hoped Will Aeton might be.

Leaving the market behind, he broke out into the courtyard where Eliad's library stood. It was quieter here, with only a few people standing around the central fountain. It looked like an ordinary fountain, but he remembered with a shiver that the water had the power to erase memories. Turning his eyes back to the library, he saw that the main steps were unoccupied and made a beeline for them. Hurrying upwards, he entered the foyer and passed through into the main room.

A few people looked down at him from balconies that were suspended around the perimeter of the room. He scowled at them and they returned to their work. Trying to keep his footsteps quiet, he passed between the first two shelves. The end was blocked off by another shelf but he gave it a gentle push. The frame swung aside to reveal a new row and he smiled to himself. At the end of the third row, he stopped in front of a ladder that led up to the balcony level. With no other route available, he began to climb. Stepping from the top rung, he looked with awe at the maze of books spreading out below.

'Never seen books before?'

He turned to see a small boy smirking at him and glowered back. The boy stuck his tongue out but James ignored him this time. From up here, he could see all the balcony study spaces, but there was no sign of Will anywhere. His gaze fell on a flight of steps to his left, half-hidden behind a pillar. A chalk line was drawn below the bottom step and he knelt to touch it. The chalk left a dusty residue on his fingers and he cleaned them on his cloak. Straightening up, he stepped over the line and craned his neck to see up the stairs.

A magnetic wave struck him in the chest, forcing him backwards. He stumbled against the balcony railing and heard the young boy laughing. Gritting his teeth, he steadied himself and approached the stairs again. This time, he latched onto the bannister and leant against the force until it eventually weakened and vanished. Free to proceed, he hurried upwards and found himself standing in a small, round room. Light shone through the circular windows and crossing over to the nearest one, James saw thousands of orbs floating beyond the glass like tiny stars.

'Who's there?'

A nervous voice rose from a dark corner of the room, making James jump. He spun around but his eyes were bruised from the brightness of the orbs.

'Who's there?' he echoed.

'James?' The voice came again, louder and more surprised. 'James Fynch?'

Rubbing his eyes, James saw the faint outline of a person emerge before him. The face looked familiar and as it came into focus, he realised who it was.

'Will!'

His friend stood just a few steps away, his face only just visible among the shadows. Dressed in everyday jeans and a jumper, he looked much the same as when James had last seen him, though perhaps a fraction taller.

'What're you doing here?' Will exclaimed.

He tossed the book he was holding onto the window seat and stepped forward to shake James' hand. Their palms locked and grinning widely, he pulled James into a hug.

'I'm glad you're here,' James confessed, ducking away from another slap on the back. 'I hoped you would be.'

'You were looking for me?' Will stepped away, his face suddenly serious. 'Why? I mean why are you here? *How* are you here?'

'Slow down!' James returned with a faint smile. 'I'll tell you

12

everything, but maybe not here.' He glanced around nervously but Will merely shrugged.

'No one comes up here. It's a private staircase as I'm sure you discovered. I come here to study. Mum doesn't know though,' he added quickly. 'She thinks I'm with my tutor.'

'Your tutor?' James made a face. 'Don't they realise that you're missing?'

'Mum would rather I have a tutor than go to school. When I got back here, after the last adventure, she was furious,' he added, lowering his voice. 'She thought I'd gone missing, like my dad. She got me a tutor to try and educate me out of wanting to travel like he did. I, however, found someone to take my place.'

'You're terrible,' James laughed. 'Are Arthur and Aralia here, in Arissel?' he continued seriously. 'Didn't they come back with you?'

Will nodded. 'They're staying just outside the city. They're not allowed inside because, well, you know.'

'Because what?'

'No documents. They're parentless and technically homeless so they can't come through the main gates.' Will began to gather up his books, trying to stuff them into an already full rucksack. 'That reminds me,' he continued. 'I have something to show you, well, all of you. I was starting to wonder if you'd ever come back.'

'Me too,' James muttered. 'How long has it been?'

'Long enough. Everything has been quiet here. It's been quite boring to be honest.'

In his mind's eye, James recalled leaving this world and passing through the cramped darkness back into his own. Everything had looked the same, as if time hadn't passed at all. When he'd returned home, to Number 7, Greenwood Avenue, his parents had acted as if he'd never been gone. It was only when he'd looked at the calendar that he'd realised time *had* passed, but no one seemed to have missed him at all. It was like the time between worlds was different, but he didn't understand how. A thudding sound at the base of the steps recalled him to the present moment. He glanced at Will who stood frozen to the spot with his ear cocked to the air.

'We should go,' Will mouthed.

He put a finger to his lips and crept towards the stairs. Signalling the all clear, he began to descend and James silently followed. At the bottom, they paused to look around but there was no one there. They passed out onto the balconies that were far more crowded than before. Clusters of school-aged children gathered around the narrow tables, poring over their books. Will and James pushed past them and clambered down a ladder to the first floor. At the foyer door, Will stopped to grab a piece of paper from a basket on the wall. He scribbled a note on it before slipping it into a black box suspended below the basket.

'For Arthur and Rai to meet us,' he briefly remarked and exited the library.

Neither of the boys spoke as they navigated their way through the packed underground streets. Will avoided making eye contact with the sellers and James followed his lead. They passed unheeded into the gated tunnel, leaving the underground city behind. Once out in the open air again, Will picked up his pace. He led the way through four identical streets before stopping outside a familiar building. It was the same one Albert had led James to when he'd first come to Arissel. The Night Inn.

'Come on in,' Will invited, holding the front door open for James to pass through.

The interior was dark but Will conjured a ball of light in his palm. It illuminated the empty tables and chairs and the bar at the end of a long room. Crossing to the far side, Will dropped his bag onto one of the tables. The light in his hand revealed the outline of a door behind one of the high-backed chairs. Releasing the orb into the air, he dragged the chair aside and opened the door.

'You coming?' He gestured for James to follow him before disappearing through.

Entering just behind him, James found himself in a small room filled with low chairs and coffee tables. An ashy fireplace stood against one wall with a pile of logs nestled beside it. Two of the walls were oak panelled but the room was otherwise plain.

'The inn will be empty for a few more hours,' Will announced, brushing ash from a padded backrest. 'Sit down if you want.' He gestured widely to the room and grinned. 'You hungry?'

James nodded. 'Starving.'

'Wait here,' Will directed. 'I'll see what I can find.'

James sat on a squashy red chair and shivered. Although the room was windowless, an icy draught was drifting in from somewhere. The chair itself was comfortable enough and he felt his eyelids starting to droop. A creak sounded at the door and he sat up sharply. Peering around the edge of his seat, he saw that the door had opened a fraction. He was just wondering whether Will had left it that way when a hand appeared around the side and pushed it fully open. He leapt to his feet as two cloaked figures entered the room, followed by Will.

'You're jumpy!' Will laughed and set a tray of biscuits on a nearby table.

Before he could respond, James found himself enveloped in a tight hug. Blonde hair filled his eyes and mouth and he disentangled himself to find Aralia smiling at him.

'You're here!' he exclaimed. 'I thought you weren't allowed in the city?' He immediately bit his tongue, wishing he hadn't made this remark.

'You're back!' Aralia returned, her voice bursting with excitement. She sat down in one of the chairs and fixed him with her blue-grey eyes. 'Never mind how we got here. How and when did *you* arrive?'

'Not long at all. A few hours.'

'Business trip?' Arthur asked wryly, stepping forward to shake his hand.

'Sort of, I suppose.' James sat back down and took a biscuit from the tray. It tasted dry and mealy but he hardly noticed as he looked around at his friends. He was sure Arthur had grown taller too and Aralia was even prettier than he remembered.

'The best I could find,' Will said with a shrug. 'The biscuits,' he clarified as James cast him a questioning frown. 'You don't look like you're enjoying them.'

'Sorry,' James muttered, swallowing a mouthful.

'I don't blame you,' Will grinned. 'We've only got a few hours 'til my mum comes back,' he continued. 'We'll have to be quick as none of you are exactly welcome here.'

'Why are we here?' Arthur asked. 'Why are *you* here?' he emphasised, turning to James.

James looked at each of them in turn. He was glad to be back with his friends but the weight of why he was here weighed heavily on him. Part of him expected Albert to appear, to tell him what to do next, but so far there was no sign of him.

'I'm not quite sure why,' he said quietly. 'There was a man following me. Well, not just me but the clockmaker too. He tried to kill the clockmaker.'

'The clockmaker?' Will leant forward, an uneaten biscuit

still in his hand.

James nodded and took the gold clock from his pocket. 'The man who sold me this.' He held it out and Will took it in his free hand, staring at it as if he'd never seen it before.

'An assassination?' Arthur asked. 'Why would someone try to kill a clockmaker?'

'To try and scare me?' James suggested. 'Or maybe…,' he trailed off, his uncertainty mounting.

'Go on,' Arthur prompted.

'I was on my way to see the clockmaker. The clock started ticking strangely last night but I didn't know why. I thought the clockmaker might help me.' He paused to brush the crumbs from his lap. 'What if he knew something that the other man didn't want me to find out?'

'Is the clockmaker alive?' Will asked, his eyes narrowing.

James nodded. 'I think so. Someone saved him. But the man, the one who tried to kill him, wasn't really there. He was a shadow of some sort, an illusion. After the incident, I realised why the clock was acting strangely. It was trying to show me that I needed to come back.'

'There are rumours of darkness spreading in the south, but everything has been quiet here,' Aralia said in a low voice. 'People don't know how powerful the Belladonna is. Most don't even know her name.'

'It won't be long,' James replied solemnly. 'There's one other thing. The man followed me here, to Arissel. Only here he wasn't just an illusion. I think he's one of them.'

The ensuing silence was broken only by the sound of Will munching a biscuit. Aralia looked at him disapprovingly before turning her gaze back to James.

'If they're moving again, the dark, then we're already at a disadvantage,' she said quietly. 'We may have stopped but they haven't. Every day they grow stronger and the Belladonna with them. Maybe it's time for us to start looking for the next crystal.'

Chapter 3

ARALIA'S words rested in the air like a challenge. No one spoke for a long time, as if doing so would be an act of acceptance. They all looked at the floor, the silence pressing heavily around them. After a long while, Will rose from his seat and turned to inspect the fireplace.

'I found something a few days ago,' he mumbled to the wall. 'I think it might be important but I'm not sure how or why.'

'What is it?' James asked, a hint of impatience in his voice.

Will turned around, his eyebrows deeply puckered. 'I can show you if you follow me. We have to go upstairs.'

He led the way across the inn's interior, past the bar and up the stairs to the first floor. James paused on the landing, trying to remember which room he'd stayed in before. Seeing Will disappear up the next flight of stairs, he tore himself away and hastily caught up. The stairs led up to the inn's third floor. It was oddly narrow, consisting of a single passage with a door at the far end. Will made straight for the door, pausing only briefly to turn a key in the lock.

Last to pass through, James paused in the doorway to observe the room in front of him. It was small and stuffy, with rows of shelves reaching from floor to ceiling. At the far end, a desk and chair stood beneath a circular window. A faint light sifted through the glass, the kind of light that belonged to early evening. Its dusky radiance fell onto the neatly arranged desk and map plastered walls. While the room appeared to be well-organised, the array of belongings created an almost claustrophobic atmosphere.

'Come in and shut the door,' Will instructed.

'Whose room is this?' James asked as he closed the door behind him.

'It's my dad's old study.' Will paused to watch a ball of light float from his hand to the ceiling. 'Mum's kept it locked ever since he disappeared. I found the key a few days ago so I've been coming in here and looking through his journals.'

'Your dad was a traveller?' Aralia asked.

'Of sorts. He was a historian and often went on research trips to different parts of the world. A few years ago he went missing and hasn't been heard of since.' Will glanced at James who offered a nod of consolation.

'I'm sorry,' Aralia uttered. 'I didn't know.'

Will shrugged and refused to meet her gaze. 'I was reading one of his journals and I came across a note. The words written on it ring a bell, but I'm not sure why.'

He crossed over to the desk and pulled a leatherbound book from one of the drawers. James, Arthur and Aralia gathered around him as he opened the stiff covers. The yellow pages were covered with scribbled words and diagrams. Will turned them over one by one until he reached the central page. A note was stuck in the top right-hand corner, bearing the words, 'The Lost Years'. An uneven triangle was drawn beside it, the apex pointing downwards.

'This journal is the last one my dad wrote,' Will said, running his fingers over the pages. 'He wrote it during a trip to Milou which is on the west coast.' He lifted the base of the note to reveal more words etched beneath it in jerky handwriting.

'The Lost Years,' Aralia read aloud, 'spanning at least a century when the renowned Dark Master was in power.'

'Dark Master?' James asked, peering at the writing more closely. He was sure he'd seen these words before, engraved in a panel of wood, but couldn't quite remember where.

'There's only ever been one Master as powerful as the Belladonna is supposed to be,' Arthur elucidated. 'People called him Jasper.'

'Jasper? That's a type of crystal isn't it?' James frowned, recalling the name as one they'd originally linked to the firestone.

Arthur shrugged. 'Everyone's taught about Jasper and his reign of terror, but it was hundreds of years ago so no one knows if it ever really happened. No one has ever found any legitimate records.'

As he spoke, James' memory of The Lost Years suddenly came into focus. They had been written in the Garian prison, etched onto the shelf where he'd found Arvad's false incarceration records. The records that had, as they'd later discovered, really belonged to Arvad's brother Ira.

'Is there anything else about The Lost Years in here?' he asked, gesturing to the journal. He couldn't help wondering if Will was right about the words having some kind of significance.

'Not in this one.' Will slipped the book onto a shelf and pulled out another. 'There are still five I haven't looked through out of about twenty. You can all help, if you're happy to.'

'We may as well,' Arthur agreed. 'Four pairs of eyes will be quicker than one.'

James cast his gaze over the surrounding shelves. The bottom rows were filled with books and the rest with an array of trinkets. A silver box caught his eye, resting on a bracket above the desk. He flipped open the lid and peered inside. It was filled with a fine green powder and he leant forward to sniff it. The sickly scent of tobacco filled his nostrils and he recoiled. Behind him, Will laughed.

'I wouldn't get too close to that.'

'What is it?' James asked, swallowing firmly.

'Jeverna Tobacco. It comes from Jeverna, a region on the north-west coast. Some villagers gave it to my dad as a gift but it smells horrible, as you've just discovered.'

'Really horrible!' James emphasised with a grin.

A small globe stood next to the tobacco box, its base engraved with the name 'Nicolas.' On the shelf above, a much larger globe stood, its surface covered with puncture marks. James spun the sphere through his fingers, watching the four continents of this world blur into one. A beam of light suddenly burst through his fingertips and he snatched his hands away as if they'd been burnt. The light emanated from one of the puncture holes and came to rest on the ceiling. Looking up at it, James saw that the white paint had come alive with colourful pictures.

'Memories,' Will said in a low voice. 'These are memories of the places and people my dad came across on his travels. I used to love lying on the floor and looking up at the pictures when I was little.'

'They're beautiful,' Aralia breathed.

Will nodded. 'The globe was a gift from an inventor in Lounasse.'

As the images began to fade, Will turned away. James wanted to ask him if he was alright, but his friends' nose was buried in one of the journals. Taking the volume Will had left on the desk for him, he too began to read.

'Day forty-eight, Muir,' he muttered under his breath. 'After docking on the shores of Davo, I was taken by a rough man dressed in furs to a hut built on nearby grassland. His family welcomed me and fed me meat and strong alcohol which chased off the cold. He didn't speak my language, but we communicated using drawings.'

'Take a look at this!' Arthur's voice cut through his mumblings. 'It says it again. The Lost Years.'

James, Will and Aralia hurried to his side. The open book in his hands displayed a crudely drawn map that was spread across two pages. An uneven circle had been traced around a small island just off the eastern coast of the northern continent. It was officially marked with the title 'Arvora' but 'The Lost Years' had been scribbled beside it by an untrained hand.

'Arvora,' Will frowned. 'I've never heard of it.'

He slipped a hand behind one of the shelves and drew out a roll of paper. Kneeling on the floor, he spread it out for everyone to see. A large map was inked across the surface, the regional divisions much clearer on this than on Will's father's drawing.

'There,' Arthur stated, pointing to the same island. 'It looks the same anyway.'

'It is the same one,' Will confirmed, 'but it's called Opoc not Arvora.' He held his hand above the map and a light glowed. The continents and regions started to spin beneath his fingers before resettling in their original positions. 'The name Arvora doesn't appear anywhere on this map,' he announced. 'It must be colloquial.'

The sound of a door banging shut somewhere below made them freeze. Will cursed under his breath and quickly rerolled the map. James, Arthur and Aralia gathered up the journals and returned them to their respective shelves under Will's

23

instruction. Once everything was in order, they exited the room and Will locked the door behind them.

'We'll have to go down the back stairs,' he hissed. 'Hurry!'

He walked down the passage on tiptoe and stopped in front of the far wall. Pulling up his left sleeve, he pressed his symbol to the white paint. The faint outline of a door appeared in the wall and he tugged it open. It led straight onto a flight of descending stairs and he gestured for James, Aralia and Arthur to follow him. Halfway down, he stopped outside another door that was fixed in the wall on their right. He opened this too and they all stepped through into the space beyond.

'I'm sorry, but you'll have to hide in here,' he whispered. 'I'll have to go and show my face so my mum doesn't worry.'

They were standing in a storeroom that was piled high with crates and sacks. At one end, a ladder led up to a raised loft. Beneath this, another door was just visible behind a stack of whiskey barrels.

'What then?' Aralia asked. 'We don't have a plan.'

'I have an idea,' Will replied, 'if everyone agrees to it. In the next town, there's an academy where my tutor works. He might be willing to help us.'

'You think he can tell us about Arvora?' Aralia brushed the dust from the lid of a nearby barrel and slid herself onto it.

Will shrugged. 'Maybe. The town is about half a day's walk from here, maybe less. If we leave tonight, we'll be able to make it by tomorrow morning.'

'I thought you'd never met your tutor,' James frowned.

'Not never,' Will replied with a wink. 'I went for a trial lesson with him a while ago. He won't remember who I am but he seemed friendly enough.'

'Well alright,' James agreed with a small grin. 'It's a start.'

Once Will had gone, James, Arthur and Aralia explored the

storehouse. They found some old apples in one of the barrels and took them up to the loft to eat. With stomachs a little less empty, they sat down amongst the piles of empty sacks that filled the loft. Clouds of dust rose from the hessian fabric, only to settle again on their hair and clothes.

'We should try to sleep,' Arthur suggested, 'otherwise it'll be a long night.'

James nodded and closed his eyes. Despite the pang of hunger lingering in his stomach, he drifted into a dreamless sleep. Someone shook him by the shoulder and he jumped awake. He was sure he'd only been asleep for a few seconds, but when he tried to move he felt stiff and cold. Opening his eyes, he saw Aralia looking down at him, her face illuminated by a light in her hand.

'Time to go,' she whispered.

She moved aside and Will appeared. He shoved a metal flask into James' hands, followed by a brown package. James thanked him and tucked both inside his bag before rising to his feet.

'Everyone ready?' Will asked.

'Ready,' James confirmed.

One by one, they clambered down from the loft. Pushing aside the whiskey barrels, Will opened the door James had spotted earlier. It led straight out onto a street that ran behind the inn and the surrounding houses. Following Will's lead, they began to walk, slipping over the cobblestones like shadows. This street led onto a second and third until they found themselves snaking alongside the city wall. At the end of this street, Will eventually came to a halt. Squinting through the darkness, James noticed a door resting between the grey stones. He recognised it as the same one he and Will had used to escape the city many months ago. Now again, he found himself leaving Arissel behind and entering the forest beyond.

'We're heading south,' Will announced. 'The town we're going to is called Idessa.'

The road they joined was well trodden, marked with many footprints. It ran parallel to the Ari Forest from which Arissel took its name. On the other side of the road, the landscape widened into a flat plain. Walking alongside his friends, James felt strangely at ease. He liked being out here in the darkness of night, not quite knowing where he was going. It gave him a sense of freedom.

The road was long and unforgiving. They talked a little as they walked but quickly grew tired. It was easier to continue in silence, accompanied only by the gentle thudding of their feet. Dawn was just breaking on the horizon when Idessa came into sight. It looked small and lonely on the flat landscape, with nothing surrounding it but dry earth. As they drew closer, James saw that the road they were on led straight up to the town gates. Two guards stood on watch but both had lowered their heads to their chests.

As James, Will, Arthur and Aralia approached, one of them straightened up and moved to block the road. He gestured for them to reveal their symbols and after a quick glance at each, waved them past. The iron gates swung open and the companions slipped through into the town beyond. Unlike Arissel, Idessa had a welcoming atmosphere. Yellowish buildings enclosed the wide streets where a number of early risers were going about their business. There were shops here too, ordinary grocers and butchers interspersed with those selling magical objects. Looking through one of the windows, James watched in fascination as two metal birds rose from their stands and fluttered against the glass.

'Look, there's an inn at the end of the road.'

Arthur's voice cut through his thoughts and he turned to

look down the street. A tall building stood on the corner, its yellow sign marked with the title, 'Academy Inn'.

'It's a bit early to go there,' Aralia said firmly. 'I don't fancy sitting with last night's drunks.'

James was about to agree when his attention was drawn to two figures sitting at the edge of the street. They were huddled under the same threadbare blanket, eyes closed against the morning. One was a middle-aged woman and the other a child whose face was partially hidden by the blanket. Not wanting to stare, he shifted his gaze away but started when a thin voice sounded close by. Turning back to the pair, he realised the woman was watching at him.

'Amar,' she said softly. 'I beg for your help.'

Beside her, the child lifted its head. The grubby face was somehow familiar and as James looked at it, he realised it belonged to the boy who had guided him through Arissel the day before. The features looked softer in this light however and he began to wonder if he was actually a girl. As she moved, her cloak slipped and she reached up to grab it. He immediately noticed that her left wrist bore no symbol and he heard Aralia gasp.

'Your eyes do not deceive you,' the woman said softly. 'She has no mark; she is without.'

'No symbol,' Aralia breathed, her eyes widening.

From the corner of his eye, James saw his friends step back. He frowned but his attention was caught by the sound of a new voice whispering deep within his mind.

'You are the seeker.'

He looked around but there was no one else in sight. The voice was unfamiliar and he turned back to the pair on the street. His eyes fell again on the girl and the voice sounded again.

'You are the wanderer.'

'Who are you?' he asked sharply. 'I know you, don't I? We met yesterday, in Arissel.'

'We have not met before,' the voice replied. 'Not in this life at least.'

James frowned. 'You must be mistaken.' As he spoke however, he began to doubt himself. The stranger in Arissel hadn't understood him, whereas this girl did.

'James, we have to go!' Arthur hissed but James ignored him.

'I know of you, wanderer,' the girl whispered. 'People whisper that name everywhere, but they don't know what it means.'

James felt his heart beat a fraction faster. He wanted to tear himself away from the girl, but his curiosity was stronger than his fear. As he continued to look at her, she smiled and lowered her eyes.

'My name is Tala, meaning wolf,' she said gently, 'and we, wanderer, will meet again.'

Chapter 4

JAMES stared at the girl for a moment longer before turning away. He let Arthur propel him through the inn door and the girl was lost from sight. The inn's interior wasn't large, nor was it decorative. It consisted of a single square room which stank of sweat and beer. Although it was early, one or two people were already sitting at the bar. The rest of the room was filled with tables that stood between several oddly placed pillars.

'Anything to drink?'

A barman approached the table where Will and Aralia had just sat down. Aralia shook her head and Will looked a little disappointed as the man turned away. James dragged a chair up to the table and sat down while Arthur joined his sister on a bench by the window.

'Are you alright, James?' Aralia asked, leaning across the table.

'I'm fine,' he replied quickly. 'Why?'

'That girl,' Aralia whispered. 'She's cursed.'

James studied a knot in the wooden table. 'I heard her voice. She didn't mean any harm.'

'She spoke to you?' Will also leant closer, his hazel eyes suddenly curious. 'What did she say?'

'She called me the seeker and the wanderer. She said her

name is Tala.' He raised his eyes to Will's face and looked at him intently. 'I've met her before, yesterday actually. She showed me the way to the underground city.'

'Your ability to hear voices in your mind is growing stronger,' Aralia warned. 'You should be careful.'

A frown threaded its way across James' forehead. 'You think I'm weird don't you?'

'Not weird,' Arthur replied gruffly, 'but unusual. Not many people our age know how to communicate like that. Rai's right, you should be careful, especially of people like that.' He jerked his head towards the door and fell silent.

'Are you really that afraid of people who don't have a symbol?' James asked. 'I didn't have one when I first came here.'

'To have no mark is a curse, James,' Aralia answered in a low voice. 'It's incredibly rare in this world. It's seen as a curse because that person doesn't belong amongst people with magic. They are considered *untouchable*.'

James nodded but chose not to disagree. 'How does someone perform magic without a symbol?'

'Symbols don't create magic,' Will explained. 'They simply give individuals an identity and allow them to belong to this world.'

His words made James feel less vulnerable somehow. The symbol on his wrist gave him the right to exist in this world, just like everyone else. He glanced around the inn and his eyes came to rest on the people at the bar. They looked just like anyone else and it was odd to think that they too could perform magic. To the right of the bar, a tall table stood supporting a large water jug and stack of glasses. As he watched, it tipped to fill a glass of its own accord. He knew this was an ordinary kind of magic, the kind that couldn't be felt in the air but simply was.

He was about to turn away, when his attention was caught by a trio of men by the inn door. All three were dressed in yellow robes, marked with an embroidered star. They crossed over to the bar, so deep in conversation that they didn't seem to realise they weren't sitting down. Under James' gaze, one of them looked up. He smiled nervously and looked between his hands where the barman had just placed a steaming cup.

'Professors,' Arthur said in a low voice. 'They must be from the academy.'

'They are,' Will confirmed. 'They're wearing academy cloaks.'

Plied with drinks, the three men left the bar and headed back out onto the street. They turned immediately left, walking away with hurried steps.

'We should follow them,' James hissed, jumping to his feet. 'Come on!'

He exited the inn with Will, Arthur and Aralia close behind him. Out on the street again, he couldn't help glancing to the corner where Tala and the woman had been. He wasn't in the least surprised to find that they were no longer there. Responding to Will's calls, he hurried to catch up with his friends who had overtaken him. They left the high street, turning down a side road as the scholars had done.

The road had a steep decline and was cut off at the base by a tall building. This rose two or three floors above the surrounding houses, its ancient brickwork set with many windows. Where the street finished, a flight of stone steps rose up to a door that was guarded on either side by stone gargoyles. The professors had already reached these and the companions hurried to catch up. The door was still open when they reached the bottom and Arthur mounted the steps in three bounds. He pushed the wooden panel aside and ushered James, Will and

Aralia through.

'What's the name of your tutor?' James whispered as he entered the academy behind Will. 'Where can we find him?'

'Now we're here, I'm not sure where I went last time,' Will replied with a shrug. 'It was a while ago and this place is huge!'

They were standing in a corridor that was lined with windows and dusty paintings. Many of the paintings featured grey-haired men in yellow robes, their faces set with a reserved boredom. Only three portrayed women and they were old too. The companions walked to the end of the corridor and stopped abruptly. A few steps ahead of them, the professors were just parting ways, each heading towards a different door. Two of them disappeared quickly but the third paused mid-step and turned to look straight at the companions.

'May I help you?'

His face was small and wrinkled and his watery eyes peered out from behind thick glasses. One heavily ringed hand rested on a walking stick and the other was curled around his coffee cup.

'Erm, yes, maybe,' James stuttered, taking a step forward.

'I recognise you,' the professor remarked, squinting at James. 'Are you a student here?' James shook his head but the professor was no longer looking. 'Four of you,' he muttered, leaning his stick against the wall. 'You'd best come into my office.' He fumbled with the door handle in front of him and stood aside to let them all through.

The room was plain, lined with cream wallpaper and set with old wooden floorboards. A desk stood against the back wall, beneath a tiny window that didn't let in much light. It was flanked by two bookshelves and each was labelled with an array of metal title plaques.

'Welcome to Goldstars Academy,' the professor began as he

settled himself behind the desk. 'My name is Samuel Atuah and I am here to guide you. This is the most prestigious academy on the Northern continent, where no pupil comes uninvited.' He spoke in a slick but bored voice, as if he'd uttered the same words hundreds of times.

Will cleared his throat and their host looked up, surprised. 'Excuse me, Sir, but I'm afraid we're not here to talk about academy places.'

Professor Atuah's surprise deepened. 'You're not? Are you perhaps visitors instead?'

James fixed his eyes on a silver fountain pen resting on the desk. 'We're here to speak to one of the professors,' he explained and turned to Will for support.

'Erm, yeah,' Will joined. 'Professor Sallow.'

'Ah, Sallow,' Professor Atuah acknowledged. 'I'm afraid he's not in today. Perhaps I can answer your questions.' He leant forward on the desk, his eyes alight with curiosity. 'Please, ask away.'

James looked at his friends for encouragement but they merely shrugged. 'We've come to ask about The Lost Years,' he began, 'and its connection with a place called Arvora.'

The professor's grey eyes widened and he shrank back in his chair. His mouth hovered half open, as if he couldn't find the words to speak. He stared at the companions for a long time before any sound came out.

'Arvora,' he breathed at last. 'I see. Why would four children want to know about a place like that? Most people don't know of it at all and those who do tend to wish they didn't.'

'You know about it then?' Will was quick to ask.

Atuah nodded slowly, as if unwilling to admit it. 'A little.' His eyes flashed defiantly. 'Arvora, you must understand, is a place of myth.'

Arthur took a step forward. He was tall for his age and the scholar shrank back as he leant over the desk. 'Myth or not, we'd like to know anything that you do,' he said sharply.

Placing a hand on her brother's arm, Aralia drew him back. 'If you'd be so kind as to help us,' she added, shooting Arthur a disapproving glance.

'Very well, I'll tell you,' Atuah said with reluctance, 'though it's not much.' He folded his fingers together and looked at each of them in turn. 'However, if I tell you, you must promise never to return to the academy. Is that clear?' The companions nodded obediently and he continued.

'It is thought that Arvora once existed on the Isle of Opoc which rests in the Eeron sea. The elders were once said to gather there to discuss high magic. In later years, Arvora became linked to terrible things. The elders fled to give way to the dark powers who thought Opoc belonged to them by right. It became known as the Dark Isle during the reign of Jasper, seven hundred years ago.'

'Jasper?' James asked. The vague connection they'd already made between Jasper and The Lost Years now seemed even more intriguing.

Atuah nodded. 'Jasper, the Master who controlled more darkness than any before him. He was said to rule the Dark Isle under the name Lord Opoc, but as the darkness grew, the isle slipped from the map into extinction.'

'You say this happened seven hundred years ago,' James pressed. 'Do The Lost Years relate to Arvora in some way?'

There was a long pause before the professor spoke again. He eyed James with a wariness that made his bearded face look pinched and sour. 'You ask questions which I shouldn't answer,' he muttered, 'but I can see you are serious in asking. Yes, I have heard of The Lost Years but I don't know how

34

closely they are connected to Arvora. They refer to the time when Jasper ruled because much life and light was lost.'

'How d'you know so much about all of this?' Will asked curiously.

Atuah laughed and his glasses slipped down his nose. 'I know only a little, the more common knowledge you might say. People know of Jasper and of the Dark Isle, but few know that it also went by the name Arvora. Even fewer know that it is now known as Opoc. Jasper's story is one of seven myths from that time, including that of the Seven Sisters and Arvad the Wanderer. These myths, in their bare form, are common knowledge to those in my profession.'

James glanced at his friends. He could see from their faces that they too were intrigued by the professor's words. 'Have you read Arvad's tale?' he questioned.

'Only the first part. There are few, if any, complete records of the story. Most people who know of Arvad have merely heard a summary of the tale from someone else.' He pushed his glasses back into place and rose from his chair. 'The school day is almost upon us and it's time that you left.'

He crossed to the door and opened it, his intentions clear. The companions passed back out into the corridor and turned to thank their informant. Atuah smiled, looking relieved to have a little more distance between himself and his uninvited guests.

'I wish you well,' he said cheerfully, but his face had returned to its natural seriousness. 'Never,' he whispered, 'repeat that it was I who told you this. It would be the end of my career.'

'We won't,' Aralia reassured him. 'Thank you.'

She turned away and James and Arthur moved with her. Only Will lingered behind, a question brimming on his lips.

'Did you... ever know a man named Nicolas Aeton?' he stuttered.

Professor Atuah looked at Will sharply. 'It seems you have revealed where you know of Arvora,' he observed. 'You must be Aeton's boy.'

Will nodded, his own face brightening. 'He had unfinished research and that's why we came. His journals mention Arvora but don't say anything about it.'

Atuah smiled and loosened his grip on the door frame. 'I only met him once, but he knew much of the world. He helped me with my own work; it's why we met. At the time, he was researching the islands off the east coast and had just come back from the River Villages. He'd heard the name Arvora mentioned by locals and was hoping to find out more about it. The only reason I know anything about Arvora and its connection with the Dark Isle was because I read his papers.' His voice trailed away and he gestured again to the corridor. 'Time moves on and you should go. I hope you find the answers you're looking for, young Aeton.'

'Thanks for all your help,' Will acknowledged.

Professor Atuah nodded politely before closing the door on them. The companions began walking back the way they had come. Turning into the long, portrait spattered corridor, they hurried along to the main door. As Will opened it, James found his attention caught by a room at the other end of the passage. The door stood ajar and through it he could see a grand room, painted in white and gold. He stepped a little closer, curious to see further inside.

'James, what're you doing?' Will hissed.

Only half listening, James stepped up to the door and peered through. The room was vast and laid with lavish carpets. It looked like the kind of room found in stately homes, only less crowded. The only furnishings were a few chairs and a long table pushed up against the back wall. Leaning in closer, he noticed two yellow robed figures standing in the back corner, deep in conversation. Afraid of being seen, he pulled his head back and knocked into Arthur.

'What's in there?' Arthur whispered at his shoulder.

'Not much,' James returned. 'We should go.' He felt a fresh sense of urgency rising in his chest but wasn't quite sure why.

As he stepped away, he couldn't help glancing through the doorway again. To his surprise, the figures had moved and were heading for the doorway. They were still deep in conversation but one of them suddenly looked up. James found himself looking into the face of the man who had tried to kill the clockmaker.

'Run,' he managed to gasp. 'Just run.'

Chapter 5

THE companions ducked as a bolt of light struck the door frame behind them. The wood splintered and the fragments scattered, filling their clothes and hair. Pushing the main door open to its full capacity, James stood aside to let Will, Arthur and Aralia hurry through. He followed them out without looking back and stumbled down the stone steps to the street.

The road leading up to the high street looked steeper from this side. With Will in the lead, the companions hurried upwards with breathless determination. At the top, they paused to assess the scene before them. The town had grown much busier while they'd been gone. It was now filled with groups of yellow robed children, all chattering in raised voices. They seemed oblivious to the everyday shoppers who pushed past them with disapproving glances.

Looking at one another for reassurance, the companions stepped amongst the throngs. One or two children turned to stare at them but most left them alone. They headed towards the end of the street where the paving stones joined a patch of grass. In the centre of this, a single tree bowed over a low bench. Ducking under the drooping branches, the companions turned to each other with nervous glances.

'Who are we running from?' Will immediately asked. 'What

happened back there?'

'It was him,' James replied breathlessly. 'He's here. The man who tried to kill the clockmaker is here.'

'At the academy?' Will leant against the tree trunk and shook his head. 'Why?'

James shrugged. 'Maybe someone tipped him off that we'd be there.'

'Impossible,' Arthur countered. 'No one else knew we were coming.'

Aralia took her brother's arm. 'Either way, it's not safe here. We should go back to Arissel.'

'I disagree,' Will said firmly. 'If we're being followed, for whatever reason, then we won't be safe there either. We should keep moving. It'll be harder for them to track us that way.'

No one spoke as his words sank in. James sat down on the bench and stared at the grass. He knew there would be eyes watching them wherever they went. He'd prepared himself for that. The part he wasn't sure about was what to do next.

'Where now?' Aralia asked, voicing his thoughts. 'We don't have any leads. We don't even know which crystal we should be looking for.'

'We have some leads,' Will replied with a shrug. 'We know that Arvad, Jasper and Arvora are all from the same time period and that Jasper is the Dark Master referenced in Arvad's tale.'

The sound of an alarm ringing somewhere close by made them all freeze. Knowing that the shrill tones came from the academy, they looked at each other with fresh urgency.

'We should go,' Arthur urged, glancing down the emptying high street. 'We're wasting time.' He turned away but Will put out a hand to stop him.

'Wait, I have an idea so just hear me out,' he entreated. He pulled a roll of paper from his pocket and opened it to reveal a map. 'Professor Atuah said that my dad was researching Arvora in the River Villages. What if we were to go there too?'

'What for?' James asked bluntly. 'I know you want to find out more about your dad, but how will going there help our quest?'

'If my dad was there researching Arvora, then the two might be linked.' Will pointed to a pair of islands on the map, drawn just off the coast of the northern continent. 'Opoc and Eeron. Professor Atuah said the villages are on the east coast, so they must be somewhere between here and Opoc.'

'Which leaves us with routes through Garia or Henlos,' Arthur concluded.

'Henlos,' Will decided. 'It can easily be reached via the trading route. We need to head through the north gate.'

Ducking back under the tree branches, they made their way across the grass. Two side alleyways joined onto it and they took the first, heading towards the town wall. The north gate was also guarded and they had to show their symbols again. They waited apprehensively while the guard checked their wrists and breathed sighs of relief when he finally let them through.

The morning was warm, promising a hot and dry afternoon. Clouds of dust rose from beneath their feet, coating their clothes with a fine layer of grime. On either side of the road, wiry grass spread out over the open landscape. Occasional glimpses of the Ari Forest appeared on the horizon, but these were scarce. The road, like the landscape, was empty, running straight and bare towards the skyline. There were no other travellers ahead or behind and the route was theirs alone to tread.

'There will be inns along this road,' Will announced after a short silence. 'We should be able to stay in one tonight.'

'Is it safe?' Aralia asked, arching her eyebrows. 'We might be better off out here in the open. Plus, an inn will cost.'

'Not my way it won't,' Will muttered under his breath. Aralia rolled her eyes and he grinned back at her. 'We should stop in the afternoon, before the road gets busy.'

Looking down the empty road, James found it hard to imagine that it was ever busy. He didn't object to Will's idea however as stopping early would give them time to plan. Reaching into his pocket, his fingers encountered the rectangular dimensions of his phone. He hadn't meant to bring it, but his escape from Victoria station hadn't left him with much time to think. Knowing it wasn't safe to have it with him, he pushed it to the bottom of his pocket and tried to forget it was there.

It wasn't long before an inn came into sight at the edge of the road. As it was only midday, Will suggested they carry on. The sun, as anticipated, was hot and dry, making the journey tough. Too thirsty to speak much, they walked on with steady determination. They soon lost track of time and were surprised when the sun suddenly disappeared behind a cloud. Looking up, James saw that the cloud was one of many, all swollen with rain. There were no other inns on the road ahead, nor any other sign of shelter.

'Maybe some rain will cool us down,' he suggested half-heartedly.

A raindrop fell on his cheek and he brushed it away. Another followed and the clouds suddenly opened, pelting them with heavy rain. It came down without remorse, soaking through their clothes in a matter of seconds. Will paused on the road and grinned as he lifted his face to the sky.

'It's been dry for days,' he laughed breathlessly.

The sound was infectious and James laughed too. Caught by a strange madness, he began to run and Will, Arthur and

Aralia raced to catch up.

'Hey, look over there,' Arthur's voice called over the sound of the rain. 'There's a building between those trees.'

Blinking the water from his eyes, James looked at the line of trees that ran alongside the road. Through the sparse branches, he could just make out the edges of a building. It seemed small and its wooden structure made it look more like an outhouse than an inn.

'Looks a little dodgy, don't you think?' He stopped in the middle of the road and waited for his friends to catch up. 'Worse than the other one we passed anyway.'

'What's your plan, Will?' Aralia asked crisply. 'How do we stay here *your* way?'

Will tapped his nose and winked. 'Come on, follow me.'

He dived off the road and into the trees. James, Aralia and Arthur followed at a more tentative pace. Will led them a little deeper into the trees before stopping with a mutter of triumph. Coming to a halt beside him, James saw that they were standing in view of a tumbledown shed. While the door and walls were warped by damp, the roof was still intact.

'This is your plan?' Aralia stared at the building and shook her head.

'Our free lodgings,' Will announced with a grin.

'Slightly worse than the inn but better than the road,' Arthur commented.

He approached the shed and tried to open the door, but it was jammed. Skirting along the wall, he pushed himself behind the building and disappeared amongst the trees. 'There's a broken window back here,' he called. 'We can climb inside.'

Pushing aside the thick branches, James found Arthur standing beneath a small window. The glass was mostly intact, with a single hairline fracture running between two corners.

Removing his sodden cloak, Arthur balled it around his fist and punched the window with all his strength. The glass shattered and the sound echoed in the trees around them. Grabbing onto the window frame, Arthur carefully hauled himself through to the other side.

'It's not so bad in here,' he reported. 'Come on.'

James clambered up next, trying to avoid the broken glass as he slid through the frame. He dropped down into the darkness on the other side and brushed the dust from his hands. Closing his eyes, he imagined a ball of light filling his palm. His left wrist prickled and opening his eyes, he saw that the shed interior was newly illuminated. It was small and musty, the floor littered with dead leaves. One corner contained a trapdoor and the remaining space was filled with piles of sacks and coiled ropes. The stench of damp was overpowering, a smell which even the draught coming under the door couldn't change.

'It'll do,' Aralia reluctantly approved. 'We can sit on these ropes at least.' She brushed Arthur aside as he tried to help her to the ground and settled herself on a fat coil.

'Looks like we're not the first to have stayed here,' Arthur announced, scraping at the floor with his foot. A layer of ash rested across the tip of his boot, omitting a smoky scent as it was stirred.

The rain had grown louder again, battering against the roof. There was a leak somewhere too that began a persistent drip. Shivering in his wet clothes, James sat down on an empty sack. His stomach rumbled and he opened his bag, searching inside for the food package Will had given him. Several biscuits were squashed next to a fat sandwich and he hungrily bit into the latter. Reaching into his bag again, he drew out two folded sheets of paper. He'd packed them several months ago, alongside his other essentials, but hadn't looked at them since.

'What've you got there?' Will asked as he sat down close by.

'They're the pages from Arvad's tale,' James returned slowly. 'I always carry them with me, just in case. I've read them so many times and haven't found anything new yet.'

'The rest of the tale must exist somewhere,' Will mused. 'Even if it isn't written down, as Professor Atuah said, someone must know the whole story.'

'What if they don't?' James finished his mouthful and brushed the crumbs from his lap. 'What if these pages are all there is? Maybe no one has ever found the crystals because they couldn't find the story first.'

'There must be other clues,' Aralia said quietly. 'The tale can't be the only record. As Will has already said, someone, somewhere, must know more.'

James nodded and tucked the pages back in his rucksack. 'We could be looking for any of the crystals. Earth, air or water but it's impossible to know which.'

'If you think about it, you didn't know you were looking for the firestone at the beginning,' Will reminded. 'It was the only one the tale spoke of, so it seemed like the obvious one to pick. Maybe it's up to you to decide which one to find next.'

'You could be right,' James supposed. 'At least we have some kind of plan. If The Lost Years are linked to Arvad and to Arvora and Jasper, then we're already closer than we were yesterday.'

The conversation lulled and they settled more comfortably on the sacks and ropes. Outside, the rain had stopped but thunder rumbled close by. Arthur stood up again and pushed some ropes across the crack in the door. He also hooked a piece of sacking over the broken window to keep out the wind.

James could already feel himself drifting into sleep, his arms protectively wrapped around his bag. Damp tingled in his nostrils and his stomach still rumbled, but he forced himself to think about Arvad and the crystals. As he passed into the realm of sleep, the air grew colder around him. Opening his eyes a fraction, he saw that the shed and his friends had completely disappeared. He was standing in a familiar place, white mist swirling all around him.

Chapter 6

AT first, James thought he was in No Man's Land, but this thought vanished when he noticed a shape emerging from the mist. As he watched, the shadowy form drew closer and he suddenly realised where he was.

'We meet again, James Fynch.'

A soft, feminine voice sounded, a voice that James knew well. It had guided him on his search for the firestone, had been there when he most needed help. For a moment, he didn't know what to say. He felt like this figure was a stranger, even though he knew her voice.

'I haven't seen you for a while,' he said at last. His voice echoed eerily around them, making him shudder.

'It has been difficult for me to reach you.' The girl stepped forward and James caught a glimpse of her pale face beneath her hood. 'In your world, you are often bound by the constraints of ordinary dreaming.'

James frowned and looked down at his invisible body. 'Am I the only one who can hear your voice in my mind?'

The girl nodded. 'You and I are bound together by our fates. We can speak where others can't.'

James looked at her intently, trying to find her eyes amongst the shadows. 'I heard someone else speak in my mind,' he began, 'another girl. How come I could hear her too?'

'Very few can speak the old language, the language of the mind and of the spirit. You and I can because we have great destinies.'

'I'm not sure I want a great destiny,' James reflected.

'Then what do you want?'

'To find the crystals before *She* does.'

The girl moved but the mist around her remained still. 'If that's true, then you do want to fulfil your destiny.'

James nodded thoughtfully. 'I suppose I do, in a way.' He tried to turn away, only to find that he couldn't. The girl stepped up to him and gently laid a hand on his arm. He blushed, even though he couldn't feel her touch.

'I am not here to tell you about your destiny,' the girl said. 'I am here to tell you that the darkness is growing stronger and you must begin the race again.'

Before James could answer, the girl's body began to flicker and fade. The mist grew thicker around her until it swallowed her altogether. James didn't call out after her, knowing that it wouldn't bring her back. Instead, he allowed the dream to fade and opened his eyes. Although it was dark, he immediately remembered where he was. Somewhere close by, he could hear the regular breathing of his friends and the drip from the leak in the roof. He lay listening to these for a long time as he thought over what the girl had said.

As he lay there, he became aware of another sound. It was faint and monotonous, like the murmuring of many voices. Sitting up sharply, he strained his ears to hear more clearly. After several unsuccessful minutes, he slid from the rope he was on and crept over to the shed door. Pushing aside the coils Arthur had left by the crack, he pressed his face to the floor and peered through. It was too dark to see anything, so he turned his ear to the gap instead. There were definitely people close by and closing his eyes, he tried to hear what they were saying.

'Hurry up and finish smoking so we can go inside.'

A male voice reached his ears, accompanied by the stinging scent of tobacco. He swallowed and pressed his ear more firmly against the crack.

'Stop hurrying me,' a female voice snapped. 'Just one more drag, that's all.'

'He's waiting,' the man hissed. 'Linus Caperna never likes to wait. You know that.'

'Well he'll just have to, won't he?' There was a long pause while the woman tried to control a coughing fit. 'Tell you what,' she eventually croaked, 'why don't you make sure the stock's in order and I'll go in and meet him. I'll explain why I was late, get the money, and then bring him out here.'

James was listening so intently that he jumped when something hit the door. It was followed by the rattling sound of a lock being shaken somewhere above his head. Jumping to his feet, he stumbled across the dark shed and began shaking the silhouettes of his friends.

'Wake up!' he urged. 'We have to get out of here.'

Muttering mild curses, Will, Arthur and Aralia stirred where they lay. James continued to shake them, horribly aware of the clattering sounds behind him.

'What's wrong?' Will mumbled. 'What's that noise?'

'Man, coming in here, will see us,' James explained breathlessly.

This time, they heard him and leapt into action. Will tore the sacking from the window and tossed their bags through. He stood aside to let Aralia clamber through before pulling himself after her. The creak of a door opening made James freeze. He looked wildly at Arthur, whose shadowy form was only halfway through the window. In a split second, Arthur jumped back inside the shed and disappeared into the far corner. Hoping he was safe, James dived behind a pile of ropes and waited.

Peering through the loose coils, he saw a bulky silhouette emerge in the doorway. The figure was accompanied by the stench of ripe ale, a scent that reminded James of his dad's breath after an office party. He pinched his nose and tried not to breathe too deeply. The stranger pushed the door shut and moments later, a light blossomed into being. James found himself looking at a dark-skinned man whose golden eyes flashed keenly around the shed interior. His gaze passed over the stack of ropes but didn't linger there. He turned instead to the pile of sacks and took one into his hands.

'Not hiding that sack, Yulan?'

A thickly accented voice broke the silence and James swung his eyes back over to the door. Another man stood there, his rough face illuminated by Yulan's orb.

'Linus Caperna,' Yulan returned with a nervous nod. 'Not hiding, Sir, just checking the stock.' He dropped the sack at his feet and took a step backwards.

Linus laughed. 'I see.' He advanced into the shed and slammed the door behind him. 'Stealing is a crime you know,' he added in a low voice. 'If you were, I might have to kill you.'

A third figure entered the shed, this time a woman. James watched as Linus grabbed her arm and flung her inside. She stumbled forward and fell onto the rope pile. Her head was just centimetres from where James sat and he could feel her breath ruffling his hair. He held still, his own breath caught in his throat.

'Open the sacks and show me the goods before I break her neck,' Linus hissed.

Yulan jumped into action, untying the cord on the nearest

sack. 'Black ones in here, quartz in the other, Sir. Where do you want them?'

'There's a covered cart just within the trees. Take them there.' Striding over to where the woman lay, Linus grabbed her by the wrists and pulled her upright. 'Take the sacks to the cart,' he growled in her ear. 'You know how I hate weakness, Isla.'

He pushed her away from him and she bent to collect two sacks before exiting the shed. Linus followed her, his own hands empty. James remained completely still. He watched with silent dread as Isla and Yulan continued to ferry sacks from the shed and out to the waiting cart. Linus stood just outside the door, hissing regular commands. Entering to collect the final two sacks, Yulan shoved aside some ropes which had fallen in his way. James felt the whole pile shift in front of him. He pressed himself against the wall, trying not to make any sound as Linus emerged in the doorway.

'Fifty racha for the work.' Linus pulled out a handful of notes from his pocket and held them out to Yulan.

'You promised one hundred,' Yulan objected. 'Notes marked with the Southern Trading Symbol are worth less in the north. It'll cost all that just to get from here to the River Villages.'

James inhaled sharply. The sound echoed in his ears but the two men didn't seem to notice. He clapped a hand over his mouth and continued to watch them intently.

'They charge you know,' Yulan continued. 'There's an extra cost to take the wagon through, and more for unloading at the docks. Our deal was for one hundred.'

'Deals change,' Linus said smoothly. His lips twisted in an ugly grimace and a vein on his temple throbbed. 'Take the money or leave it.'

'A deal's a deal,' Yulan insisted. 'Have some honour.'

'Alright,' Linus agreed, his voice rising. 'I can quite easily get Isla to take them for me instead. Perhaps it's easier for me not to keep you around.'

Yulan uttered a strange whimper and tried to duck around Linus. A burst of light flung him backwards and he hit the shed wall with a force that sent him reeling forward again. He tumbled to the floor, face squashed in the dust, and lay still. Brushing his hands together, Linus picked up the final two sacks and exited the shed. The orb of light faded behind him and everything went dark. James sat rooted to the spot, unable to take his eyes from the place where Yulan lay. Even though he couldn't see the body, the knowledge was enough to numb him.

It was a long time before he could move, but he eventually dragged himself upright. A scraping sound made him start. It was quickly followed by a light that sparked to life in the far corner. Arthur's pale face emerged behind it and James breathed a sigh of relief. The light floated across the shed and settled above Yulan's body. Without further delay, Arthur knelt beside the limp frame and felt for a pulse. After several long seconds, he looked up with a nod of relief.

'Still breathing. James, we need Rai. She'll know how to help.'

James hurried across to the broken window and peered out into the night. There was no sign of Will or Aralia anywhere and he called their names into the darkness. The silence was then broken by the sound of rustling and Will and Aralia emerged from between the trees.

'You're alright!' Will whispered in a relieved tone.

James nodded. 'The door's open. Come quickly.'

He left them at the window and hurried to greet them at the

door. They both darted inside but stopped short at the sight of Arthur kneeling over Yulan's body.

'Who is that?' Aralia whispered. 'Is he dead?'

Arthur shook his head. 'No, but you need to look at him, Rai. His name is Yulan.'

She nodded and knelt beside her brother without hesitation. Removing her small shoulder bag, she rummaged inside and drew out two glass bottles. Lit by the orb above her head, she prised Yulan's lips open and poured in liquid from one of the bottles. His eyelids twitched in response and eventually opened. He looked up at Aralia uncertainly, his lips trying to form words.

'Who are you?' he croaked. 'Are you dead? Am *I* dead?'

Aralia laid a hand on his arm. 'Not yet, but you should drink more of this.' She held the bottle to his lips again and he gulped the liquid down.

James opened his mouth to speak, but before he could say anything, Yulan rolled onto his side and vomited. Aralia patted his back and shifted herself away from the liquid pooling on the floor.

'Try to lie still,' she instructed.

Kneeling beside her, James looked into Yulan's pained face. 'Who d'you work for?' he asked gently. 'Who is Linus?'

Yulan coughed and a trickle of vomit dribbled down his chin. James swallowed his own nausea and held the stranger's gaze.

'I work for anyone who wants my trade. I am a trader. Linus is too.'

'What did he want?' James pressed. 'What was in the sacks?' Aralia looked at him reproachfully but he carried on anyway. 'Please, we need to know.'

Yulan's eyes rolled in his head, but he forced them to focus on James again. 'Jet and quartz,' he whispered. 'Crystals.'

'Crystals? What for?' Will hovered just above Yulan, blocking the light with his head.

'I don't know. Please, do not think me a bad man. I do it for my family. Without this money, we would not survive.'

His breath grew shallow and his eyes rolled again. A thin stream of saliva dangled from his lips as his head rolled to the side. Aralia grabbed the second glass bottle from Arthur and let three drops of liquid fall into Yulan's mouth.

'I'm losing him,' she whispered desperately. 'Will, take off your cloak and put it under his head.'

Will did as he was told, removing his cloak and tucking it under the patient's head. Yulan's eyes were flickering here and there, as if he was looking at something no one else could see.

'His ribs are broken. I don't think I can save him.' Aralia's eyes grew misty and she bowed her head. 'I don't know how.' Her voice came out in a hopeless gasp.

'Shouldn't we fetch help?' James asked. 'We can't just let him die here.'

Aralia slowly shook her head. 'It's too late. He's fading more quickly than I anticipated. There isn't time to fetch anyone so the best thing we can do is sit with him.'

Arthur wrapped an arm around his sister and held her tightly. James remained kneeling, his head respectfully bent, and Will sat down beside him. A deep gloom filled the space around them. Aralia held Yulan's hand in her own as he passed in and out of consciousness. They remained by his side in silence until his body stopped shaking and a peaceful expression came into his eyes. Extracting her hand from his limp fingers, Aralia bowed her head.

'No one deserves to die,' she whispered. 'Your family were lucky to have someone who cared. Rest well now, I'm sorry I couldn't save you.'

She fell silent and tears rolled down her cheeks. Arthur drew her away before leaning forward to close Yulan's eyes.

Chapter 7

'WHAT do we do now?'

Aralia's voice cut through the silence like a knife. Yulan's body lay on the floor in front of them, still and cold. Its presence cast a shadow over each of them, numbing them to the outside world. James, Will and Arthur looked at Aralia, but no one said a word. Time ticked on meaninglessly while they just sat there, waiting.

'We should go,' Will said at last. 'We can't just sit here.' He rose to his feet and moved to open the shed door. Pre-dawn light crept into the shed, accompanied by a faint gust of wind. 'We should go,' he repeated.

James stood too and joined Will at the door. The early air was fresh and he breathed it in deeply, trying to clear the damp from his lungs.

'You're right, we should go,' he echoed. 'If we hurry, we can catch up with them.'

'Catch up with who?' Aralia tore her eyes from Yulan's face but still didn't move away.

'There were two other traders here. They were taking the sacks to the River Villages.'

'The River Villages?' Will's eyes widened. 'Why would they be trading crystals there?'

James shrugged. 'I'm not sure. The other man who was in here, Linus, tried to pay Yulan less than he'd promised for the journey. Yulan tried to object and that's why he was…'

'I heard the same,' Arthur interrupted. 'If they are going to the villages then it can't hurt to follow. It'll be quicker than finding our own route, but they've had a head start so we'll have to hurry.'

Aralia turned back to Yulan, her face pained. 'What do we do with him?' she asked softly. 'We can't just leave him here.'

Arthur leant across her and gently removed Will's cloak from under Yulan's head. 'There's nothing we can do, Rai. It's best to leave him here, where he can be found. We can't lose any more time and we don't want to be caught with a body.'

Pulling back her sleeve, Aralia unfastened a silver bracelet wrapped around her wrist. She laid it on Yulan's chest and bowed her head briefly before standing up and hurrying from the shed. Arthur, Will and James also bowed their heads before following her out. They retrieved their bags from beneath the broken window and made their way back towards the road. Pausing on the verge, they looked at the wheel tracks that were clearly printed in the muddy earth.

'The tracks look fresh,' James commented. 'If they came from the trading cart then it can't be that far ahead of us.'

A faint whining noise made them all freeze. It was rasping but gentle, sounding almost like the wind. Tilting his head to listen, Arthur stepped back between the trees lining the road. Aralia opened her mouth to protest but Will put a finger to his lips and hurried after him. Glancing at Aralia, James shrugged before moving to follow. Pushing through the needled branches, he saw Will and Arthur had stopped just ahead of him. A long, low building stood a short distance in front of them, resting parallel to the inn which was just visible through the trees.

'What're you all doing?' Aralia hissed, coming up behind James. 'I thought we didn't want to be seen.'

As the words left her lips, the whining sound came again. It was coming from inside the building and Will turned to Arthur with a mysterious grin.

'Ferastia,' he whispered.

Crossing over to the building, he tugged the door open and slipped through. Arthur followed, with James and Aralia close behind. The interior was filled with rows of animal stalls. Only five out of ten were occupied and James couldn't help staring at the animals inside. They looked like horses, only much taller. Their skin was a pale silvery colour, like that of the pre-dawn sky. It seemed to shimmer across their bodies which rippled with fine muscles.

'Never seen one up close?' Will held his hand out to the closest creature and it bent to nuzzle him.

James shook his head. 'Never.'

Will grinned. 'You're about to have a quick introduction. On a ferastia, we can easily catch up with the trading wagon.'

'We could just take two and share,' Arthur suggested.

Opening the stall gate, Will stood aside to let the ferastia out. The beast sniffed the air before tentatively stepping into the main stable. Arthur led out a second animal and the pair nosed each other curiously.

'Here, use this to climb onto its back,' Arthur commanded. He placed an upturned crate next to one of the animals and gestured to it.

James nodded, feeling small beside the huge beasts. He had never even ridden a horse before and the size of the ferastia unnerved him a little. Standing back, he watched as Aralia jumped onto the box and swung herself gracefully aloft.

'It's easy,' she encouraged, smiling down at him.

Following her lead, he stepped onto the crate and grabbed the ferastia's mane. With one great heave, he swung himself onto the animal's back and let his legs fall on either side. Its flesh felt cold and scaly beneath his fingers and he kept one hand firmly wrapped around its mane. Mounting the second animal behind Arthur, Will slapped its side but it refused to move.

'Come on,' he urged. 'We don't have time to hang around.'

'Ferastia are loyal to their owners, aren't they?' Aralia said softly. 'They won't respond to us in the ordinary way.'

Will stared at her. 'What?'

'I think they're loyal to their owners,' she repeated.

'I heard you,' Will snapped, 'but why didn't you say something before?' He stroked the beast's neck and sighed. 'If they won't move, then there's no point in us being here.'

A noise outside the stable door made them all freeze. The ferastia began stamping again, their eyes wide and alert. Before anyone had time to think, a figure appeared in the doorway. His broad, leather clad body blocked the exit, eliminating any chance of escape.

'No move,' he hissed. He raised his palm towards them and a light began threading its way between his fingers.

Two more men appeared behind him. They too stood with outstretched hands, waiting for the right moment to pounce. James raised his hand in automatic response, but too late. A flash of light burst from the doorway and struck the tip of his shoe. Another bolt followed, shooting across the stable with lightning speed. This time, it struck his ferastia directly in the chest and the beast let out a terrible scream. Head bent, it charged towards its assailants. James felt Aralia grab onto his cloak as the animal burst through the doorway and into the trees beyond.

It didn't stop there. Eyes wide with terror, it sped past the inn and out onto the road. Its speed was dizzying and James looked at his hands to stop his head from spinning. He could feel the animal rippling beneath him, running with smooth strides. Despite its speed, he felt safe in his position behind its neck. Aralia however moved her arms around his waist and held on tightly. It felt like a long time before their pace began to slow. The ferastia settled into a loping trot and feeling less dizzy, James turned to look back down the road.

'That's Will and Art,' Aralia announced. She withdrew her hands from James' waist and pointed to the blurry shape racing towards them.

'We should keep going,' James replied urgently. 'We need to outrun those men.'

Aralia nodded. 'The ferastia will respond to us now. Their last rider is always their master.' She dug her heels into the beast's side and it broke into a canter.

It was no longer necessary to hold on tightly and James focused his attention on the surrounding landscape. There were more trees than before and the ground wasn't quite as flat. A few flowers pricked the grass, yellow petals facing towards the absent sun. The gentle rolling of the ferastia's stride quickly lulled James into a false sense of comfort. The cloudy morning sky left a heavy feeling in the air and his eyes began to droop. He was lost in deep thought when Aralia's voice sounded in his ear.

'Arthur and I have been to Henlos before, you know.'

James dragged his eyes open again. He nodded but said nothing, waiting for Aralia to continue of her own accord.

'There's a region called Rivel, on the east coast,' she soon obliged. 'It shares a border with Henlos. There's a forest there, right by the sea. We lived there for a while, but I don't remember much of it.'

'Is that where you were born?' James asked, his senses gradually returning.

'We stayed there until I was four and Arthur five.'

James suppressed a yawn. 'Have you ever wanted to go back, to find your parents?' His question was met with a long pause and for a moment he thought he'd offended her.

'Why do you ask that?' she then asked.

'Doesn't everyone want to know where they come from?'

'We tried once, not long before we first came to Arissel.' Aralia lowered her voice and James sensed her unease. 'We were told both our parents had died and that the Silene family name had been cursed. There's nothing to go back for now.'

James looked down at his hands. He'd never heard Aralia mention her surname before and he now understood why. A new question was forming in his mind, but he wasn't quite sure if he could ask it.

'What was it like living with dryads?' The question felt strange on his tongue. Most of the time, he forgot that Aralia wasn't fully human.

'It's alright, you're allowed to ask me that,' she murmured. 'It was normal. It felt like that was how life should be. Dryads aren't so different from everyone else. They're shy and have knowledge of natural magic, but they look like humans, apart from their paler skin. Art and I are more human than dryad now.' She paused and James could feel her eyes on his back. 'What about you?' she asked. 'You hardly ever speak of your world or your family.'

James lowered his head, unsure of what to say. 'I live with my parents in a country called England,' he began with a shrug. 'We have countries, not regions,' he quickly added.

'Did you ever want a brother or sister?'

James fiddled with the corners of his cloak. He usually said no when people asked if he had or wanted siblings, but he didn't want to lie to Aralia. 'She died before I was born,' he said simply. 'I don't even know her name.'

'I'm sorry,' Aralia returned softly.

Silence fell between them but Aralia's hand strayed over to rest on his arm. The ferastia continued to carry them forward and day grew darker around them. Suddenly, Aralia uttered a soft cry and pointed to the road ahead. Following her gesture, James saw the shape of a carriage on a distant bend. It was unlike any he'd seen before, two storeys high and completely black. Two metal panniers, shaped into solid balls, hung from either side, disrupting the balance of the vehicle and causing it to sway.

'Is that the trader's cart?' he asked in disbelief. 'It's a carriage, to start with.'

'That's what the trading wagons look like.' Will's voice sounded close by and turning, James saw he and Arthur had managed to catch up.

Hooves sounded on the road behind them and they glanced fearfully at one another. Just a few metres away, at a bend in the road, stood three sweating ferastia. Each carried a rider, dressed in leather hunting clothes and wielding whips of light above their heads. The companions looked at each other desperately. Caught between the trading carriage and the hunters, there was nowhere to hide. Not on the road at least. James looked at Will and saw the same thought flash over his friend's face. With a mutual nod, both dug their heels into the ferastias' sides. Spurred into action, the animals leapt from the road as light burst in the air behind them.

Chapter 8

THE ferastia rode hard and the landscape flashed past in dizzying swathes. Light continued to streak through the air behind them, but it was impossible to tell how close it was. The animals grew more skittish with each flare, racing over the uneven ground with whinnies of distress. Taking a hand from his animal's mane, James pressed his palm to the sky. A soft light formed on his fingertips, growing to the size of a tennis ball. Pulling back his arm, he flung it away from him and watched as it was taken by the rush of air that accompanied the ferastia's gallop.

There was no time to see where it landed before the ferastia abruptly changed direction. He grabbed onto the scaly flesh and felt Aralia latch onto his arm. Just as suddenly, the animal stopped dead in its tracks. The force of this movement flung James from its back and he landed on the grass with a thud. He lay winded for a moment before sitting up to survey the landscape. Everything lay still and there was no sign of their pursuers anywhere. Turning his head, he saw Aralia lying on the ground nearby. Just behind her, Will and Arthur were just dismounting from their own ferastia.

'Whoa,' Will eased, stroking the distressed animal on its neck. 'You're alright.'

'Did we outrun them?' James jumped to his feet and shook out his stiff limbs.

'There was too much going on to tell what actually happened,' Arthur replied as he bent to lend Aralia a hand. 'Either we outran them or they gave up.'

'We're miles from the road now,' Aralia sighed, brushing mud from her cloak. 'We won't catch up with the cart again.'

'If we keep moving, we might get back to the road before it rains again.' Will glanced up at the sky, where the clouds were conspiring to create another rainstorm.

Latching on to the mane of his ferastia, James pulled himself back into the scaly saddle. His limbs were aching but he settled himself as best he could while Aralia jumped up behind him. He dug his heels into the ferastia's sides and it began to trot forward. Will and Arthur's beast moved alongside it with the same, swaying pace. The repetitive movements once again lulled James into a state of drowsiness. He closed his eyes but his mind was too wired to switch off completely.

Some time passed before he opened them again. There was still no sign of the road but the sky had grown darker. Low clouds hung on the horizon, rippled with dark grey. Turning, he saw that Will and Arthur were hunched over with fatigue. As if sensing James' gaze, Arthur looked up. He glanced at the sky and wiped a raindrop from his forehead before turning back to James.

'Looks like we're going to get caught out again,' he remarked. 'We should stop soon and try to find some shelter. The ferastia should rest too.'

He patted his steed on the neck and it slowed to a steady walk. James did the same and the two animals turned to nuzzle one another. Behind Arthur, Will stirred and raised his head. He too looked up at the sky and frowned as the misty rain struck his face.

'Are we stopping?'

'For now,' Arthur replied. 'The ferastia need to rest.'

'We haven't reached the road,' Will objected. 'We should be nearly there.'

'We are there.' Aralia spoke and the boys turned to her, surprised. She pointed ahead of them to where the grass grew long and wild. 'It's on the other side of that grass,' she continued. 'We're just a few steps away.'

'If you're right, then let's keep going,' James instructed.

They encouraged the ferastia to walk a few more metres. The road soon came into view, winding its way through the marshy grass. On the other side of the road, two trees stood close together, their branches forming a rough arch. Their roots also joined together, creating gnarled bumps and hollows. There was no other sign of shelter on the horizon and the companions guided the ferastia to rest beneath the leafy branches.

'Let's hope it doesn't rain too hard,' Will said, sliding from the ferastia's back.

Dismounting, James turned his gaze to the sky. It was vast and gloomy, filled with universal powers which he still didn't quite understand. The space reminded him of the difficult task ahead and he sat down on a gnarled root with a sigh.

'I know we have a plan, but there's still so much we're not sure about,' he said quietly. 'How do we know which crystal to look for without knowing the rest of Arvad's story?'

'Maybe it's up to us to work it out.' Will sat down too and leant back against one of the trees. 'We know the names of the elements at least.'

James nodded but said nothing. He wished they had a clearer plan, one that would give them a better chance of defeating the Belladonna. Even the thought of her made him shudder and he turned his attention back to his friends. Will's eyes were now closed and Arthur and Aralia were huddled against the second tree. The sound of deep breathing suggested that all three of them had fallen asleep where they sat.

Glancing cautiously around him, James drew out his phone. The smooth frame felt comforting beneath his fingers and he pressed the on button. The screen lit up and he automatically checked the time. It hovered at ten to midnight and he frowned, remembering that his phone clock didn't align with the hours in this world. His thoughts turned back to the power cut which had struck on his fourteenth birthday. The time had read ten to midnight then too, the moment of his birth.

His mum had once told him about the power cut that occurred on the night he was born. The midwife had only known the time because her old-fashioned watch had rung an early alarm. That was really the beginning of it all, but no one had known it then. Leaning his head against the tree trunk, he felt a wave of fatigue wash over him. His mind felt fuzzy, as if he were about to pass out, but his vision was still clear. Closing his eyes, he tried to focus his brain but everything was spinning. Somewhere in the depths, a voice began whispering but he couldn't hear what it was saying.

'Is someone there?' he asked.

No one answered but the whispering grew louder. From the swirling depths of sound, a distinctive voice then spoke.

'James Fynch.'

Behind his eyelids, James saw a white mist emerge. He felt himself sinking into it, even though he knew he was still awake. Looking down, he found that his body had disappeared. The only visible form was that of a cloaked figure, standing just in front of him. As he watched, the figure raised its head and he found himself looking at a familiar face.

'Albert!' he exclaimed in disbelief. 'What're you doing here?'

Albert smiled a friendly, all-knowing smile. 'It's good to see you again, James. I'm afraid I couldn't give you any warning.'

'Where are we?' James looked around at the swirling mist but had a feeling he already knew.

'Still just as curious,' Albert observed. 'It has taken me a while to reach you. You haven't been letting me in.'

'*Letting* you? I didn't even know I could talk to you like this.'

'Well, that's just it, you didn't know so you didn't believe. Holding a conversation in your mind takes concentration and openness. Perhaps you aren't quite old enough yet. It's rare for someone so young to have such an ability.'

'I'll be fifteen before too long,' James objected. 'Well, I think I will be at least.' He paused and looked down at where his feet should be. 'Time seems to pass quicker in my world than it does here,' he said quietly. 'Is that true?'

Albert looked at him for a long time before answering. 'Time is a matter of perception,' he said at last. 'It may seem like there is a distortion between the two worlds, but everything is really happening simultaneously.'

James frowned. 'I'm not sure I understand. You see, when I got back to my world, time had passed, but my parents didn't seem to realise I'd been gone.'

'Time is nothing but the present moment,' Albert replied. 'Imagine a universe without time. Do you think events would happen in order, or would they all happen at the same time?'

'At the same time,' James answered promptly, 'but…'

'The two worlds rest across time from each other,' Albert cut in. 'I believe I have told you that before. When you pass between worlds, you aren't travelling in time. You are simply continuing to exist in your own reality. Time isn't separate from you. You are time itself, just like everybody else.'

'But what about my parents?' James asked.

'Those left in your world continue to experience their own realities, with or without you. When you return, it is like you have always been there.'

'That doesn't make sense,' James replied. 'If someone travelled to the moon without telling anyone, people would still notice that they were gone.'

'Does it have to make sense? Magic isn't bound to scientific fact, but it still exists. Humans have a limited perception of reality. In an absolute reality, all time disappears and the universe is limitless. One day, you will come to understand that.'

James nodded, trying to calm his spinning thoughts. 'I can hear others in my mind, you know,' he said, changing the topic. 'There's a girl…'

'Your destiny fooled even the wisest of us James,' Albert returned. 'You had to meet her eventually. You, James, have crossed one of the greatest boundaries of all, second only to death. You have moved between worlds and all boundaries are open to you if you let yourself cross them.'

James sighed, whether aloud or in his head he didn't know. 'You know who she is then?'

'I know her destiny is joined to yours.'

'I see her in a mist too.' James looked up to find Albert watching him. 'Are we in No Man's Land?' he added.

Albert shook his head. 'We are nowhere in particular. You see, a mist is a neutral place, where two minds can connect, or where boundaries meet. The mist you see now is something your mind has created. It's why you can't see your own form.'

'How is your body here then?'

'The person who seeks out the mind of another may hold on to their physical form.'

James felt the urge to turn away but stopped himself. 'Why are you here now, inside my mind?'

'I came to give you a warning.' Albert let the smile fade from his face before continuing. 'The darkness is growing stronger. It seeps into every corner like a shadow, invisible but waiting. People talk of a second wanderer, but they don't know what it means. The race has begun again.'

'I'm already on it,' James said firmly, 'but I'm not quite sure where to go. Do you know what happens in the rest of Arvad's tale?'

'I'm afraid I don't,' Albert replied. 'The crystals aren't meant to be found in a certain order. Like all magic, they stand apart from structure and logic. You found the firestone and your path to the others will become clear.'

'What if I fail?'

Albert looked away into the swirling mist. 'Failure teaches us lessons. It shows us that there's more than one way to succeed. Just because one road has ended doesn't mean there isn't another. The crystals may belong to nature, but Arvad's magic was human. That is why his quest belongs to you.'

James tried to respond, but his mind grew fuzzy again. Albert faded away and he felt himself returning to the real world. Opening his eyes, he saw that he was back on the roadside with his friends. The sky had mostly cleared but a few clouds still hung on the horizon, rippled with the purple flecks of evening. A gentle creaking startled him. It sounded far away, but not too far to be indecipherable. Jumping to his feet, he peered down the road. In the distance, a bulky silhouette was just disappearing behind a bend. Hurrying back to the trees, he bent to shake Will awake.

'There are wheels on the road,' he whispered. Arthur and Aralia stirred at the sound of his voice and he shook them too.

'Traders?' Will sat up, suddenly alert.

'I think so,' James replied. 'We should go.'

It took them just a few minutes to collect their bags and remount the ferastia. The animals didn't seem to mind, softening their knees to make the process easier. Arthur and Aralia travelled together this time and Will rode with James. They all sat in silent drowsiness as the beasts carried them back onto the road. James found himself turning over Albert's words in his mind. Part of him wondered if he'd imagined the whole conversation, but the other part knew that couldn't be true.

'Not tired?' Will's voice startled him and he looked up.

'I can't stop thinking,' he said quietly. 'While you were all sleeping, I had a sort of dream. Albert was there, in my mind, talking to me.'

'Albert?' Will asked frowningly. 'Why?'

'He said he'd come to warn me of the spreading darkness.'

Will hissed through his teeth. 'I know they're out there, but where? No one ever speaks of the darkness and it's like it doesn't really exist.'

James shrugged and looked up at the darkening sky. 'She's building her forces. They're everywhere, lurking in the shadows where we can't see them.' His eyes found a tiny star, far away in the twilight haze. He thought how the star was like his own world in a way, in the same universe but too far away to easily reach.

'I've been thinking,' Will began after a long pause. 'The firestone came from a fire which was made eternal by the gift. What if all the crystals and gifts are bound to something eternal?'

James dropped his eyes to the ferastia's mane and slowly nodded. A few steps ahead, Arthur and Aralia turned to look back, their pale faces strangely alike.

'Nothing is truly eternal,' Aralia said softly. 'All elements shift and change.'

'Not if they're aided by magic,' Will responded. 'No fire is eternal, but the one which held the firestone was made eternal by the coin.'

'Surely all elements are eternal, even without magic?' Arthur's deep voice contradicted. 'Humans, in fact all living things, depend on them for survival. Earth, air, water, and fire; we need them all.'

'That's true,' James joined. 'Most things on earth are dependent on the elements. They shift and change, as Aralia said, but they don't disappear completely.'

'Fires burn out, water dries up, the earth moves, and air can become polluted,' Arthur continued. 'They each have their own cycle. None of them are completely eternal, but they've all been around in some form since time began.'

'And with magic, an element can be made eternal in one state for thousands of years or more,' Will added with a grin.

'If that's true, then we're looking for a gift that can make one of the other elements eternal,' James concluded. He grinned back at Will but his mind was already on the next stage of their journey.

A thoughtful peace settled between them. Eternity, the thread that tied the crystals together. It was so simple, yet none of them had thought of it before. Straightening his back, James breathed in the cool night air. In the fading gloom, his eyes fell on two stone bollards resting on either side of the road. Nudging Will, he pointed wordlessly towards them.

'It's the border,' Will announced sharply. 'We've made it to Henlos.'

Chapter 9

THE ferastia came to a halt and the companions dismounted. Leaving the animals nibbling at the grass, they walked over to the stone plinths. Both were waist height and engraved with climbing roses. Delicate stems wound around the circumference of each, spattered with blooming flowers. The stones were joined by a swathe of wild grass that formed a natural border.

'Henlos,' Arthur uttered, reflecting Will's earlier announcement.

'Do the roses symbolise anything?' James asked, running his fingers over a stony vine.

'Every region has a symbolic crest,' Will explained, moving to stand beside him. 'This one belongs to Henlos, the region of warriors. Camil is the region of knowledge, marked by a lotus.'

'It shouldn't take us long to reach the villages,' Will interrupted. He spread his map over the pillar and tapped two inky lines with his nail. 'These rivers are the Garin and Garone. They're the only two that go towards the east coast.'

'So you think the River Villages must be somewhere along those two rivers?' James queried.

A soft whining made him turn. For the first time in their journey, the ferastia looked physically tired. Their long necks hung limp and their eyes looked dull. Pulling her water flask from her bag, Aralia poured a little into her palm and let both animals drink.

'We should let them rest again,' she said softly. 'I know we haven't made much progress, but they're tired.'

She patted both ferastia, encouraging them to leave the road and find shelter amongst the undergrowth. They settled on a patch of grass to the side of the road, hidden behind low bramble bushes. The companions left them to rest and moved to sit a short distance away. Opening his bag, Will pulled out his sandwich and took a large bite. The scent of dried meat made James' stomach rumble and he drew out his own food packet. He tore the remaining sandwich in half, trying not to imagine roast dinners and pizza as he ate. A thudding sound made him turn. Will, Arthur and Aralia heard it too and they all looked towards the road.

'Traders,' Will warned. 'Stay low.'

They ducked and held themselves flat to the grass. Footsteps sounded on the road nearby and someone began shouting commands. These were delivered in a steady stream, the words merging together in a vicious tirade. After several long minutes, the voice fell quiet. In the ensuing silence, James pressed his face to the grass and tried to calm his thudding heart. It sounded loud in his ears and he was sure the traders would be able to hear it.

Suddenly, one of the ferastia let out a whinny. The companions cast each other anxious glances and held still. After what felt like a long time, the stillness was broken by a rustling sound. Turning his head a fraction, James saw two figures pushing their way between the brambles. The taller of the two sported a beard but his companion's face was hidden beneath a hood. Both saw the ferastia and stopped short before bending down to inspect the animals. For a moment, James thought he, Will, Arthur and Aralia wouldn't be seen in the gathering darkness, but the man then turned around.

'Arama ista min?' He stepped towards them, his heavy footfall causing the ground to tremble. His clothes stank of sweat and animal skins and James suppressed a gag.

'Ferra kin etts ferastia!'

A female voice spoke and the second trader stepped forward. Her hood fell back a fraction, revealing a pair of tattooed eyebrows. In one swift movement, she bent down and grabbed Aralia by the arm. Arthur reached out to pull her back but the woman kicked him in the chest. He fell on his back and she pinned him down with her foot.

'Espe utek?' the man barked.

The woman shook Aralia firmly. 'He ask question,' she said roughly. 'Where you go?' Aralia kept her lips stubbornly sealed and tried to wriggle away. 'I say, where you go?' the woman snapped and delivered a sharp slap to Aralia's cheek.

'The village,' Will interrupted desperately. 'We're going to the village.'

The woman rounded on him as he jumped to his feet. 'Village?'

Will nodded and the tips of his ears turned pink. 'A village east of here, M...'

'Mercy,' Aralia cut in. Her cheek was burning from the slap but she made no attempt to nurse it. 'We're going to Mercy, in the Rivel region.'

'Why you go there?' the woman demanded.

'My father lives there.' Aralia shook herself free from her captor's grasp and backed steadily away from her.

The man moved to block her path. 'You brought friends?' he asked. His accent was so thick that the words were barely intelligible. 'Is this boyfriend?' He kicked James in the shin and laughed.

'My friend,' Aralia answered sharply. 'I come with friends and my brother.' She pointed to Arthur who tried to respond but the woman pressed her heel more firmly into his chest.

'Elt maha idillih,' the woman hissed to her companion. 'We move.' She stepped away from Arthur and made another swipe at Aralia. 'You, take animal,' she commanded.

Kneeling beside the ferastia, Aralia gently stroked their necks. They rose at her touch and turned instinctively towards the road. The woman followed them and Aralia, Will, Arthur and James trailed behind. Emerging onto the road again, they stopped to stare. A small group of people stood clustered together at the border, all dressed in shabby brown cloaks. One or two looked up as the traders approached but most continued to stare at the ground. Their haunted expressions bothered James, but he wasn't quite sure why.

'Maha!' The man trader uttered a sharp bark and landed a fist in James' back. Wincing, James hurried to the ragged group behind his friends.

Another man emerged on the roadside, dressed as the other traders were. He approached the companions with a self-assured air and gestured for them to hold out their wrists. Left with no option, the companions stood helplessly as he bound each of their wrists together. Turning his eyes on the other captives, James saw that none of their hands were bound. For a moment, he thought this was strange but a realisation gradually dawned on him. He looked at his friends with horrified eyes but their expressions told him they already knew.

'Slaves,' he breathed. 'They're trading slaves.'

At the head of the group, the female trader mounted a ferastia and began gathering the slaves behind her. The two male traders brought up the rear, with the second ferastia sandwiched between them. While waiting for the next command, James let his eyes wander amongst the captives. There were eleven of them altogether, some old and some young. Five men took the lead, closely followed by four women, a young girl and a boy. As he stood looking, the boy suddenly turned around. He found himself being scrutinized by a pair of dark eyes and turned awkwardly away.

'Who are you looking at?' Will whispered.

'No one really,' James returned with a dismissive shrug.

The group began to move and he found his eyes wandering back to the boy. He had the strange feeling that he'd looked into those eyes before, but couldn't remember where. On several occasions, he noticed the boy staring too and became increasingly convinced that he knew him. Curious to find out if this was the case, he quickened his pace until he fell into step beside the boy. Several of the slaves shrank away from him but the boy kept walking at a steady pace.

'Remember you.'

The boy's voice was soft but strained and he kept his eyes fixed on the road ahead. The sound triggered a memory in James' mind and he suddenly knew where he'd seen the boy before.

'You're from the slave town,' he said in a low voice. 'In Garia.'

The boy nodded. 'We call Arima. It mean City of Souls.'

James recalled the rancid smoke that had filled the slave town. Someone had said it came from the burning bodies that were cremated in the towers. He hadn't known the town name then, but City of Souls seemed appropriate.

'What're you doing in Henlos?' he asked tentatively. 'Where're you going?'

'I ask same.'

James looked at the ground, unsure if he could trust the boy. 'We're travelling to the River Villages,' he divulged after a pause. 'We've come from Arissel, in Camil.' From the corner of his eye, he saw Will, Arthur and Aralia move in behind him but didn't turn to look at them.

'Long journey,' the boy said. 'I never see Camil. Only Garia and Henlos.'

'You're going there too.' Aralia's soft voice sounded behind them and the boy turned around. 'They're taking you to the River Villages,' she continued. 'Why?'

'I don't know where we go,' the boy replied. 'Journey has no end.'

'All journeys have to end eventually,' James pointed out.

The boy shrugged, a gesture that threatened to break his thin shoulders. 'We walk without knowledge. Journey never end for traveller. Not until we die. We walk or die.'

He sealed his lips, bringing the conversation to an abrupt end. James hovered by his side for a moment longer before stepping back to join his friends. They looked at him, searching for an explanation, but he said nothing. Turning his eyes to the road ahead, he realised that the boy was looking at him again.

'We walk lonely road,' he whispered. 'Darkness waits. Be careful.'

He turned away again and James was left to stare at his back. Feeling faintly uneasy, James slipped a hand into his trouser pocket, searching for the gold clock. His fingers met instead with the smooth surface of his phone and he gripped it tightly, trying to find some comfort in its touch. A sudden vibration trembled beneath his fingertips and he dropped the phone as if he'd been burnt. It was the staggered buzzing of a call and he instinctively knew that it would be from an unknown caller.

Chapter 10

THE clock ticked continually against James' chest. He could feel it counting his heartbeats as he walked, tucked in a hidden fold of his cloak. His phone was silent now, pressed deep into his trouser pocket. He didn't dare check if the call really was from the unknown caller and tried to forget the insistent vibration that had disturbed him just moments before.

Despite the persistent ticking of the clock, he lost track of time as they walked. The sky grew light and then dark again above the road but the traders never stopped to rest. Although the slaves were weak, they kept moving, driven forward by the invisible shackles that bound them to their fate. Occasionally, the traders tossed a water gourd between them but this quickly ran dry. The companions had finished their own supplies too and trailed behind the group with parched mouths and rumbling stomachs.

After many hours on the road, the landscape began to change. The dry, brambled verges opened out into a rolling green landscape. Low slopes stretched to the horizon, scattered with gnarled trees. Lush grass sprouted everywhere, sprinkled with colourful flowers. The air was warm under the unsheltered sky, a welcome change after the damp chill of the past few days.

'Eka xito!' The female trader brought her ferastia to a halt and turned to glare at the slaves. 'Eka xito,' she repeated. 'Hurry up. We reach village before dark.'

Her words sent a fresh wave of exhaustion over the group. It was as if they had been physically struck and several of the slaves dropped to their knees in the dirt. The two male traders dragged them to their feet again, spitting in their faces and pushing them forward. Watching the scene, James felt a deep admiration for the captives. They walked with a controlled effort that was born from a desperation to survive. Straightening his shoulders, he tried to shake off the fatigue that signalled an imminent end to the journey.

As the travellers drew closer to their destination, a breathless silence descended. It wasn't the tired silence which had so far accompanied them, but an anticipatory hush. The atmosphere tingled with it and James wondered if the slaves knew something that he didn't. He glanced at Will, but his friend had his eyes fixed on the road ahead. The sky was on the cusp of evening when the village came into sight. Tucked into the side of a low slope, it welcomed them towards it with its twinkling lights. The sight of it brought fresh energy to the group and their pace automatically quickened.

It didn't take them long to reach the first row of stilted houses. Several of the villagers came out to stand on their balconies, staring down at the travellers as they stumbled past. The traders eventually stopped outside a large, unstilted house that had thick shutters over the windows. Dismounting her ferastia, the female trader rapped sharply on the door. It opened instantly, held by an ancient woman dressed in grey robes. She stood aside to let the traders pass through but held out a hand to stop the slaves from following. One by one, they held out their symbolled wrists and she waved them inside. Her eyes narrowed as they fell on the companions but she glanced only briefly at their wrists before letting them pass.

They found themselves in a dimly lit corridor that was lined on either side with closed doors. At the far end, a set of steps led down to another door which stood open. The slaves were slowly filtering through this entrance and the companions hurried after them, driven forward by their grey robed host. On the other side of the door was a large room. It was low ceilinged and windowless and furnished with rows of neatly made beds. Stepping into it, James noted how like army barracks it looked. Unnerved by this observation, he turned instinctively back to the door. Out in the corridor, someone reached for the handle and the room suddenly went dark.

'Have they locked us in?' Will's voice came through the darkness, loud and indignant.

'Keep your voice down,' Arthur hissed. 'What did you expect?'

Holding out his palm, James let a small light form there. It illuminated the faces of his friends and they looked anxiously back at him. Stepping over to the nearest bed, he sat down on the thin mattress. The sheets stank of smoke and sweat but he swallowed his nausea and tried not to breathe in too deeply. The mattress dipped as Will sat down beside him. Arthur and Aralia perched themselves on the next bed along and tucked their bags between their feet.

'I don't think we'll get much sleep here,' Aralia whispered. 'I'm not lying down on this!' She prodded the greasy sheets and wrinkled her nose in disgust.

'You wouldn't do well in prison then,' Will remarked. 'Best not break any laws.' His attempt at light-heartedness fell flat as Aralia rolled her eyes at him.

'What is this place?' James quickly asked. 'An asylum?'

'More like a checkpoint I think.' Will dropped his bag onto

his lap and trapped it between his knees. 'It must be a place to keep the slaves, and us, until it's time to move on again.'

'Move on where I wonder?' Aralia mused.

'This is trading inn.'

A husky female voice rose from the darkness. James held up his light and squinted across the room, searching for the speaker. A thin shadow shifted on a nearby bed and slowly moved towards them.

'Who's there?' James challenged.

The shadow took on the shape of a woman. She came to a halt at the end of his bed and he saw a dark pair of eyes looking back at him.

'I 'ave no name,' the woman whispered. 'I am slave.'

Her accent sounded slightly French and James wondered if there was an equivalent region in this world. Holding his light higher, he searched for her face amongst the shadows. He found it just beyond the glowing circle, pale skinned and framed by a halo of grey hair. A faint smile played about her lips and her eyes sparkled despite the fatigue that was causing her back to bend.

'How long have you been here?' Aralia asked, her voice soft with concern.

The woman sighed and leant on the closest bed frame. 'Two day, maybe more.'

'Two days!' Will exclaimed. 'Do they feed you?'

'It's alright,' the woman replied gently. 'They want us alive. I was brought 'ere by private master, from Milou on west coast. Not many slave come from there; most come from towns in east.'

'Towns?' Aralia's eyes widened. 'As in slave towns? Are there more than one?'

'Towns all over world. Many from north continent come

80

past here, past trading inn.'

'What happens then?' Arthur asked bluntly. 'What do they want you here for?'

The woman looked at him curiously. James thought he detected suspicion in her eyes but the look was fleeting.

'You aren't slave,' she said simply. "Ow could you understand?'

'We're not slaves, but we're travellers,' Will said, leaning forward on the bed. 'We're on our way to the River Villages.'

'River Villages?' The woman's voice sounded suddenly tense. 'Road lead from 'ere, mouth of river Garin, to there. Villages are dark places. Slave go there too.'

'Why dark?' Aralia asked intently.

'Slave disappear.' A second voice spoke. Turning, James saw the slave boy who had travelled with them clambering out of his bed. His hair was tousled but his eyes were wide and alert. 'Taken by boat into sea,' he continued. 'I hear tale.'

A thought flashed across James' mind, one which he didn't dare believe. He looked at the boy with wide eyes and felt his heart leap in his chest.

'In these tales, is the name Arvora ever spoken?'

An uneasy silence fell over the room. Even the sound of gentle breathing seemed to stop. The boy and the woman looked at James fearfully and he felt the hairs on his neck prickling.

'We not speak this name,' the woman whispered.

James looked from her to the boy and back again. He'd never seen two people so afraid of a word before. He wanted to ask them more, but both turned away and slunk back to the shadows of their beds. Left alone, the companions looked at one another but said nothing. Here, amongst the slaves they had to be careful. Exhausted from the long journey, they moved into separate beds and reluctantly lay down. James let his light go out and wrapped his cloak tightly around him. The smell of the sheets was so terrible that he lay awake for a long time until his eyes forced themselves shut.

He woke up to the sound of whispering. Sitting up, he tried to bring the darkness into focus. His eyes fell on a shadowy figure standing beside Aralia's bed. A thin light shone out over the mattress, revealing the dark frame of the slave boy's face. Aralia sat looking up at him, her pale face contrasting his. They were whispering together and James tried not to listen, but their voices were oddly loud in the surrounding silence.

'You go, all go,' the boy whispered. 'Don't belong here.'

Aralia shivered and pulled her cloak tightly around her. 'Neither do you. We can't leave you here.'

'You cannot help,' the boy returned. 'This our life, our death. We bound by magic of generation.' To James' surprise, he leant down and took Aralia's hand in his own. She flinched, but didn't pull away. 'You not like us,' the boy continued. 'You not slave.'

As if sensing another presence, he turned to look at James. Their eyes met and James opened his mouth to speak. 'We might not be slaves, but we're trapped here like you,' he began.

'You not slave,' the boy repeated, shaking his head determinedly. 'I know way, you go. Please, you trust me,' he urged. 'Come, follow.'

James looked at Aralia and she nodded before slipping from her bed. She moved to shake Arthur and James turned to wake up Will. When they were all ready, the boy beckoned to them and they followed him across to the far corner of the room where an empty bed stood against the wall.

'Move,' the boy commanded, pointing at the rusty frame. 'Need to move.'

The companions each took a corner of the frame and lifted it aside. A pile of compressed earth rested beneath it and kneeling on the ground, the boy began digging it with his bare hands.

'What're you doing?' Will asked incredulously.

'Tunnel, under here,' the boy replied. 'Dug by slave for many century. He show me.' He gestured to a nearby bed where an old man lay sleeping. 'He know many tale.'

Aralia knelt beside the boy and looked at him intently. 'A tunnel? Are you sure?'

'Slave dig tunnel, but bound by magic and can't escape.' The boy sat back on his heels and brushed the dirt from his hands. 'Look.'

An opening had appeared in the ground in front of him. It was small and dark but undeniably real. Squatting beside it, James formed a new light and held it over the entrance.

'Any idea where it goes?' he asked.

The boy shrugged. 'You find out. Go. No waste time.'

James looked at his friends and they nodded in acceptance. Letting his light float down first, he lowered himself in after it. The opening was tight and the earth crumbled around him as he squeezed through. Before shifting his torso to join his legs, he reached out to shake the slave boy's hand. The boy nodded at him but didn't extend his own hand in return. James nodded back before pushing the rest of his body into the tunnel. The light revealed a narrow passageway that was only just wide enough to crawl through. He began inching forward, leaving enough room for his friends to squeeze down behind him.

Rounding a sharp bend, James suddenly found himself at a dead end. He ran his fingers over the earthy wall in front of him, hoping to find an opening. A thin layer of dust rubbed off on his fingertips but the wall was otherwise solid. Balancing on his knees, he reached up to the tunnel feel roof. His hands met with a smooth panel that felt like a trapdoor of some kind. Little by little, he felt his way across the surface until his fingers met with a thin gap. Pressing his fingers into this crack, he jerked his hands upwards but the panel didn't move.

'What's going on?' Will hissed from behind him. 'You're suffocating us with all this dust.'

Pulling himself into a ball, James smashed his shoulder upwards with full force. There was a soft thud somewhere above as the panel came loose. Rubbing dust from his eyes, he latched his hands onto the edge of the opening he'd created and hauled himself upwards. He found himself sitting in a small room that was empty apart from a fireplace. The light from the tunnel illuminated peeling walls, cracked skirting boards and a threadbare carpet.

'There's a room up here,' he announced a little too loudly. 'Come out.' Scrambling to his feet, he stepped away from the trapdoor and waited for his friends to join him.

'We're still in the building then,' Will said as he hauled himself from the tunnel. 'Clearly they didn't think to dig a tunnel outside.'

'I don't think they could,' Aralia's voice drifted up behind him. 'Slaves are confined to the limits of the building.'

Crossing the room, James peered around the edge of the open door. His eyes fell on the main hallway that they'd walked down a few hours before. It was for the moment empty and he gestured for Will, Arthur and Aralia to join him. The sound of voices suddenly startled them. Will extinguished the light and they stood frozen in the darkness. Watching the hallway, James saw one of the male traders emerge from a doorway. He paused to take a swig from the glass in his hand before stumbling down the passage. The female trader appeared behind him. She followed in his wake as he stumbled down the steps towards the dormitory.

'We should go now,' James whispered. 'They're going into the dormitory.'

Before they could move, the woman's voice sounded again. 'Aram Morvel,' she barked. 'Visti iego?'

'They know,' Aralia gasped. 'They know we've escaped. Aram means gone. What d'we do?'

James slipped out into the hallway but a hiss from Will drew him back. 'Hey wait, here's another door back here.'

There was a soft thud as someone knocked over a chair. No one stopped to retrieve it however as they followed each other's shadows across the room. A soft click suggested that the door had been opened and a wave of fresh air brushed against their faces.

'Not so fast.'

An unfamiliar voice paralysed them mid-movement. A light glimmered nearby and James gasped as a wrinkled, barely feminine face appeared just centimetres from his own. He stumbled backwards as the floating visage bared a row of rotting teeth. As his eyes adjusted, he realised that the face belonged to their ancient host.

'I think you don't run,' the woman croaked. 'You stay here.'

'Don't listen to her,' Arthur called from the doorway. 'Run!'

James stepped towards the exit but a gurgling sound made him turn again. His heart dropped as he saw the woman standing with her hand fixed around Aralia's throat.

'I scream, they come,' she jeered. 'She scream, she die.' She tightened her grip on Aralia's neck, causing her to choke.

'Rai, fight her!' Arthur shouted.

He burst back into the room and locked eyes with his sister. A beam of light burst from his fingers and in the same moment,

Aralia cracked her head against the woman's face. Surprised, the old lady let go and Aralia ran for the door. Arthur and James hurried after her, ducking as a bright stream of light rushed in from the hallway.

Chapter 11

JAMES tried to ignore the staring faces of the villagers as he, Will, Arthur and Aralia ran into the street. No one spoke to them or offered them any help, they just stood staring down from their balconies. The street was in reality a grassy path that ran through the centre of the village. It cut a direct line between the houses and disappeared into the darkness beyond.

The companions ran blindly, all sense of direction erased by their need to escape. Light flashed from the inn doorway behind them, a streak of red that burst against a nearby house. Several of the occupants screamed and this was followed by the sound of a door slamming shut. The companions kept to the path at first but with the traders close behind them, they darted behind the houses. A voice suddenly called out through the darkness. It was a wordless cry and came from somewhere above them.

'Issa mayha.' The voice sounded again. It had a feminine tone but the accent was harsh. 'Issa mayha. This way.'

A beam of light flashed directly behind the companions. The residual glow revealed the outline of a house in front of them. Wooden steps led up to a balcony where a stranger stood waiting. Left with no choice, they began to climb. A white hot flare struck the bottom step, causing the whole frame to shake.

It fizzled out just behind James' feet but he managed to dodge out of the way. On reaching the balcony, the stranger grabbed him by the arm and pulled him through an open doorway. He found himself thrust into more darkness and heard the door slam shut behind him.

He stood absolutely still, waiting for some kind of signal. A soft light then began to fill the surrounding space and he looked up. His eyes fell first on Will, Arthur and Aralia, but quickly moved to observe the woman standing by the door. She was tall but her face and hands were finely boned. Her sharp eyes flicked between her guests, gentle but searching. Stepping away from the door, she gestured for the companions to follow her. They left the sparsely furnished front room behind and entered an adjoining kitchen. The woman gestured for them to sit at the table before turning away to place a kettle on the stove.

'Home,' she said over her shoulder. 'Safe here.'

She waved her hand and the stove lit up. Delicious smells began seeping from a pan on the hob, a mixture of cinnamon and other spices. The woman didn't speak as she stirred the contents and the companions simply watched her work. The kettle whistled and she whisked it from the hob. She poured the steaming water into four cups and set them on the table.

'Please, drink,' she urged.

Returning to the stove, she began spooning the deliciously scented food into bowls before placing them on the table alongside the mugs. Before anyone could thank her, she disappeared into the front room. Glancing at each other, the companions picked up their spoons and began to eat. The food was some kind of sweet stew that reminded James of rice pudding. It was warm and quite pleasant apart from the lumpy consistency.

By the time the woman re-entered the kitchen, all four

bowls were empty. James, Will, Arthur and Aralia turned to greet her, only to find she was no longer alone. A young boy and girl hovered behind her, both wrapped in blankets. They stared at the companions but didn't step any closer. The woman moved to clear away the bowls, leaving the children standing in the doorway.

'Can I help?' Aralia queried, half rising from her chair. She picked up her cup but the woman took it from her.

'You sit,' she commanded with the flicker of a smile. 'Look tired. I give you bed.'

'Why are you helping us?' Will asked bluntly. 'You don't know us.'

'You don't know me, but you came in.' The woman sat down at the table and the little girl jumped onto her lap. 'This Flora, my daughter,' she said, stroking the girl's hair. 'Come,' she instructed the boy but he stuck out his tongue and ran into the front room. 'My son, Mikkel,' she continued with a smile. 'I am Ella, from the Kurn family.'

'James, from the Fynch family and Will, from the Aeton family,' Arthur announced, gesturing to both of them respectively. 'I'm Arthur, from the Silene family and this is my sister, Aralia.'

Ella smiled again but her eyes narrowed. 'I know what inn is for,' she said softly. 'We see slave come and go. You are not first to run from them and you will not be last.'

'How d'you know we came from the inn?' Aralia asked, carefully detaching Flora's fingers from her hair.

'Why else were you running?'

'We were captured by traders at the Henlan border,' James quietly confirmed.

'You not first people I help,' Ella said. 'It is why I understand your language. I learn from people.' Pushing Flora from her lap, she moved to stand in the doorway. 'Come now, I give you blankets. You must be tired.'

Leading them into the front room, she gestured to a pile of cushions in the corner. A few blankets had been placed on a chair beside them, along with a patchwork quilt.

'Here, use these,' she offered. 'Washroom is through here.' She pointed to a door in the kitchen which was currently blocked by Flora and Mikkel who stood tossing a ball of light between them. 'I sleep above with the children,' she continued. 'You stay here, it is your home tonight.' She turned towards the stairs which were almost invisible in the shadow of a large alcove.

'How far is it to the River Villages?' James spoke quietly but Ella heard him and froze.

'Why you ask?' She kept her face to the stairs, her posture rigid.

'That's where we're going.'

Ella spun around, her eyes darting across the room to where her children stood. 'You wait,' she said sharply. 'Will put children to bed, then talk.'

James, Will, Arthur and Aralia returned to the kitchen table and sat in silence. Ella joined them several minutes later, crossing over to the stove to brew a fresh pot of tea.

'You go to River Village.' She sat down at the table and looked at each of them in turn. 'Why?'

'We're hoping to meet a friend there,' Arthur replied, his voice low and serious. 'We don't know the way.'

Ella's expression warmed. 'It must be special friend for you to travel there.' She rose again and poured the tea before continuing. 'This village, Senya, is first of seven. It take a day or two to reach next, Eriphas.'

'Why are slaves brought here, to the villages?' James leant

forward on the table, his hands clasped around his steaming cup.

A nervous expression flickered across Ella's features. 'No one really know. They come, they go and are never seen again.'

'How often do they come through here?' Will asked, wiping a dribble of tea from his chin. 'You speak like you know more about them.'

'I know little. They come every seven day, maybe more. Not many like you.' She rose abruptly from her chair and gestured to the doorway. 'You must rest before morning,' she commanded. 'In Henlos, we say God Tsov, meaning good sleep.'

'God Tsov,' Aralia returned as Ella left the room.

They heard her climbing the stairs and everything went quiet. Leaving their unfinished drinks on the table, they moved into the front room. Aralia distributed the blankets and cushions before constructing her own makeshift bed on the floor.

'Definitely more comfortable than the roadside,' she murmured, more to herself than anyone else.

'Only a day or two to the next village,' James whispered as he wrapped himself in an orange blanket. The wool was itchy, but he was grateful for the warmth.

'Right now, I don't ever want to think about walking again,' Will muttered.

'Let's not then,' Arthur said. He extinguished the orb that had followed them in from the kitchen and the room went dark.

'God Tsov,' James whispered and Will, Arthur and Aralia returned the expression in chorus.

Closing his eyes, James felt a calm drowsiness wash over him. Too tired to even think about using the washroom, he buried his face in the orange blanket and drifted into a deep slumber. He was lost in the depths of some imaginary world when a loud banging caused him to stir. At first he thought he was still dreaming, but he quickly realised the noise was coming from somewhere nearby. Eyes still closed, he reached for his phone. His hand fell on wooden floorboards and he sat up sharply, suddenly remembering where he was.

'What's that?' Will sat up too and rubbed the sleep from his eyes. 'Is it morning already?'

'There's someone at the door,' James replied tensely. A harsh shout accompanied the banging and he looked nervously at Will. 'We can't have been asleep for long. It's only just getting light.' He gestured to the curtained window, the edges of which were illuminated by the faint light of morning.

'We should get out of here,' Will uttered, throwing off his blanket. 'It must be the traders.'

Another sound disturbed them and they turned to see Ella stumbling down the stairs. She was dressed in a shabby green dressing gown and her hair had formed a frazzled halo about her face. She looked from the companions to the door and back again, her eyes burning. Pressing a finger to her lips, she crept over to the window and peered through the curtains.

'Who is it?' Arthur sat bolt upright and looked at Ella with dazed eyes. 'Are they here for us?'

'It is my husband.' Ella turned to them but couldn't meet their eyes.

'Your husband?' Aralia gasped. She stumbled to her feet, her blanket still draped about her shoulders. 'Can't he let himself in?'

Ella slowly shook her head and a soft flush spread across her cheeks. 'I lock door from inside. He…' She paused and let the curtain slip from between her fingers. 'He is trader.'

'A trader!' Will hissed accusingly. 'I thought you wanted to help us.'

'I do,' Ella stammered, shrinking back against the wall. 'You must believe me. I never know when he come home. He work abroad, in South.'

'Did you know he was in the village last night?' James asked, his tone a fraction too harsh.

The door began shaking violently and Ella stepped away from it, her eyes cool and frightened. 'I want to help you,' she whispered. 'Come, I show you way out of here, then maybe you believe me.' She led the way into the kitchen and opened the door she had pointed to earlier that night. It was dark on the other side but a wave of fresh air wafted through. 'Stairs lead to washroom and storeroom,' she continued. 'Door there will take you to road.'

Aralia reached out to grasp Ella's hand. 'Thank you for helping us. We do believe you, really.'

'I understand,' Ella returned. 'Be safe now on your journey. Hygge Eise. It mean good travels.'

As these words left her lips, the front door flew open. Ella waved them onto the storeroom stairs and slammed the kitchen door shut behind them. Thrust into darkness, James, Will, Arthur and Aralia stood still and listened. A man began shouting again and Ella tried to calm him with her soft tones. Eventually, she succeeded and everything went quiet. Igniting a small light, Will started down the stairs. James, Arthur and Aralia followed him, descending into the room below. They found themselves standing in a draughty space filled with sacks and barrels. Dried herbs and meat hung from the ceiling, adding a musty tinge to the air. Lifting the lid off one of the barrels, Will plunged his hand inside and drew out two apples.

'For the road,' he explained.

Encouraged, Arthur and James took some fruit too. Aralia watched them reproachfully but eventually joined in. They took just enough food to supply them for a few days and filled their water bottles from the jug in the washroom. They each took turns to wash their faces before meeting at the base of the stairs. The outside door opened onto the central village path that lay empty under the early morning sky. The companions crept out in single file, scanning their surroundings for any signs of danger.

They kept to the shadows where they could, even though no one was about. Freedom was not yet theirs, not until they'd left the village behind them. Their route soon joined the trading road which wound its way across the sloping landscape. Keen to leave the village behind, they picked up their pace and headed towards the brightening horizon. It wasn't long before the village was swallowed by the hills and they turned to one another with relieved expressions.

'We were lucky this time,' Arthur said quietly.

They hadn't been walking long when Will uttered a soft exclamation and stopped in his tracks. He pointed down the slope to their right, his eyes alight with excitement. Far below, where the landscape flattened out, a silvery ribbon glittered in the morning sunlight. Its meandering form stretched as far as the eye could see, slithering through the countryside like a shimmering snake.

'Is that one of the rivers?' Aralia asked.

Will nodded. 'The Garin. We're one step closer already.'

Keen to reach the river before evening, they veered off the road and began clambering down the slope. The ground was uneven, making the going tough, but they pushed on anyway. Time slipped by around them and James began to feel dizzy from concentrating so hard on his feet.

The sun was already high in the sky by the time they reached the base of the slope. It carried no warmth but it chased away the shadows from the surrounding landscape. The silver band transformed into a great swathe of water, rippling calmly between the low banks.

'We made it!' Will exclaimed, coming to an abrupt halt. 'Here.' He took the map from his pocket and spread it out on the grass. 'This is where we are,' he continued, pointing to a thin line. 'The next village must lie somewhere along the river.'

'If we stay close to it, we'll be able to trace our route more accurately,' Arthur added.

Flinging his bag onto the grass, James breathed the fresh air deep into his lungs. The river glistened invitingly and he felt the urge to throw himself in. Kneeling at the water's edge, he dipped his hands beneath the cooling surface. Will joined him on the bank and James flicked some droplets in his direction. Shrinking away in mock horror, Will scooped up a large handful and dropped it over James' head. With a sudden whoop, Arthur charged past them both and plunged into the water. Bursting through the surface, he called for them to join him. Needing little encouragement, they removed their shoes and outer layers before diving in.

'Come on Rai, join us!' Arthur shouted.

She shook her head but removed her shoes and sat on the bank with her feet in the water. Arthur ducked beneath the surface and suddenly she was in the river too, gasping for air. Her squeals of protest turned to laughter as she chased her brother into deeper territory. Once they were suitably freezing, the companions pulled themselves from the water. Taking an apple from his bag, James sat with his feet trailing in the shallows.

A faint buzzing disturbed his thoughts and he batted the

surrounding air, suspecting a fly. It was only on the fourth vibration that he realised where it was coming from and his stomach dropped. Throwing his apple core away, he reached into his pocket and drew his phone. The screen was black, as if the battery had died, but the unknown caller continued to ring.

Chapter 12

JAMES shivered but it wasn't from the cold. He knew that he shouldn't have brought his phone with him to this world but there hadn't been time to think. By the time he'd realised, it was too late. Part of him had hoped that it wouldn't be a problem, even though he knew this wouldn't be the case. Pulling his feet from the water, he gripped the device tightly in his hand. His fingertips trembled with the monotonous vibrations, going on and on like the drone of an enraged wasp.

'James, what is it?' Aralia sat down beside him, her damp hair spraying him with water droplets. 'You look like you've seen a ghost.'

James turned to look at her, his expression serious. 'We have to go,' he said tensely. 'Now.'

'What's happened?' Aralia persisted. 'What's changed your mood so quickly?'

Fixing his gaze on the rippling water, James opened his hand. The phone had stopped vibrating, but he was afraid the caller might try again.

'A phone?' Will came closer, his cloak wrapped tightly around his shivering body. 'Why d'you have it with you?' He leant in to take a better look but didn't try to touch it.

'I didn't really mean to bring it,' James shrugged. 'It's been ringing, like it did before.'

Will's eyes narrowed. 'Ringing? Why?'

'I don't know.'

'What if it's them?' Will let his words hang in the air for a moment before continuing. 'The dark, I mean. What if they're using it to follow you, like they did before?' He took the device from James' palm and placed it on the ground. 'You have to destroy it.'

James nodded slowly. He knew Will was right but felt reluctant nonetheless. His parents wouldn't be pleased if he brought home another broken phone. Rising to his feet, he stood looking down at the black rectangle lying in the grass. Will stood just a few steps away with Aralia and Arthur flanking him.

'Do it now,' Arthur encouraged. 'If you can't, I will.'

Prising a stone from the earth, James held it above the pristine screen. The device was too new to have anything saved on it but it still seemed like a waste. Stretching his arm to its full height, he paused for just a second longer before plunging his hand downwards. The stone smashed the glass instantly and the case buckled under the pressure. James brought the shard down one more time before bending to gather up the broken pieces.

'Well, there you go,' he muttered. 'Job done.' He tucked the pieces at the bottom of his bag where they could be forgotten.

'Alright,' Will stated. 'We should start moving again.'

They began walking in a bedraggled line along the riverbank. Patches of bramble occasionally blocked their path but the route was mostly straight. The river gradually widened alongside them, stretching out to touch the opposite bank. At times, an uneven bed was visible through the shallow water, a mixture of rocks and scattered shale. The sinking sun had transformed the water into a golden mirror. It was almost too bright to look at, the smooth surface burning with light.

'The golden hour,' Aralia announced to no one in particular.

Shading his eyes, James looked to where the gleaming ribbon rounded a nearby bend. There, the surface appeared to change, the water driven forward by a faster current. A myriad of whirlpools danced against the bank, spun out of control by the river's undertow. James found his gaze continually drawn to these glittering eddies, even though the brightness blotted his vision. Mesmerised, his feet pounded a regular rhythm on the grass and he became lost in thought.

He was brought to a sudden halt by Will who had stopped in front of him. Blinking bruised colours from his eyes, he brought himself back to the present moment. Under the deepening clouds of evening, the water had changed again. An even stronger current now gripped it from below, turning the gentle ripples into a heaving swell. The writhing mass was both majestic and malicious, becoming more powerful as it rounded another bend. Spray filled the surrounding air, turned pink and orange by the blossoming sunset.

'Incredible!' Will called over the sound of roaring water.

'Can we check out the map?' Arthur shouted back.

Will pulled the roll of paper from his pocket and opened it out. Arthur, Aralia and James gathered around him, focusing their attention on the area surrounding the Garin.

'Here, look!' Will pointed to a cluster of dots on the opposite side of the river. 'These weren't there before,' he continued excitedly. 'I didn't even know the map could do that. What d'you think?'

Peering at the crumpled paper, James concentrated on the group of black dots beneath Will's fingernail. They were drawn beside the Garin, almost too small to see, but not quite.

'Are they houses?' James was close enough to Will to not have to shout above the noise of the river.

'I think so,' Will replied. 'The fact that they've just appeared on the map must mean they're close. I think they must belong to the next village.'

'Eriphas,' Aralia remembered. 'That's the name Ella gave us.'

'The houses are on the opposite side of the river to us,' Arthur observed. 'We'll have to cross it.' He looked uneasily at the rushing water tugging against the bank. 'There must be a boat or at least a bridge.'

'Let's walk a little further and find out,' Will suggested.

They wandered along the bank, scanning the river for any sign of a boat or bridge. The brightness of the water made it difficult to see and they were forced to shade their eyes. Arthur was the first to spot something up ahead. He stopped abruptly and pointed to where the water joined the horizon. A dark silhouette lay across the river and the companions hurried eagerly towards it. As they drew closer, it became apparent that the silhouette was a bridge, or the remains of one at least. The rotting frame stretched across most of the river but broke away just before it reached the opposite bank.

'Well, it's something,' Arthur remarked.

'We can't cross that,' Will objected. 'We'd be signing our own death warrants. Look how fierce the current is.'

'There must be another way,' James agreed.

'Shame your dad didn't write about how he got to the village,' Arthur said sarcastically.

'Don't blame my dad for this,' Will snapped. 'Maybe we should've crossed the river when we first joined it.'

James lowered his bag to the ground, wishing he could sit down beside it. 'It doesn't look so bad,' he levelled.

'Come on James, you'd be an idiot to even consider it,' Will returned. 'Even if we did manage to cross the bridge, we'd still have to jump the last bit.'

Aralia stepped between the boys, arms folded across her chest. 'It seems we have three options,' she said evenly. 'We could try to cross the bridge, but that does come with a risk. Alternatively, we could go back to where we started, but that would waste time. Finally, we could not go to Eriphas at all. It's only one out of five other villages.'

The boys stared at her, their animosity forgotten. 'We can't go back,' Arthur said eventually. 'We really would be wasting time.'

'We don't know how far it is to the next village,' Will added. 'We don't know its name either.'

'Then I suppose that leaves us with one option,' Aralia concluded. 'We cross the bridge.'

James looked across the foaming river. The distance between the end of the broken bridge and the bank was little more than a grown man's stride, but the current was treacherous. He could feel fresh urgency swelling in his chest and swiftly made up his mind.

'We cross the bridge,' he said, echoing Aralia's words. 'What's the worst that could happen?'

No one responded and he was glad. The answer lay in the raging current that pounded between both banks. Walking over to where the bridge met the grass, he stepped carefully onto the wooden planks. These creaked beneath his weight and he grabbed onto the railing for support. Much of the frame was missing but he walked carefully forward, keeping his eyes fixed on his feet. The bridge trembled beneath him and turning, he saw Will, Arthur and Aralia tentatively stepping onto the planks behind him.

It felt like a long time before he reached the end of the bridge. Standing close to the edge, he removed his bag and launched it into the air. It sailed over the boiling water and landed safely on the other side. Swallowing his fear, he looked over his shoulder again. Arthur had stopped just behind him and was lowering his own bag onto the decaying planks. Rummaging inside, he pulled out a length of rope and held it out to James, gesturing for him to tie it around his waist.

'Just in case,' he shouted. 'Use two half hitch knots.'

Nodding, James took the rope and tied it around himself with shaking fingers. He still remembered how to tie half hitch knots, having learnt them once at school. Once the rope was secured, he passed the free end to Arthur before turning to face the opposite bank. Taking a few steps back, he braced himself before running forward and leaping from the bridge. Time seemed to slow down as he sailed across the river and landed with a thud on the other side. Scrambling to his feet, he watched as Arthur lashed the other end of the rope around his own waist and jumped. He landed heavily on the grass beside James and untied the rope again before throwing it across to Will.

Will tied the rope around himself with deft fingers before thrusting himself from the bridge. His feet left the planks but he lost momentum almost instantly. Flailing in mid-air, he tried to grab onto a loose plank but too late. His legs hit the water and the current quickly sucked him under. The rope around James' waist gave a sudden jerk, pulling him towards the river.

'Come on,' he shouted to Arthur. 'Help me pull him in.'

He ran a little way along the bank, trying to resist the tug of the current. Undoing the knot at his waist, he pulled the rope free and passed a section of it to Arthur. In the centre of the river, Will's head emerged above the swell. Desperate to help him, James and Arthur began to pull at the rope, but the current was too strong. It tugged at the narrow cord, threatening to drag them into the river too.

'The ground's too soft,' James called. 'We're slipping.'

A powerful jerk suddenly tightened the rope. It was powerful but neither James nor Arthur had time to turn around and see what had caused it. The wrench came again, dragging Will swiftly towards the bank. As soon as he was close enough, he reached for a grassy tuft and tried to pull himself free from the current. James moved to help but a dark cloaked figure pushed past him and bent to heave Will from the water. Lying on the grass, Will coughed up a mouthful of water and the stranger turned him onto his side.

Dropping the rope, Arthur and James knelt beside him. The stranger however picked up the coil and tossed it across the water to where Aralia stood anxiously waiting. She caught it and secured it to her person before leaping across the river. Although her stride was powerful, she fell against the bank and the stranger hurried to her rescue. After making sure she was safe, the mysterious figure finally turned around.

'Rivisa elor ubrika emba,' a male voice uttered. Beneath the hood, a pair of gold flecked eyes looked outwards from a dusky skinned face.

'I'm sorry, but we don't understand your language,' Aralia said gently. 'We've come from Camil.'

The man acknowledged her apology with a nod. 'You risked your lives,' he said reproachfully. 'You are not the first to try and cross the river unaided.' He spoke with his hands, his mannerisms soft and inoffensive.

'How are people meant to cross?' James asked. 'We couldn't find another way.'

'They travel by boat. Few try to cross the bridge. Those who do often drown.'

James shivered and bent to gather up the rope. 'Thank you for helping us,' he said as he straightened up again. 'The outcome clearly could have been different.'

'Oede,' the stranger revealed, gesturing to himself. 'My name is Oede.'

'I'm James and these are my friends, Will, Arthur and Aralia.' James noticed how Oede didn't mention his family name and couldn't help wondering why.

'Greetings, strangers,' Oede said and stepped forward to shake each of their hands in turn.

Looking away from the river for the first time, James saw the faint outline of houses on the horizon. In the gathering gloom of early evening, they had become mere shadows on the marshy landscape.

'Do you live over there, in the village?' Aralia asked, speaking before James had the chance. 'Your accent isn't Henlan.'

Oede's golden eyes turned on her and he smiled. 'Your ear is good. Here I live and work, but I come from Garia. I have not been here long.' He gestured towards the houses and his smile widened. 'You have come tonight to join many others. On this night, people travel from across the northern regions to celebrate the light. It gives me great pleasure to welcome you to Eriphas, to the Bakkaran Festival of Fire.'

Chapter 13

OEDE led the companions away from the river. The rushing water grew quieter as they walked towards the village, soon fading to a gentle rumble. Another sound then replaced it, a murmur that rose from amongst the shadowy houses. Straining his ears, James realised it was the drone of many voices.

Most of the houses were two or three storeys high and built from uneven planks. The imperfect nature of each build gave the village an unconventional appearance. It looked as if it might belong more comfortably in a fairytale than here, in trading territory. The houses cast long shadows onto the surrounding grass. These were disturbed by hundreds of twinkling orbs that hung between the windows. The light revealed a narrow pathway between the buildings and Oede led the way onto it.

The path was brought to an end by an archway. The delicate metal frame curved to meet a reverse triangle that rested right at the top. On the other side of the arch, a cobbled courtyard lay between the houses. It was connected to the surrounding village by more paths that lay around its circumference. In the centre of the courtyard, a huge bonfire stack stood waiting. It was as yet unlit, but four fiery braziers were fixed around it.

'What is this festival exactly?' James asked, turning to Oede who had stopped at the edge of the courtyard. 'Why are there so many people?'

The voices they'd heard from outside the village came from crowds of people filling the courtyard. They were everywhere, their individual tones merging to create a mellow hum. Sounds mingled with scents as wafts of sizzling meat, salt, and caramel drifted through the air. The smell was both satisfying and sickening, reminding James of the country fairs he'd been to as a child. The aromas came from stalls which lined the courtyard, open tents decorated with orbs and colourful streamers.

'You do not know what happens here?'

Oede glanced towards the bonfire and James followed his gaze. He noticed for the first time that many people in the crowd were holding books. Some only held one or two while others bore stacks of five or more. He turned to Oede who looked back at him with solemn eyes.

'Perhaps you have answered your own question,' Oede observed.

'They're here to burn books,' Will said incredulously. 'Why?'

'You do not know?' Oede repeated, his eyes narrowing. 'Why are you here, if not for the burning?'

'We're heading to Mercy, in Rivel,' Aralia quickly lied. 'We thought we'd stop here for the night.' She nibbled a fingernail and glanced at the boys for support.

Oede nodded but his eyes still looked at them searchingly. 'You cannot be here without a book. All villagers and travellers bring books to the burning.'

'Why?' Will repeated. 'What's the burning for?'

'It happens every seventh year.' Oede waved his hands and looked upward, as if trying to find the right words. 'Dark magic,' he said eventually. 'They burn dark magic.'

No one said anything. Oede's voice floated menacingly

around them, waiting to answer questions that no one dared ask. It felt like a long time before Oede stepped away from the archway they had paused beneath and beckoned for them to follow him. He began threading his way through the milling throngs and the companions hurried to catch up. A few people turned to stare as the group pushed past, as if sensing the presence of strangers. Oede kept up a smooth pace until he'd reached the safety of another archway. Passing into the street beyond, he slowed down but still didn't stop.

'Book burning began a long time ago,' he explained on an outward breath. 'The last Dark Master wanted all evidence of light magic to be destroyed. After his death however, people began burning dark magic. Today, they burn dark magic to make light.'

'A Dark Master?' James asked, taking a double step to keep pace. 'D'you mean Jasper?'

'Only when books burn do we say his name,' Oede returned harshly. 'He was born here, in Eriphas, where we now condemn him to a second death and call for the light. We pray that never again will there be one like him.'

James watched Oede closely as he spoke. He was fiddling with a waxed thread around his neck at the end of which was a small, green stone.

'Jasper,' he heard Aralia whisper.

Oede turned on her, his golden eyes burning. 'To speak his name, you cannot know of his darkness,' he hissed and let the necklace fall beneath his cloak.

His words created a tense silence. James glanced at his friends. Will caught his eye and nodded in recognition of the same thought. The mention of Jasper and his connection with the River Villages confirmed their earlier theories. If Arvora did exist here, Arvad had to fit in somewhere too. If he did, then they were once again gaining speed in the race against the dark.

'Here, stop.'

Oede's voice brought the companions to a halt. They'd reached the end of the street and were standing outside a narrow building. The door stood open and Oede stepped aside to wave them through.

'You'll find books in here,' he gruffly informed them.

On the other side of the door, a large room greeted them. Faded furniture lined the edges, stacked precariously against the walls. Wooden crates filled the remaining spaces, stuffed with an array of fabrics, tableware and paintings. The space had a vintage smell, a mixture of moth-eaten clothes and old attics. It reminded James of an antique shop, only much less organised. Nothing was labelled and there was no one there to answer questions.

Just behind the front door, the base section of a stairway peeped from behind a heavy curtain. Intrigued, James pushed the dusty fabric aside and peered upwards. There appeared to be another room at the top and he began to climb. The final tread met with a small room. It was more orderly than the one below but just as crowded. Rows of display cases lined the walls, all filled with silver trinkets.

'Strange place to have a shop.'

James turned to find Will behind him and nodded. 'They must sell to the villagers and traders.'

He slipped a ring from a nearby stand and tried it on. The silver band, set with a tiny yellow gemstone, only just fitted around his little finger. He put it back on the stand before turning his attention to a display of nautical instruments.

'Ida era?'

He spun around to see who had spoken. An old man stood in the doorless frame of an adjacent room, his watery eyes staring at them through a pair of thick lensed glasses.

'Ida era?' he repeated.

'Oh, erm, we're looking for some books,' James tried.

'For the burning,' Will added, waggling his fingers like flames.

The man pulled a white hair from his jumper and shook his head. 'Hire one Henlos, ise su?' He pointed to his lips on which a bead of saliva was forming.

'He only speaks Henlan.' Aralia's voice sounded and pushing past Will and James, she folded her hands as if reading a book. James noticed that she wore a ring on her finger, the same one he'd tried on moments before.

The man's face lit up. 'Brene?' he asked and beckoned for them all to follow him into the next room.

'Elia hos impala flora.' Oede appeared in the doorway, followed by Arthur, and the old man grinned widely.

'Oede! Ah, ita.' He gestured widely to the room they had entered. It was filled with shelves which were packed with endless rows of books. 'Impala flora,' he continued. 'Itu Iudia.'

'These are cheap, you can take some for the burning,' Oede quickly translated as the man continued to speak. 'All villagers and many travellers and traders come here for books on this day. This is the owner, Ongra. He lives here with his wife Maira. They have seen eleven burnings.'

'He must have lived here all his life,' Will calculated.

'Where do all the books come from?' James asked, pulling one from a nearby shelf. 'Can you ask if he's ever heard of a story called Arvad the Wanderer?'

'The books come from all over the world,' Oede relayed after a brief conversation with Ongra. 'Strangers bring them and swap them for others or just leave them here. As for the tale you speak of, he knows of it but says there are no copies here.'

Before anyone could speak again, a great shout rose from the courtyard. It was the sound of many voices cheering, a mixture of celebratory joy and greedy anticipation. It was the kind of shout that belonged to ancient amphitheatres in expectation of watching violence and bloodshed.

'The burning soon begins,' Oede announced. 'The fire will be lit in the last moment of twilight. We must hurry.'

Will scraped together a few coins and paid for the books. Aralia added in a little money of her own for the ring she'd selected. Once change had been exchanged, Oede led the way downstairs and back onto the street. Out here, the chanting voices were much more oppressive. The closer they were to the courtyard, the worse it became. It was hot too, the fiery braziers adding to the heat of human bodies. Many people now held their own torches too, wooden poles that glowed with unnatural flames.

Oede forged the way through the crowd and the companions followed him. He didn't stop until they'd reached the centre of the courtyard where the bonfire barriers began. They huddled together in what little space was available, standing just metres away from the unlit stack. The chanting voices had reached a new and unbearable pitch. Across the courtyard, people held their books to the sky, waiting for the fire to be lit. Their voices rose in a wave of tuneless sound and crashed over the village.

'Do what they do,' Oede instructed. 'It is part of the ritual.'

A man was shouting somewhere nearby, hidden behind the bonfire, and the people began cheering in response. This was accompanied by the appearance of four figures, all holding burning torches. They approached the bonfire in single file and held the flames against the stack of wood. It caught alight instantly, fire rushing up through the centre and bursting against the sky. Huge flames shot into the air and the crowd screamed with fresh hysteria. Oede and the companions ducked as a wave of heat struck them. The crowd rushed forward, desperate to feed the burning monster with their offerings.

'This is mad!' Will yelled.

'It is fiercer than I imagined,' Oede returned. 'Something is wrong.'

From the milling masses, there came a new shout. The sound triggered a strange hush over the crowd as everyone stopped to listen. From behind the flames, three black cloaked figures emerged. People cleared the way for them as they headed straight for the bonfire. Their shouts turned into a forceful chant which rang ominously around the silent courtyard.

'What is it, what's going on?' James hissed in Oede's ear.

'There were rumours, but it can't be true.'

'What can't? Who are they?' James asked desperately, but he had a feeling he already knew.

Before Oede could answer, a fresh blaze burst from the bonfire. The flames shot higher than before and the heat intensified. The black cloaked figures raised their hands to the sky and James saw that they too carried books. He watched with growing dread as they dropped the volumes into the flames. The fire suddenly lowered to half its original height, its golden glow turning to a deep, smoky red. The surrounding crowds stood still, watching and waiting.

As he stood there, James became aware of movement somewhere close by. Turning his head a fraction, he spotted someone moving through the crowd. They were forcing their way through the packed rows, making a hurried escape. Watching them go, James felt an inexplicable urge to follow. He tried to catch Will's attention but his friend wasn't looking. Turning away, he began pushing against the people behind him. No one looked up or made a sound until suddenly someone started screaming.

Chapter 14

THE screaming went on and on but James didn't stop moving. He could hear Will calling his name but kept pushing forward through the rows of people. All around him, the crowd began to boil and heave. He lost sight of the figure he was chasing and allowed his instincts to take over. Fighting against the panicked onlookers, he headed for the closest path out of the village.

After what felt like a long time, he reached the edge of the courtyard. The final, scattered row of people peeled away, leaving him free to escape. Pausing beneath an archway, he turned to observe the scene behind him. Panicked people surged around the bonfire which was blazing again. From a distance, it looked like the scene of an apocalypse. His gaze then fell on three figures who were fighting against the crowd. He recognised the faces of his friends beneath the hoods and relief washed over him. Hoping they would catch up with him, he turned away again.

The path in front of him was wrapped in shadow and he began to walk along it. He recognised it as the same path Oede had led them down earlier that evening. Emerging from between the houses, he found himself standing on open grassland. Driven by the inexplicable instinct, he started towards the river, the light from the village showing him the way. Squinting through the half-darkness, he saw a shadowy figure standing on the bank. He stopped in his tracks, not wishing to startle them. They were only just visible against the inky water and stood completely still, as if waiting for someone.

'I can see you there, you know.'

A voice sounded in the darkness, causing James to jump. It was harsh and feminine and there was no doubt that it belonged to the shadowy figure.

'Who are you?' she demanded. 'Why are you following me?'

'Erm… I…,' James stuttered, his words momentarily evading him. 'I don't know,' he finally managed.

'You don't know?' the woman continued icily. 'Do I have to force it out of you?'

James was sure her voice sounded vaguely familiar, but quickly dismissed the thought. 'I'm not sure why I followed you,' he replied honestly. 'Maybe because you were the only person trying to escape.'

'Apart from you,' she returned sharply. 'What's your name?'

Before James could answer, a light appeared in the woman's hand. Although faint, it enabled him to see her face. A loose strand of red hair had fallen across her features, but beneath it he could see a pair of green eyes watching him. The eyes, like the voice, were familiar and he suddenly remembered who the woman was.

'It's you,' he said disbelievingly, 'from the Hidden City.'

'James Fynch.' She glared at him, her eyes boring into his own. 'I never thought to see you again.'

Watching her closely, James noticed her gaze waver. It hovered just past his shoulder and he instinctively turned around. Three shadowy forms flitted over the grass and skidded to a halt just behind him. Will, Aralia and Arthur stepped into the circle of light, their eyes fixed on the woman with evident suspicion.

'Dina,' Aralia said disbelievingly. 'From the Hidden City.'

'At least someone remembers my name,' Dina replied fiercely.

'What're you doing here?' Will asked with emphasis.

'I could ask the same of you.'

'We're looking for the same thing as before.' James spoke quickly, as if delaying his answer would make him doubt the truth of it.

'A book?' Dina queried, her eyes dancing across his features.

'More like part of a story.' His own gaze subconsciously flickered to the volume she held in her hand.

'Did you think I might have it?' Dina held the book to her chest and the folds of her cloak fell over it. 'Is that why you followed me?' James opened his mouth to answer, but she continued. 'Why come here, to this village?'

'Because of The Lost Years,' Will suddenly snapped.

Dina looked at him sharply. 'The Lost Years? What could you possibly want to know about them?'

'We want to learn more about a place called Arvora.' Arthur spoke quietly and his voice could only just be heard above the noise of the river.

A soft gasp sounded behind them and Oede stepped into their circle. His eyes flashed in the light and his lips were drawn into a tight line. He didn't look at the companions and turned instead towards Dina. A silent message seemed to pass between their eyes before either of them spoke.

'The place you speak of is no more.' Oede moved to stand beside Dina, his voice gentle but firm. 'It is no more,' he repeated.

'If it doesn't exist anymore, then it must have once,' Arthur calculated.

Oede twisted the jasper pendant at his neck. 'It is said to once have existed on an island just off the Henlan coast.'

'Opoc,' Will offered.

Oede inclined his head. 'Not much is known about it but some records still exist.'

'Records?' James looked from Oede to Dina and back again. 'Are there any here?'

Dina cast Oede a fiery glance. 'You said it was dangerous,' she snapped. 'You can't.'

Her eyes locked with his, green and gold in a silent war. The companions stood waiting, observing a conversation they could not hear.

'I will take you,' Oede said at last. 'I can show you the records. There is a vault on the banks of the Garone, built deep into the earth. Many books are hidden there. We must be swift and quiet, like shadows.'

'What's happening there, in the village?' James asked. In his mind's eye, he recalled the shadowy figure standing on the platform at Victoria station and shuddered.

'They wish to punish us for burning the darkness.' Oede turned away and his voice was drowned by the river.

'People will fight back,' Dina surmised. 'These so-called followers of darkness believe themselves to be serving a great cause. In reality, they possess ordinary powers, just like the rest of us.'

James opened his mouth to object but Aralia pinched his arm and he swallowed his words. He sensed Dina was watching him again and turned away, wondering if she had guessed what he was thinking.

'I will take you to the records.' Oede broke spun around to face them. 'We can't go tonight. There is a law against being outside the village after dark. We can go in the morning.'

He turned towards the village and the companions followed him. Dina came on behind, keeping a clear distance. They crossed the grassland quickly and slipped back down the path that led to the courtyard. The village was strangely empty now and only a few people wandered between the market stalls. Burnt books and discarded food littered the ground all the way up to the bonfire. The flames had died away completely, leaving partially burnt logs behind. Smoke still seeped from the cracks, filling the courtyard with a bitter scent.

'There is a place to stay at the end of the next street,' Oede offered. 'Go through that arch,' he added, pointing to a nearby structure. 'Give them my name. Stay there all night and don't leave until morning. Then meet me here.'

He held out his hand for each of them to grasp before walking away. Dina nodded to them briefly before hurrying after him. Left alone at the edge of the courtyard, the companions turned to one another questioningly.

'What now?' Will asked.

James looked towards the dying bonfire. The thought of a warm bed was appealing but he forced the image away.

'We go to the vault of course.'

Will raised an eyebrow. 'You heard Oede. It's illegal to leave the village after dark. Plus, I wouldn't mind going to sleep.'

'The law? That hasn't stopped us before,' James replied. The scent of sizzling meat reached his nostrils and his stomach grumbled. 'We could eat first though,' he added more reasonably.

They wandered over to a nearby stall where an aproned man stood leaning over a red-hot grill. He greeted them in his own tongue and handed over four loaded skewers in exchange for a few coins.

'What happened here?' Aralia asked. 'Where is everyone?'

117

The man wiped his hands on his apron and sighed. 'Where?' he asked. 'Men go, disappear. People run home.'

James cast a nervous glance around the courtyard. 'Disappeared?'

'Gone.' The man pushed his well-greased hands apart. 'Pouf!' He shook his head and turned away to serve another stray customer.

'Pouf!' Will repeated through a mouthful of meat. 'Descriptive.'

Pulling him away from the stall, James shrugged. 'They could be anywhere. We'll have to be careful if we go down to the river.' He took a bite of sticky meat before continuing. 'Listen, one of those people...'

A grunt near his elbow made him look down. His gaze fell on an elderly woman sitting cross legged on the cobbles. A holey blanket was draped around her shoulders and her hair fell across it in matted strands. She stared solemnly up at James, her eyes bleary with partial blindness.

'I would'na go to river at this time o' night. In the dark hour before dawn, that's when they come. Ships from hell I call 'em. The ships on which they leave and ne'er come back.'

The companions gaped at her, letting her words sink in. She looked back at them, her eyes narrowed into sightless slits.

'Ships?' James frowned.

'Oh yes, I seen 'em. Every seventh night they come and go fro' docks. Quietly slip in, silently go out, taking their cargo with 'em.'

'Cargo?' Will queried, wiping a dribble of fat from his chin. 'What cargo?'

'More importantly, what ships?' Arthur added.

The woman closed her eyes and for a moment, James thought she'd gone to sleep. She then spoke again, her voice low and rasping.

'Nobody knows where they go. To some dark place. As for their cargo, slaves.' She shook her head but her eyes remained closed. 'Tonight they move again.' She fell silent and her breathing deepened. James gave her a gentle shake but she didn't respond.

'They're going to Arvora,' Aralia whispered. 'The ships are going to Arvora.'

James turned to her, his heart racing. 'I suppose it makes sense,' he said quickly. 'The boy in the inn told us about the slaves that disappear. They are taken by ship to Arvora, a place that no one believes to exist. As soon as they reach it, they also stop existing. It's clever, if you think about it.'

'I'm not sure I want to,' Aralia muttered.

'If the ships leave tonight, we can see them for ourselves,' Arthur suggested. 'If we're going to find the vaults, then we may as well see if we can find the docks.'

'I suppose it's better than wasting time in a warm bed,' Will sarcastically agreed.

Rejoining the familiar path, they left the courtyard behind them. Breaking out onto the grassland again, they turned their backs to the Garin and, with Will's map to guide them, started walking towards the Garone. It was much darker and quieter on this side of the village. Where the houses ended, a steep bank sloped downwards into unknown territory. It was too dark to see more than a short way ahead and Will ignited a small light despite protestations from the others. The beam was just bright enough to show them where it was safe to tread.

They stopped when the ground levelled out again at the base of the bank. A short way ahead of them, Will's light caught on a strip of dark water. The reflection hardly wavered, held prisoner by the unmoving current. The opposite bank was hidden in shadow, but the silhouettes of several trees stood out against the sky. On this side of the river, a muddy path ran parallel to the water, its meandering form also shrouded by the night.

'It's so quiet,' Aralia whispered.

James nodded distractedly. His attention had been caught by a mark in the mud and he bent to inspect it more closely. Half of it was missing, but the fanned indents suggested it had been made by a shoe.

'A footprint,' he announced. 'Someone's been here quite recently. The mark looks fresh.' He straightened up and took a step forward on the path. 'Come on, let's go along here and see if there are more.'

He took the lead, taking care to avoid the rocks protruding from the mud. Will's light only just reached him, meaning he had to squint at the way ahead. He hadn't walked far when he stumbled against something solid. Will collided with him and the light went out, plunging them into complete darkness.

'What is it?' Will hissed. 'What's wrong?'

'The path is blocked.' Exploring the air in front of him, James felt his fingers brush against cold stone.

Light glowed again and he adjusted his eyes. A large stone slab stood blocking the path, one side leaning against a rocky outcrop to their right. The stone was smooth apart from a vertical fracture on the left hand side. James ran his hands over the crack. It cut a straight line through the stone which spread out unevenly on either side. One side was slightly raised above the other and stood back to take a closer look.

'The slabs don't match up properly.' Will's voice sounded loud in his ear. 'The fracture isn't natural; it's been manmade.'

'It's a door!' Arthur said suddenly. 'Look, there's another cut on the other side but it's much smaller. I think it might be open

120

already. Try it, James.'

Pressing his fingers into the crack, James jerked his arms towards his chest. The slab resisted at first but as he strained against it, something moved. He found himself stumbling backwards as the heavy door scraped open.

Will peered over his shoulder, holding the light up to the dark entrance. 'It must lead to the vaults,' he speculated. 'There's another footprint next to the door so someone must already be here. We should be careful.'

Led by James, they passed through the doorway. A small flight of steps greeted them, leading steeply downwards. A musty, bookish scent hit their nostrils as they descended. This grew gradually stronger, undeterred by the fresh air that followed them in from the riverside. The stairs led straight into a large room that was filled from top to bottom with shelves and drawers. Even though every space was crammed with books, every section was neatly labelled.

'We're looking for anything about Arvad, Arvora, Jasper, or The Lost Years,' James directed.

A faint thud made them freeze. The sound came from behind a door in the far corner of the room. Creeping up to it, Will pressed his ear to the panels. He straightened up with a shrug and slowly turned the handle. For a moment, the door blocked him from view but he popped his head back round.

'It's empty in here,' he whispered, 'and there are loads more books.'

James, Arthur and Aralia followed him into the room. It was smaller than the first but equally organised. Three out of four walls were lined with books while the final section was filled with drawers.

'Maybe we should've come with Oede,' James murmured. 'None of us can speak Henlan.'

'Art and I used to know a little,' Aralia replied, 'but not enough to understand all this.' She took a book from its shelf and brushed dust from the cover. 'Arvora might be a universal name. Maybe we'll recognise it anyway.'

James nodded. 'All we need is confirmation that it's real.'

'It is.' A voice sounded at the doorway and they all spun around. A figure was standing there, strands of red hair spilling from beneath its hood.

'Dina!' Will exclaimed.

'We should stop running into each other,' she replied, eyes flashing. 'I should have guessed you'd come here.'

'It seems you've broken in too,' James retorted. 'We followed your footprints and found the door open.'

A frown threaded its way across Dina's forehead. 'I didn't leave the door open,' she said sharply. 'I made sure to close it.'

James felt his stomach drop. 'If that's the case, then who did leave it open?'

'Follow me,' Dina hissed. 'If someone else is here, we should all leave.'

She led the way into the main room and back up the stairs to the riverbank. Rather than continuing down the path, she turned to face the rocky outcrop to their left. Hooking her fingers onto the jagged surface, she began to climb.

'Come on,' she commanded. 'Don't just stand there.'

In three movements, she had pulled herself on top of the vault. James, Will, Arthur and Aralia clambered up behind her and she extended an arm to help them over the final ridge. A thud sounded just below them. It was followed by a scraping noise, like that of stone on stone. Moments later, someone appeared on the pathway. They were dressed entirely in black and disappeared like a shadow into the night. As soon as they had gone, Dina's voice sounded through the darkness.

'I know why you're really here,' she said quietly. 'This is the seventh night, the night when the Arvorian ships pass by the River Villages.' There was a long pause before she spoke again. 'I am also here for the ships. If you are mad enough to join me, I leave for Arvora tonight.'

Chapter 15

DINA'S words hung heavily in the air. James, Will, Arthur and Aralia stared at her with a mixture of excitement and uncertainty. She looked back at them, her gaze defiant.

'You're actually going?' Will asked. 'You're that sure Arvora is real.'

'Yes,' she replied firmly. 'Aren't you?' She rose to her feet, taking the light with her. 'Perhaps I guessed wrong. I can easily go alone.'

'No, wait!' James jumped up to face her. 'Tell us what we need to do.'

Dina's eyes narrowed. 'Alright. Follow me.'

Sliding from the roof of the vault, she rejoined the path. James, Will, Arthur and Aralia slithered down behind her. They began walking back along the river, taking care to avoid the muddiest parts.

'We should cover our tracks,' Dina whispered. 'Walk on in front of me.'

Holding her palm to the earth, she let a trail of light sweep along the ground behind her, erasing their prints as they went. After several long minutes, she called for them to stop. The path ahead was interrupted by an archway, marked with an upside down triangle. On the other side of it, the silhouette of a jetty rested on the water, joined to a building that might have been a boathouse.

'Is this the dock?' Will made a face and moved to stand under the archway.

'Expect something grander?' Dina returned. 'It was originally built for traders moving between villages, but they've now constructed a much larger one further up the river.'

'What does the triangle symbol mean?' James asked, pointing to the arch. 'I saw it in the village too.'

'It's the mark of the River Villages and one of the most common alchemical symbols for water.' Dina paused to clear her throat. 'I'm afraid I have to leave you for a while, but I'll come back.'

'Leave?' Will turned to face her. 'Where're you going? You'll miss the ships.'

Dina glanced in the direction of the village. 'I have to see someone before I go. I'll be back, I promise.'

She turned away before anyone could object and disappeared into the night. Her light went with her and the companions watched it gradually fade away. Closing his eyes, James imagined a light forming in his own hand. It glowed brightly through his eyelids and he moved to hide it beneath the folds of his cloak. Stepping through the archway behind Will, he wandered towards the jetty. Although it was dark, the faint light in the sky indicated that much of the night had passed and dawn would soon follow. He'd only taken a few steps when he bumped into something solid. Looking down, he saw a wooden crate blocking his path. It was one of many, scattered across the riverbank.

'Shipping crates,' Arthur commented. 'They must belong to the traders.'

'I guess the ships trade more than just slaves.' Will bent to prise one open but the lid was jammed shut.

James sat down on one of the crates and surveyed his surroundings. From here he could see both the river and the slope that led up to the village. Will and Arthur came to join him but Aralia lingered behind. Tying her cloak at the waist, she squatted in the mud and began tracing her finger through it.

'Rai, what're you doing?' Arthur stood up again and moved to join her by the arch.

She looked up at him, her eyes bright. 'I'm working things out.'

'Working out what?'

'Links and solutions,' she replied and turned her gaze back to the ground. 'Dina said the upside down triangle is the mark of the River Villages and of water. Look at the spelling of Eriphas.'

James and Will hurried over to join the siblings. Aralia had written the word *Eriphas* in the mud, the letters uneven but otherwise ordinary.

'Are you sure it's spelled like that?' Arthur asked.

Aralia cast him a withering glance. 'Yes, I'm sure. It was written on one of the papers in the vault. Try reading it backwards.'

James focused on the word, reading it as instructed. The letters danced in front of his eyes, refusing to make much sense. He squinted at them determinedly and a word began to form in his mind.

'Sapphire,' he read aloud. 'It says sapphire. Well, almost.'

'Exactly,' Aralia confirmed. 'Do you know what a sapphire is?'

'A gemstone,' Will offered.

'It's not just any gemstone.' Aralia stood up and tried to

brush the mud from her fingers. 'Sapphires, at least some of them, are connected to the element of water.'

James, Will and Arthur stared at her. She folded her arms and looked back defiantly, as if waiting for one of them to contradict her.

'It all connects,' Will said at last. A deep frown spread across his forehead before he spoke again. 'My dad's notes, Arvora, Eriphas, the crystals. The crystal for water must be a sapphire.'

'The crystal for water must be a sapphire,' James repeated, his tone disbelieving. 'We're looking for a sapphire.' The words sounded strange on his tongue and he mouthed them again.

His gaze was drawn to the upper bank on which a glimmer of light had appeared. It was moving along a line of trees, carried by a shadowy figure. As he looked, a second light appeared, held by another figure. The two individuals came together in what might have been an embrace and he looked away, suddenly embarrassed. He focused his attention on the river, watching the gentle ripples spread across its surface. The slap of footsteps on the muddy path made them all turn. A light glowed on the path and Dina's face appeared behind it.

'You came back,' James whispered.

'Did you doubt me?' she flashed. Brushing past him, she went to stand at the base of the jetty.

'His name is Kaedon,' she continued, as if reading their thoughts. 'He doesn't know we're here.'

'Why *are* you here?' Will asked sharply. 'You haven't actually told us why you want to go to Arvora. There must be a reason.'

Dina nodded but didn't turn to look at him. 'I made a promise to save someone who I believe has been taken to Arvora.' She sighed and the light in her hand dimmed.

'To save someone? Who?' Will watched her expectantly but

when she didn't immediately answer, he turned his eyes to the ground.

'My sister.' Dina's body went rigid and she tilted her head, as if listening.

'The ships!' she announced. 'We must hurry.'

'Hurry where?' Will asked, looking around for inspiration.

Dina darted over to one of the crates. She placed her hand on the lid and a light glowed. There was a soft popping sound and she swiftly opened the crate.

'We hide in the containers,' she said simply.

'Won't they be opened before loading?' Arthur queried.

'Nothing is left on this dock that shouldn't be here. Plus, many of the crates are empty. They'll only be opened once they reach Arvora. That's when we have to worry.'

She removed the lids of four other crates before gesturing for the companions to climb inside. Having no better plan themselves, they pressed themselves inside the crates as she instructed.

'Stay quiet and don't open the lids until we're on the boat,' Dina warned. 'If we're split up, be careful.'

Settling himself into his crate, James pulled the lid back over the top. The space was cramped but the air coming through the uneven slats made it bearable. He wrapped his arms around his bag and tried not to move. Out on the docks, Dina's light finally went out and everything went dark. Although the air was cool, James felt strangely warm. For a moment, he wished he had his phone to look at, but quickly dismissed this desire. He let his mind wander instead and soon found his thoughts turning to the sapphire. Part of him wondered if the crystal was hidden in Arvora but the other part of him deemed this outcome highly unlikely. Unable to decide which option would be better, he sat contemplating both while time ticked by around him.

A soft thud startled him from his thoughts. Squinting through the wooden slats, he tried to see what was happening on the dockside. Lights flashed near the jetty, accompanied by low whispers and the scraping sound of crates being moved. Sitting as still as possible, he held his breath and waited. He sat there for a long time, anxiously waiting for someone to lift up his crate. His mind began to grow drowsy but the thudding beat of his heart kept him from falling asleep. Torn between fatigue and fear, he stared at the wooden sides of the crate and counted the dark knots over and over again.

It was only when he noticed grey light sifting through the slats that he realised something was wrong. Shifting his numb body, he listened for the sound of voices but the docks lay silent. Cursing to himself, he pushed against the crate lid. It popped open and uncurling his stiff limbs, he peered over the rim. Outside, the world lay still and for a moment he just sat staring. The dock lay completely empty and if it wasn't for his own crate, he would have doubted that the containers had ever been here.

'They're gone!' he exclaimed. 'You idiot!'

The morning was still new and the grey sky cast a dingy sheen over the river. No sound came from the village but he instinctively knew that it wouldn't be safe to return there. As he clambered out of the crate, his eyes fell on the boathouse. It looked smaller and older in the morning light, leaning clumsily against a cluster of undergrowth. Grabbing his bag, he hurriedly approached the building. Seeing no door on this side, he fought his way through the brambles to the back. Finding no door here either, he came to a standstill and cursed again.

Looking up to the roof, he noted that several of the planks were loose. The climb didn't look difficult, but there wasn't much to grip on to. Digging his fingers into the cracks in the wall, he heaved himself upwards. Splinters dug beneath his fingernails but he clung on, desperate to reach the top. Forced to let go with one hand in order to climb higher, his grip loosened and he fell back to the ground. Securing his shoes more firmly against the wall, he tried again. This time, he managed to grab onto the edge of the roof and with one final effort, pulled himself on top.

From up here, he could see the river winding away from the dock in a gentle bend. He briefly admired the view before lowering himself onto his stomach. Peering between the rotten roof panels, he found himself staring down into the belly of a rowing boat. It was all he could see from this angle and sitting back on his heels, he gave one of the planks a tug. There was a tearing sound as the wood came away and the force knocked him backwards. He heard an ominous crack beneath him and suddenly found himself plummeting through the roof.

The fall was not far and he landed in the base of the rowing boat. Winded, he lay still for several seconds before hauling himself upright. His eyes immediately fell on a set of double doors at the end of the building. Clutching his bruised stomach, he clambered from the boat and stumbled across to them. He gave one side a push and it fell open to reveal the river swirling directly below. Gripped by a fresh madness, he hurried back to the boat. Taking it, he dragged it across to the open doorway before pausing to reconsider what he was about to do.

'I wouldn't touch that if I were you.'

He spun around to see a man standing at the far end of the boathouse. A door stood open behind him and James stared, wondering how he had missed it.

'Who are you?' he asked sharply.

'None of your business.'

The man bared his teeth and took a step closer. His leather trousers and jacket matched his dark hair, giving him a menacing appearance. As he turned his head to observe the broken roof, James noticed an earring pierced through his right ear.

'I'll have to stop you taking that boat,' the man continued. His eyes flashed dangerously, the blue irises abnormally bright beneath his thick eyebrows.

James glanced at the rowing boat teetering on the edge of the boathouse. He knew the current was in his favour and it would take just one push. The man saw his look and began striding towards him. Left without a choice, James reached forward and gave the vessel a gentle shove. It fell into the water with a splash and bracing himself, he jumped in after it. Caught by the current, the boat spun out into the centre of the river, taking him with it.

Forced to his knees, James didn't have time to grab the oars before the vessel spiralled out of control. Gripping onto the gunwale, he managed to haul himself onto the bench in front of him. Holding on with one hand, he reached for an oar with the other. As the boat levelled out, he dipped the oar into the water, trying to slow its pace. A shout sounded behind him and he glanced over his shoulder. The man from the boathouse had jumped into the water and was swimming towards him with powerful strokes.

'Did you think you could handle the boat on your own?' he called. 'The water is deceptive. It may look calm but the current is treacherous. You won't make it past the bend.'

His words made James shiver but he didn't want to stop. He had no idea whether his friends were safe and he knew he had to catch up with them. The boat however had a will of its own and it was all he could do to keep it away from the bank.

Dipping the oar in again, he shovelled the water aside and the vessel raced forward. The bow caught in an eddy and suddenly spun sideways. Surprised, James let go of the oar and the current dragged it away from the boat. He tried to grab it but his pursuer reached it first. Taking hold of the shaft, he threw it back inside the boat and heaved himself in after it.

'We're going back,' he commanded. Grabbing the second oar from its pivot, he began to row.

James shook his head firmly, his nerves gradually dissipating. 'We can't go back,' he protested. 'My friends are out here. They're on a ship to Arvora.'

The effect was instant. The man froze, oars poised above the water. 'Arvora?'

'They're all on board except me,' James continued, encouraged by the man's reaction. 'I got left behind and now I have to follow them.'

The stranger gripped the oars more tightly, his broad arms straining against the current as he held the boat still. His eyes flickered to the shore and James followed his gaze. Another man stood on the bank, hovering at the edge as if wondering whether to jump.

'Who is on this ship?' the man asked with sudden ferocity. 'Who are your friends? Tell me, was a woman named Dina with them?' He searched James' face, his eyes bright and piercing.

'You know her?' James asked.

'Damn her ignorance,' the man cursed, his jaw tensing. 'Damn her.' He looked back towards the bank and waved to the stranger waiting there.

There was a second splash as the man dived into the river. James shifted aside to make more room as the sodden figure clambered aboard. Ignoring James, both men began talking to one another in their own tongue. When at last the new arrival turned around, James found himself looking into a familiar pair of eyes.

'Oede,' he faltered. 'What're you doing here?' Oede didn't answer and James felt his ears grow hot. 'You know each other,' he continued, looking between both men. 'You both know Dina.'

Slowly, calmly, Oede inclined his head. 'I have known her since childhood and Kaedon for a little less time.'

Kaedon. James recognised the name as the same one Dina had mentioned by the docks. He looked carefully at the stranger, observing how the anger in his expression betrayed his affection for her.

'Did Dina tell you that she wanted to go to Arvora?' James asked, even though he already knew the answer.

'It is like her to vanish like this and forget that there are people who care about her,' Oede answered.

James let a brief silence descend before speaking again. 'If you are worried about her, then you must want to follow her,' he assumed. 'Are you going to come with me?'

'Come with you?' Kaedon laughed. 'These waters are dangerous; you'd never survive alone.'

The boat gave a sudden tug and James was thrown against the side of the boat. Water sprayed across his face but he didn't dare let go to wipe it away.

'Hold on,' Kaedon commanded. 'We're approaching the Sulobai Rapids, or Devil's Rapids, where the two rivers join. I'm going to raise the oars.'

The boat lurched again and James watched as the oars were drawn in. Kaedon and Oede then slithered from the bench into the belly of the boat and pulled James down with them. Within moments, the vessel lost all control. The river churned beneath it, tossing it from side to side at terrifying angles. Through the sound of crashing water, Kaedon started shouting.

'Don't let go. We're going to capsize.'

Any other words were lost as the boat rode upwards on a white wave and tipped. James felt his mouth and nose filling with water as the twin rivers consumed him. The current tugged at his clothes and despite his efforts to fight the force, his hands slipped from the side of the boat.

Chapter 16

FLOUNDERING in the water, James tried to fight against the current. He could taste mud in his mouth, stinging the back of his throat as he tried to swallow. Water filled his nose and his eyes, temporarily blinding him. He tried to hold his breath but the longer he was submerged, the harder it became. The current was powerful, rolling him over and over as if he were a toy. He tried to swim against it, pushing towards the surface, but the water kept forcing him down again.

An image was fighting for space in his mind but he tried to block it out, afraid that it meant he was drowning. The harder he tried to push it away, the more persistent it became. Too tired to resist this as well as the current, he let his arms fall by his sides. He had no time to alter his decision before the force of the water dragged him further beneath the surface. As he sank downwards, the image settled in the forefront of his mind. He let it in without resistance, no longer caring what it meant.

The river lay beneath him, calm and dark. Although there was no current, he could see the silhouette of a ship moving through the water. It was as if he were floating above the river, rather than beneath it. The feeling was familiar but he couldn't remember why. He didn't even know whether it was a memory at all or just a hallucination. Curious to know if the ship itself was real, he reached out towards it. A hand grabbed his arm and he tried to shake it off, but it held on. Before he knew what was happening, he found himself being dragged upwards through the water and a wave of fresh air struck him.

'He's breathing.'

Oede's voice sounded beside him and he opened his eyes. Daylight hit his eyes and he saw Oede's face floating just below the clouds.

'The ship,' he croaked. 'I saw it.'

'The ship?' Oede's lips barely moved as he spoke.

'It was there, in my mind,' James said quickly. 'We're close.'

'You had water in your lungs,' Kaedon growled. 'You were hallucinating.'

James turned to look at him. He was sitting on the central bench, an oar balanced in each hand. Neither one was in the water and the boat drifted along of its own accord. The river now lay quiet, the surface glassy once again.

'I saw it,' James protested. 'It's happened to me before.'

'Visions?' Oede asked.

James nodded. 'It's like I can see the way ahead in my mind.'

Oede glanced at Kaedon who muttered something under his breath. Both men stared at James and he looked back, wondering if they thought he was mad. As he turned away, his eyes fell on the spot where his bag had previously been. There was no sign of it now and he looked around the boat, desperate to locate it.

'Where is it?' he asked. 'Where's my bag?'

Oede reached under the bench and drew out the bag. The fabric was dark with water and dripped continuously as Oede handed it over. Unzipping it, James searched for the pages of Arvad's tale. They were stuck firmly together and the ancient ink had bled. He tried to peel the paper apart, but it ripped at the edges and he was forced to give up.

'Those pages are important to you?' Oede asked.

Unable to find the right words, James simply nodded. He returned the pages to his bag and leant his back against the side of the boat.

'Who are you exactly?' Kaedon didn't turn around as he spoke but his voice gave away his suspicion. 'Why are you going to Arvora? You must have a reason to go there.'

James lowered his gaze, wondering how best to reply. 'I'm James, from the Fynch family,' he began. 'My friend's dad went missing on one of his explorations nearly five years ago and we're trying to find out what happened to him.'

'You would risk your life for a little knowledge?' Kaedon asked.

'I guess knowing is better than not knowing,' James returned, thinking briefly of the sister he had never met.

'To find family is where the heart goes,' Oede murmured, 'but even the bravest men wouldn't dare enter Arvora.'

'And yet you would go there to find Dina.'

James turned away to look at the river and silence fell. Even though his clothes were wet, he didn't feel cold. A shy sun had come out, causing the water to steam as it warmed. It created an eerie atmosphere, like those present in a film or dream. It didn't last for long as evening clouds soon crept over the horizon, blotting out the sun. The daylight gradually faded, leaving trails of red and pink reflected across the water.

'I've never been to this part of the river before,' Kaedon said into the silence. 'The people of Eriphas say it is dangerous to go beyond the Sulobai Rapids. They believe the water is cursed.'

James was about to respond when Oede uttered a soft exclamation. Leaning over the gunwale, he pointed steadily towards the horizon.

'Movement,' he announced. 'Look.'

Squinting through the gathering darkness, James searched for shapes on the water. He could see the silhouettes of trees wavering in the distance but nothing moved on the river itself.

'I don't see anything,' he whispered.

'Look where the water meets the sky,' Oede replied. 'Do you see?'

Glancing across the twilight ripples, James let his gaze rest on the horizon. A faint shadow quivered on the water, its form barely visible against the darkening sky.

'It must be the ship,' Kaedon stated. 'It seems you were right.' He turned towards James, but his face was hidden in shadow.

'We should raise the oars again,' Oede proposed.

Kaedon agreed and swung the oars to rest along the gunwales. The boat drifted towards the bank and embedded itself amongst the willow branches that trailed in the water.

'What're you doing?' James asked. 'We need to catch up with the ship.'

'We wait,' Oede replied quietly. 'We wait for the cover of night.'

James turned to look at the darkening river. The ship was still visible in the distance and he hardly dared blink for fear of losing it in the gloom. As soon as the last patch of sky was covered by the clouds, Kaedon picked up the oars and began to row again. The boat slithered across the water, hardly making a sound. The scenery had regained its eerie quality, the river and trees transformed into menacing shadows. Closing his eyes, James allowed himself to be lulled by the rhythm of the oars. He had almost fallen asleep when Oede jabbed him in the ribs.

'Wake up. Take the mooring rope.' The boat wobbled as Oede shifted his weight and pressed a rough coil into James' hands. 'Hold on tight,' he ordered.

'How d'you know where to go?' James asked, directing his question at Kaedon's silhouette. 'It's so dark.'

A soft laugh came back to him. 'I feel it. I feel the water. Stay quiet now, we're about to move alongside the ship.'

Surprised, James looked at the river ahead. A black shape rose from the water, a fraction darker than the shadows surrounding it. It made no sound, skimming through the water with swan-like grace. The shape wasn't wide but it was tall, made so by a set of masts. Looking at these, James knew without doubt that he was looking at an Arvorian ship. As he stared at it, he realised the whole vessel was surrounded by a faint light. It was so pale that it wasn't so much visible but rather a sensation of it being there. He'd seen this light before, on the canal boats in the Hidden City, and knew it was a sign of magic.

'We'll have to row along the starboard side and tuck in there,' Kaedon commented. 'These ships usually have a mooring point for tenders.'

'You seem familiar with them,' James said.

There was a long pause before Kaedon replied. 'I work at the main dock, but I also oversee the preparation of cargo for the trading ships.'

'That's how you know about Arvora, then,' James said incredulously. 'Did *you* know?' He turned to Oede but received no reply.

They were so close to the ship now that he could almost touch it. While Kaedon rowed, he kept watch for any sign of a mooring space. It was difficult to see at first but he soon realised that he could use the faint light surrounding the vessel to his advantage. As they slid along the starboard side, he became aware of several black dots pricking at his eyes. He tried to rub them away but they persisted, dancing over his pupils. Blinking hard in an attempt to dislodge them, he suddenly realised that he was looking at a series of large portholes.

'Look,' he whispered. 'Portholes.'

'They're not portholes,' Kaedon replied. 'They're used for loading cargo. The tender deck must be somewhere close.' He drove the oars into the water and let their boat run close alongside the mother ship. 'There,' he hissed.

James looked to where he thought Kaedon was pointing. A hollow was visible in the ship's side, just large enough to hold a smaller boat. Kaedon rowed closer, trying to nose the bow of their vessel into the available space.

'If I can't moor it, we'll have to jump,' he muttered. 'The ships aren't usually moving when transfers are made.'

James felt his heart skip a beat, whether from nerves or excitement he couldn't tell. He waited quietly while Kaedon manoeuvred the boat alongside the ship and held it still. Oede took the mooring rope from James and threw it overboard. There was a small plop as it landed in the water, followed by a sigh.

'The ship is moving too fast,' Oede reported.

He muttered something in his own tongue but Kaedon didn't answer. While waiting for an order, James slung his bag onto his shoulders and looked over the side of the boat at the water. It was uninvitingly dark but he was grateful that the current was still.

'We'll have to jump,' Kaedon suddenly ordered. 'When I say so, you jump. Oede first, then you, James. You will have to move quickly when I say the word. Understand?'

Silence descended while he steadied the boat. Even the rippling water seemed to fall still. James squatted beside the bench on which Kaedon sat, anxiously waiting for the next order. It came quickly and sharply. Oede stood up hurriedly, causing the boat to wobble, and leapt from the side. A soft thud confirmed his landing and James breathed a sigh of relief.

'Are you ready?' Kaedon asked.

James said nothing. When the command came, he clambered onto the bench and launched himself over the side of the boat. It was too dark to see what he was aiming for but he fell against a hard surface. He grappled around for something to grab onto and his fingers latched onto a strand of rope. Steadying himself, he looked around for Oede. A shadow moved on a ridge just above him and wrapping the rope around his wrist, he heaved himself up to join it. Looking down at the river, he waited as Kaedon drew towards the ship one final time. At the last moment, he too jumped and the boat spun away behind him.

'We move,' Oede whispered. 'Follow me.'

The ledge they were on was just wide enough to walk along with one foot in front of the other. The river lay no more than a metre below them, its presence given away by a faint whispering. They inched their way along the ridge for several minutes before Oede came to an abrupt halt. A small light appeared just inches from his face, floating from his hand to hover against his chest. It lit up a large opening in the side of the ship, looking a little like a porthole but much larger and covered with a wire mesh.

Oede hooked his fingers into the mesh and pulled. There was a pop as it came away and he placed it by his feet. Holding onto the rim of the opening, he swung his legs inside. With only his torso and head showing, he pushed himself forward and disappeared. Feeling a prod in his back, James hurried to follow. Copying Oede's movements, he climbed inside the opening and slid into the dark space beyond. It was a tight fit but he managed to push himself forward. He felt someone grab his legs and start pulling him through.

'Quickly,' Oede's voice urged from the other side.

James slipped out of the porthole to join him and stood aside to give Kaedon enough space to come through. Straightening himself out, he turned to survey the surrounding space. They were standing in an empty cabin that smelled of mould and damp. An empty bucket stood in one corner but apart from that the space was empty. Crossing over to the door, Kaedon flung it open and peered out into the passageway beyond.

'Let's move,' he commanded.

The passage was dark and they passed quietly into it. At the far end, a set of stairs led upwards to another deck. Kaedon took these two at a time and James and Oede hurried to follow. At the top, an almost identical passageway greeted them. It was lined with cabin doors, some of which were fitted with windows. Pressing his face to one, James peered inside. The space was filled with piles of crates and he gave the door a gentle push. Entering the cabin, he began calling for Will, Arthur and Aralia but there was no answer.

Door after door opened onto the same scene. James whispered the names of his friends in every cabin but no one ever answered. The whole ship seemed devoid of people and this made him increasingly nervous. At the end of the passageway, they were greeted by another flight of steps. Leaving Kaedon and Oede to converse at the base, James hurried upwards. He moved to look through another cabin window, pressing his face to the glass. On the other side, rows of people sat on wooden benches. None of them talked but sat staring blankly at the wall.

'They're not the first, nor will they be the last,' Kaedon said over his shoulder.

James turned away, feeling slightly sick. His eyes fell on Oede who was gazing through a window on the opposite side of the passageway. Moving to join him, James peered through the glass. This cabin was filled with more people but his eyes were instantly drawn to a black cloaked trio in the corner. They were huddled together, heads bent inwards as if in conversation. As Oede stepped aside, all three figures looked up and James found himself staring into the anxious faces of Will, Arthur and Aralia.

Chapter 17

'THAT'S them,' James hissed, tapping on the glass. 'My friends are in there.'

'Dina isn't with them,' Oede returned quietly.

Pushing James aside, he shook the door. The handle rattled but there was no hopeful sound of a lock popping open. Oede stepped away with a shrug and turned to speak with Kaedon. Pressing his face to the glass again, James looked at his friends. He waved vigorously at them but none of them responded.

'Can they not see me?' he asked, spinning around to face Oede.

'I imagine not.' Kaedon drew him aside and pressed his own face to the window. 'I have an idea,' he whispered, 'but first we must get a message to them.' He drew a piece of paper from his pocket and handed it to James. 'Write them a message. Tell them to go to the head and wait. Make sure they know it's from you but don't sign your name.'

'The head?' James asked. 'What's that?'

'The ship's lavatory,' Kaedon elucidated. 'Write that instead if you wish.' He slipped a pencil from behind his ear and handed it over.

Kneeling on the hard floor, James began scribbling a note. He made it brief and left it unsigned as ordered. In the top corner however, he drew a tiny diagram of a numberless clock, hoping his friends would know what it meant.

'D'we just stand here and wait for them to notice it?' James pushed the slip of paper under the and stood up, brushing dust from his fingertips.

'We wait, but not here,' Kaedon replied. 'Come with me.' He muttered something to Oede before grabbing James by the arm and pulling him towards the stairs.

Back on the lower deck, they began retracing their steps. Letting go of James' arm, Kaedon stopped outside a cabin door which already stood ajar. A rancid smell drifted through the opening, much worse than that which pervaded the rest of the ship.

'In here,' Kaedon ordered.

'It smells like sewage,' James objected as he entered the cabin. 'What're we doing in here anyway?'

Kaedon pointed at the ceiling and James cast his eyes upwards. A circular vent was fixed between the wooden panels, covered with metal grating. A pipe ran to the right of it, passing down the wall and through the floor below.

'Waste pipes, linked to a ventilation system,' Kaedon explained. 'The waste from the cabins above comes down these pipes and into self-disposing tanks under the ship. It so happens that this vent is linked to the cabin your friends are trapped in.'

'You want them to climb down it?' James looked up through the mesh and wrinkled his nose. The vent was dark and didn't look wide enough to squeeze a person through.

'If they follow your note, they should know what to do.'

A faint thud echoed somewhere above. It was followed by the sound of metal scraping against metal. Something hard landed on the vent, causing the mesh to shake. James and Kaedon stepped aside as dust rained down from between the holes. Another thud sounded and the mesh suddenly caved inwards. There was a groan on the other side, followed by silence.

'Here, stand on my shoulders and pull the mesh from this side,' Kaedon commanded.

He knelt on the floor and James clambered onto his back. Straightening up, he lifted James towards the ceiling until he was close enough to reach the vent. Hooking his fingers between the holes, James pulled with all his strength. The metal came away in his hands and he dropped it to the floor. Before he had time to duck, a pair of legs swung from the vent and knocked him in the head. Surprised, he let go of Kaedon's shoulders and found himself plummeting to the floor. Someone fell across his chest and he gasped for air.

'Sorry!' Will's voice apologised. 'Wasn't ready for that.' He rolled away from James and sat up, brushing the dust from his hair.

Scrambling to his feet, James hurried across to the vent where another pair of legs had emerged. He took hold of one foot while Kaedon secured the other and together they lowered Aralia to the floor. She beamed at James and drew him into a tight hug.

'What happened to you?' she queried as Arthur slid to the floor beside them. 'We've been out of our minds wondering if you were alright.'

'Where is Dina?' Kaedon cut in. 'Why isn't she with you?'

Aralia frowned at him, as if wondering who he was. 'We don't know. She wasn't there when we opened the crates. We tried to track her down but, well...'

Kaedon's eyes flashed. 'You all need to stay here, in one place. Oede and I will find Dina and then we'll get off this ship. Understand?'

James nodded and Kaedon exited the cabin, pulling the door shut behind him. The companions were left standing in the darkness, waiting for someone to break the silence.

'It stinks in here,' Will said eventually.

James smothered a smile and created a small light in his palm. 'What happened to all of you?' he asked. 'How did you get caught?'

'We weren't caught exactly,' Arthur began. 'When we found out you were missing, we didn't know what to do. One option was to try and get off the ship, but we weren't sure if you were on it or not. We tried exploring, but there were guards everywhere.'

'We joined a group of prisoners and began asking around, but no one had seen you,' Will took over. 'Before we had a chance to leave the cabin again, they locked the doors. In the end, we decided it was probably safer to blend in rather than try to escape.'

'What about you?' Aralia turned to James, her expression curious. 'D'you know that man?' She flicked her eyes to the doorway and held them there.

'His name is Kaedon.' James let his light drift up towards the vent. 'I met him by the boathouse after my crate got left at the docks.'

'Kaedon, as in Dina's boyfriend?' Will asked.

James nodded. 'He knows Oede too. They helped me reach this ship.'

'Now that we're together again, we should probably work out what to do next,' Arthur suggested. 'We're not going to stay in here are we?' He looked at James who shrugged.

'I wasn't planning on it. We should explore and find out anything we can about this ship.'

Will opened the cabin door and passed out into the

passageway. He signalled the all clear and James, Arthur and Aralia hurried to join him. In single file, they crept to the end of the passage. A short flight of steps met them and they climbed these two at a time. At the top, they came face to face with two closed doors. One was marked with a symbol of an anchor and flower and the other with a black diamond and circle. The companions stopped short and stood looking between the doors with puzzled expressions.

'Which one?' Will asked.

'I didn't realise there were prisoners on board as well as slaves.' Aralia paused on the top step and pointed to the diamond on the second door. 'We've seen this symbol before.'

James nodded and felt the hairs on his arms prickle uncomfortably. 'We've seen both. I mean we've seen both the circle and the diamond.' He stepped up to the door and traced each symbol with his fingers. 'The circle for eternal slavery and the diamond Burn of Death.'

'From the slave town and the Garian prison,' Will added. 'All those marked with either are condemned to die. Which door should we take?'

'The first one,' James said firmly. He didn't know why he felt so certain, but the unfamiliar symbols of the anchor and flower intrigued him.

'Agreed,' Arthur confirmed and Aralia nodded in consent.

Opening the door, they found themselves facing another passageway. Just like the rest of the ship, it was empty and dark and James held his light out in front of him as he stepped through. There were only two doors along the walls which were curved to fit the shape of the ship. The companions crept quietly along the passage, curious to see how far it went. Rounding a gentle bend, they came to an abrupt halt. A white wall blocked their path, set with a door of the same colour.

Where the handle should have been, a white plaque rested, its surface engraved with an anchor and flower.

'Does it open?' Will whispered.

James brushed the metal with his fingertips. It felt hot to the touch and he whipped his hand away. The pads of his fingers glowed red and he quickly rubbed them on his cloak.

'Identity magic,' Will said incredulously. He bent to inspect the plaque but kept his own hands firmly at his sides. 'This must be the captain's cabin.'

'You could have warned me before I burnt my fingers,' James protested. 'What d'you mean by identity magic anyway?'

'You've seen it before, in the Garian prison. It's used to keep out unwanted intruders.' Will tapped the plaque with a fingernail before straightening up. 'Not all identity magic is the same. Certain types will only respond to recognised symbols. With others, there are ways to break through them. Like in the prison.'

'Where you forgot to tell us about it,' Arthur muttered.

'What ways?' James cut in. 'Are you saying we can get inside the cabin?'

Setting his bag between his feet, Will reached inside and drew out a black book. It was the size of his palm and wafer thin. Carefully turning the pages, he came to rest on one covered with a myriad of diagrams.

'My dad drew these,' he explained. 'I'm not sure why, but it may help us. The diagrams relate to a type of identity magic that can be impersonated using an illusion. It can't be traced for up to an hour.'

'D'you know how to do it?' James took the book as it was handed to him and concentrated on the tiny drawings. The lines and equations meant nothing to him and he looked at his friend for further explanation.

'I could try,' Will answered with a shrug.

'What happens when the hour is up?' Aralia seized the book from James and peered at the open page. 'Is it worth the risk?'

'The trace becomes permanent.' Will rolled up his sleeves, revealing his symbol of a semicircle shot through with a diagonal line. 'The diagrams suggest that someone has to burn their symbol onto the door. Access is then granted, but a person's own symbol will disappear until the hour has passed.'

'We'd essentially be committing identity fraud,' Arthur posited.

James looked at the door, feeling a rush of adrenaline in his chest. He was aware of the risks, but couldn't help feeling curious about what lay on the other side.

'If we go through with it, we all have to agree,' he said slowly. 'We have to stick together.'

'I'll do it.'

A deep voice sounded and they all turned. Kaedon stood in the passageway behind him and Oede hovered at his elbow. There was no sign of Dina with them and James felt his heart sink.

'Where Dina?' he asked aloud.

'I told you not to move,' Kaedon reprimanded. 'What part of that could you not understand?'

'We couldn't stay,' James replied honestly. 'We couldn't just stand there and wait.'

Kaedon's forehead crinkled. 'I know you're not exactly who you say you are, James Fynch. Perhaps sometime you'll tell me what you're really doing here.' He strode across to the door and gently pushed Will aside.

James looked at his friends and then back at Kaedon. 'We're here because we have a quest to complete, a quest linked to the myth of Arvad the Wanderer.'

A flicker of uncertainty passed over Kaedon's features but he said nothing. Instead, he rolled up his sleeves and turned to face the metal plaque. He raised his left wrist towards it, revealing a circular symbol filled with compass-like marks. James leapt forward to stop him, but too late. Kaedon pressed his symbol to the plaque and the metal glowed white. He held it still, his expression unreadable until the light faded away. Only then did he draw back to look at his blank wrist as the cabin door swung open.

Chapter 18

PASSING through the door behind Kaedon, James stopped to stare. The cabin interior was unlike anywhere he'd seen before, large but somehow crowded. It was shaped to fit the bow of the ship, the walls curving to meet at the front in a gentle point. On either side of this, two portholes looked out into the black night.

The whole cabin was brimming with nautical paraphernalia, all laid out upon rows of shelves. Any free wall space was plastered with maps, either displaying the world as a whole or sections of sea. Several of these were nautical charts and were etched with an array of lines and numbers. Finding himself unable to take everything in with one glance, James blinked. He stood aside as Will nudged past him and the light in his hand escaped to join Kaedon's against the ceiling.

'We do not have long,' Oede urged from the doorway. 'I will keep watch.'

The air inside the cabin smelled salty but this was not unpleasant. It was how James imagined a ship should smell, of the sea, of adventure and discovery. Sucking the scent into his lungs, he wandered further into the cabin. His attention was caught by a bronze telescope resting on one of the shelves. Carefully picking it up, he held the smaller end to his eye. A dark circle appeared and he blinked, wondering if he had forgotten to remove the cap on the other end. He was about to lower the instrument when he noticed several pinpricks of light swim into his eyeline and blinked again.

'The stars,' he whispered. 'I can see the stars.'

He turned his head a fraction and the scene moved with him. Thousands of stars filled the space before him, tiny but brilliant in their complex formations. He recognised the jagged shape of the plough to his left but didn't know the names of any others. Spinning around to his right, he found himself staring at a cluster of seven stars. They looked brighter than their companions, resting close together while remaining independent. He had the feeling that he'd seen them before, but wasn't quite sure why. Feeling a tap on his shoulder, he lowered the telescope and re-focused his eyes on Will.

'It's an Ondero,' Will explained, tilting his head to inspect the instrument. 'A reflective telescope,' he added as James raised a questioning eyebrow. 'I've heard of these but never seen one. Can I?'

James passed the Ondero to him. 'The stars are the same in my world as in yours,' he observed. 'I suppose it makes sense if both worlds are in the same universe.'

Will nodded but kept his eyes fixed on the stars. 'I suppose so, although I'm not sure your world makes much sense at all. I'm still baffled as to how two places can coexist so closely and yet never cross.'

'Well, not never.' James picked up a magnifying glass and held it up to one of the maps. 'What confuses me is that the time in my world is different. It seems to pass more quickly there than it does here. Albert says it's an illusion, because time doesn't really exist at all.'

'There are many theories used to explain the movement of

time across different spaces,' Will said. 'Dad always used to say it's more complex than a theory, but some people are unable to understand the universe without one.'

'Maybe some things just can't be explained, with or without a theory,' James suggested. He had never found physics interesting at school but this concept intrigued him. He hoped that he would understand it a little better one day, as Albert had anticipated.

Returning the magnifying glass to its shelf, he looked for something else to inspect. Spinning globes, binoculars, and other unrecognisable objects glittered in the mellow light, calling for him to pick them up. The cabin looked like a fairytale place, where science and magic came together to create a cave of treasures. In here, it was easy to forget the horrors that the rest of the ship contained.

'Here, take a look at this.'

Will reappeared at his elbow and pressed an open book into his hands. Looking through the translucent pages, James saw swathes of water swirling beneath them. The sensation was disconcerting, making him feel as if he were in it and above it at the same time. It was the same feeling he'd experienced on beach holidays as a child, standing in the sea with his back to the waves.

'It makes you part of the story,' Will explained. 'You can imagine whatever you want and it makes you feel like you're there.'

James nodded. The dizzying illusion also reminded him of the bridges he'd seen on the internet, where you could walk over deadly gorges on pathways of glass. He'd always wanted to try one, but now he wasn't so sure. A loud creaking startled him and he turned to see Oede stiffen at his watch post. The sound came again and again, each time longer than the last.

'Ropes in the wind,' Oede eventually whispered. 'That is all.' His shoulders relaxed but his expression remained unchanged.

'Here, take a look at this!' Arthur's urgent voice drifted across the cabin. He was standing between the porthole windows, his body curved over a table of charts.

Discarding the magical book, James hurried to join him. Will and Aralia crowded in behind him as he leant over Arthur's shoulder. A large chart lay across the table, the paper warped by years of salt exposure. Despite this, the lines were still clear, threading their way across inky seas. Scanning the surrounding continents, James couldn't help but stare. Beneath his gaze, sections of the map expanded as if held beneath a magnifying glass. When he looked away again, the same parts contracted, leaving the map as it had been before.

'Can you see that?' he asked in amazement. 'It moves.'

'Watch what happens when I touch it,' Arthur replied with a grin. He pressed a fingertip against the outline of a river and a light glowed. A new line appeared beside it, drawn in fresh red ink. 'It represents our route,' he explained. 'It shows the captain where the ship is heading.'

James leant across Arthur and touched the line himself. 'Are you saying that this line shows the way to Arvora?' He withdrew his fingers from the map only to find that they were damp.

'If I'm right about the purpose of the line, then yes,' Arthur answered.

'It's still several days until we reach the sea,' Kaedon growled behind them. 'This type of chart is common on ships and like all the others, it doesn't show Arvora.'

'It shows Opoc though,' Arthur pointed out. 'We seem to be heading in the right direction but then the line just stops. Why?'

Kaedon's expression darkened. 'It means that only the captain knows the precise location of Arvora.'

'How perceptive of you.'

A lightly accented voice sounded behind them. They all turned around, scanning their surroundings in search of the intruder. A woman was standing in a doorway at the back of the cabin. The white frame blended seamlessly into the walls, making it almost invisible. The woman smirked as everyone turned towards her and her sharp eyes flickered between their worried faces.

'Only the captain knows the precise location of Arvora,' she mimicked. 'It is one of the many privileges given to the Arvorian captains.'

Breaking from her stiff pose, she marched across the cabin towards the table of charts. The companions cleared the way for her but Kaedon stood firm.

'Who are you?' he snarled.

The woman paused with her face turned away from him. Without warning, she spun around and grabbed his left arm. He made no move to fight back as she pulled up his sleeve to reveal the smooth skin where his symbol should have been.

'You risked your life to break in here,' she remarked. 'Why?'

'Why do you think?' Kaedon's eyes flashed and he whipped back his arm.

'You're the captain, aren't you?' Will asked before the woman had time to answer. 'This is your ship, but...'

'Well congratulations,' she interrupted. 'But what? Were you expecting a man?'

Will shook his head but turned faintly pink as her sharp eyes bored into him. Her blue irises clashed with the green of her robe, giving her a mismatched appearance. The robe itself was short, giving her trousered legs freedom to move. Her attire was completed by a triangular cap which perched awkwardly on her short silver hair.

'Your persistence is admirable,' she continued, turning to look at James. 'The Belladonna is the oldest of the Arvorian ships and the most secure. I imagine from your faces that the name isn't unfamiliar to you.' She lowered her voice until it became almost too quiet to hear. 'She is the mistress of all ships; queen of the seas.'

James shuddered. The ambiguity of her words made him nervous. He was no longer sure if she was referring to the ship or the Belladonna herself. Before he could decide which, the captain clicked her fingers and two men appeared in the doorway behind her. Light flashed and James suddenly found his hands bound together behind his back. Before he had time to protest, one of the men strode across the cabin and grabbed him by the arm. He tried to wriggle free but the man was strong and propelled him towards the exit.

'Aca ari marlian?' The man paused in the doorway to look back at the captain.

'Aca an,' she snapped. 'Biranca.'

The man pushed James through another cabin and into the passageway beyond. It was the same one they'd walked along less than an hour before. Craning over his shoulder, James saw that his friends had also been restrained. Kaedon and Oede walked behind them, closely attended by the other guard. On reaching the doorway marked with the anchor and flower, the group came to a halt. The man holding James let go and moved to open the second door, the one marked with the Burn of Death.

It was dark on the other side and they entered a passageway lined with doors. The guards hurried along at a quick pace but eventually stopped outside one of the doors. The taller of the two tugged it open and James found himself being pushed through. Entering the cabin on the other side, he became aware of many faces staring at him. Rows of benches lined the walls, all occupied by shabbily dressed people. They turned their glazed expression towards him, watching but never judging.

Scanning the interior, James estimated there to be around thirty occupants. The air smelled of sweat and urine and he covered his mouth with one hand. Someone kicked him in the shin and he stumbled. His hands came free of their invisible bonds and he grabbed onto Will to steady himself. He caught sight of Kaedon and Oede still standing on the other side of the door. Neither were looking at him and he tried to catch their attention. One of the guards pushed them both down the passage and the cabin door suddenly slammed shut.

'Where're they going?' James asked desperately. He turned to Will, Arthur and Aralia who looked back at him with solemn expressions.

'I can't believe this is happening,' Will groaned.

Aralia pressed her fingers to her eyes. 'They'll be killed and we'll be next. What were we thinking?'

'It's a bit late to wonder that now,' Will snapped. 'Maybe they won't kill us.'

'We should work out a plan instead of fighting,' James pleaded.

Spotting a few empty seats at the far end of the cab, he made his way towards them. The slaves continued to stare as he went past, only turning away when he sat down amongst them. Will, Arthur and Aralia squeezed onto the bench beside him. No one spoke, instead turning their attention to the surrounding cabin. Many of the captives were asleep or lost in a wakeful trance. They sat hunched over themselves, simply existing.

James could feel the gold clock ticking against his chest and began to count the seconds.

At around one hundred he gave up and slipped into a tired daydream. He wanted to sleep, but the clock kept reminding him of the passing time. It held him in a strange state of wakefulness that made him feel restless. He remembered his mum telling him once, in a rare moment of closeness, that time is what humans make of it. To sit here feeling frustrated was worthless and wasted no one's time but his own. Smiling at the memory, he closed his eyes and let his mind go blank.

He woke up because something was different. Will was sitting slumped against him but he knew that wasn't it. The cabin itself was the same but the atmosphere had changed. It was as if the air was moving but there was of course no wind. Many of the slaves were sitting up straighter, their eyes open and alert. He stared at them for several seconds but none of them looked back. Although everything inside the cabin was still, he felt as if he was moving. The sensation was calming, lulling him back into a state of sleep.

'Can you feel it?'

He opened his eyes again to see Aralia looking at him from across Will's sleeping form.

'Feel what?' he mumbled.

'The sea.' She turned away from him, her eyes darting across the walls as if she could see the water through them. 'We've reached the Eeron sea.'

On the other side of the cabin, someone turned towards them. James saw the movement from the corner of his eye and tried not to turn around too quickly. He moved his head slowly until his eyes came to rest on a woman. She was watching him closely, her green eyes bright and intelligent unlike those of her fellow captives.

'Who is that?' Aralia asked.

'I don't know,' James shrugged. As he looked, the woman jerked her head as if inviting him to join her. 'What d'you think she wants?' he asked carefully.

'I think she wants you to go over there.' Will raised his tousled head and grinned. 'Go on.'

Ears burning, James stood up and made his way along the rows. The woman shifted aside to give him more room and he squashed himself beside her. From up close, her skin looked pale and sickly. The hollows around her eyes were dark and sunken, but her pupils glittered with life. Looking into them, James frowned, experiencing the strange sensation that he'd seen these eyes before.

'You're the boy,' the woman whispered after a brief silence.

'What boy?' James asked.

'The one looking for the Hidden City.'

He stared at her, suddenly realising who she was. She'd been in the Garian prison at the time of their break-in and had helped them in their search for the firestone.

'You recognise me,' she continued softly. 'I am the nameless one.'

James frowned. 'You carry the Burn of Death, the black diamond.'

'I do not know your names.' While the woman didn't directly ask, she turned to look curiously at Will, Arthur and Aralia.

'Maybe it should stay that way,' James suggested. 'That way we can be equal.'

The woman nodded but didn't meet his gaze. 'Did you find what you were looking for before? Did you find the Hidden City?'

'Yes. We found it with your help.'

The woman smiled. The way her face lit up was familiar somehow. James began to realise that it wasn't just because they'd met before but because she reminded him of someone else.

'You lived there once, in the Hidden City, didn't you?' He twisted his fingers together awkwardly but refused to drop his gaze.

'You remember,' she said quietly and her smile widened. 'Yes, I lived there. I know every alley, courtyard and canal like the back of my hand. My sister and I used to explore it all when we were young.'

A pained look came into her eyes and James took a deep breath. 'Your sister,' he began, 'does she look like you?'

'Darker and fiercer, but much the same.'

James swallowed and the woman looked at him uncertainly. He noticed her pulse fluttering in her neck and focused his attention on its irregular beat.

'She's here.'

The woman looked at him in disbelief. Her mouth moved but no words came and she grabbed onto James' hand instead.

'She's here,' James repeated, 'on this ship. She's looking for you.'

Still the woman stared. Her lips moved again and this time a small sound came out. 'Dina?'

Her cheeks flushed as if she'd been slapped and her eyes were a paradox of water and fire.

Thrown off guard, James pulled his hand away and shrank back in his seat. 'It's true,' he said quietly. 'We met your sister in the Hidden City. She's come to help you.' He paused before continuing. 'Why are you here? Why are they taking you to Arvora?'

The woman's eyes grew misty. 'My sister,' she murmured.

'My sister is here.'

The door at the end of the cabin suddenly flew open. Startled, the woman turned away from James and her face went blank. James looked at his friends and then at the door, his own heart racing. A wild haired woman entered the cabin, accompanied by a giant of a man. He could barely stand in the cramped space, his sleek scalp brushing against the roof. Neither came any closer but placed themselves on either side of the door. Another figure emerged, dressed from head to toe in black. Staring at the shadows beneath the hood, James felt his skin grow cold. The stranger's face was marred by a white scar that ran from his eyebrow to the top of his lip.

Chapter 19

THE blemish on the man's face instantly gave him away. James had never seen anyone who bore such an aggressive mark and it made him shudder. The man was someone he'd hoped to never see again, a servant of the darkness who answered to the name Kedran.

'Besha im!' A deep voice boomed across the cabin. The giant-like man took a step towards the captives and they shrank back in their seats. 'Besha im!' he bellowed again. 'Kri iama; stand up!'

All around the cabin, slaves and prisoners rose to their feet. James stood too, casting a sidelong look at his friends to check they were doing the same. Amidst the frightened silence, Kedran strode across the cabin and stopped beside the first row of captives. The guards moved with him, always hovering a few inches behind him. He looked small in their shadow but his aggressive expression left no doubt as to who was in charge.

'Arm, eran, el,' he commanded in three different languages.

The nearby captives extended their left wrists towards him. He grabbed the woman in front of him and pulled her out into the aisle. She flinched but didn't cry out as he gripped her wrist between his fingers. Light flashed across her skin but she held still. James drew himself up to his full height, trying to see what had happened, but the woman covered her wrist and sat down. Kedran moved along the row to the next captive and repeated the same process.

James watched with growing dread as Kedran drew closer. A small part of him hoped that he wouldn't be recognised, but he knew that was too much to wish for. From the corner of his eye, he saw Will pull up his sleeve. He wanted to turn and run but instead took a deep breath and laid his own wrist bare. Light flashed at the end of his row and he realised that he was now close enough to see what was going on. Everyone was being branded with a new symbol, printed onto their skin with black ink. As the old marks of imprisonment faded away, they were replaced with the emblem of Arvora.

Halfway down the bench, an old man stood leaning on his neighbour for support. Stopping in front of him, Kedran sneered before spitting at his feet. The man didn't move but regarded Kedran carefully with his watery eyes. Annoyed by this, Kedran hissed to the male guard who stepped forward to jab the captive in the ribs. Still he made no complaint and tried to stand a little straighter. The effort was too much for him however and his legs buckled beneath him.

'Stand up,' Kedran barked. 'Besha im; ikri ama.' He too prodded the man in the ribs and laughed.

The man looked back at him, his tired eyes half closed. He tried to straighten up again but couldn't quite manage it.

'I said stand,' Kedran snapped. He aimed a kick at the man's shins but missed by a fraction.

'Leave him alone.'

A feminine voice echoed across the cabin and Kedran whipped around. All heads were bent and the brave individual didn't speak again. James lowered his own eyes to the floor but he knew to whom the voice belonged. It had sounded right beside him, quiet but determined. Daring to glance sideways, he saw that Kedran's knuckles had turned white. Eyes flashing angrily, he reached out and slashed the old man across the cheek. The victim made no sound as blood trickled between his lips but the woman beside him gasped. Kedran immediately turned on her and grabbed her by the throat.

'Dare to cry out?' he barked.

The woman looked back at him with fearful eyes. Kedran held her for a moment longer before pushing her away. Light flashed from his fingertips and hit her wrist. The inky circle faded away and was instantly replaced by the mark of the anchor and flower. Another flash followed and the woman cried out as it struck her in the chest. She crumpled to the floor where she shuddered once and then lay still.

For an awful moment, James caught Kedran's eye. He felt darkness close in on his chest, slowly suffocating him. Standing just inches away from the woman's lifeless form, he hung his head and didn't dare look up again. Somewhere in his mind, a familiar voice was trying to reach him. He knew it was the girl with whom he shared a fate, but the darkness was clouding her out. Fearful that Kedran might be able to hear her, he pushed her away until she fell silent.

Kedran now stood just a few steps away, leering at the captives. His clothes stank of sweat but he stood with the confidence of a king. James watched anxiously as he leant back to whisper something in the ear of the male guard. The man smirked and reached James' side in two strides. Grabbing his wrists, he bound them behind his back and turned him towards the door. James tried to protest, but found that his lips had also been sealed.

'Hey, get off her!'

He turned to see Arthur trying to pull the female guard's

hands from Aralia's arm. His attempts got him nowhere as he too was grabbed and pushed towards the door. Stepping into the passageway outside the cabin, James noticed the surroundings growing hazy. He wasn't sure if the lights were dimming or whether it was just his eyes. Blinking hard, he tried to clear his vision but everything went dark.

He knew he was conscious because he was still walking. Someone punched him in the back and he quickened his pace. He could feel a familiar fear rising in his chest but tried to fight it back. Closing his eyes, he imagined a light in his mind and held it there while he continued to walk. After several minutes, he felt the air grow cooler. He tried not to think about where they were going but couldn't help wondering if this was it. This thought scared him less than he'd thought it would and he walked on with a more confident step. His movements became rhythmic and after a while he stopped thinking at all.

Someone pushed him from behind and he stumbled forward. Tripping over something solid, he lost his balance and skidded to his knees. Surprised by the fall, he sat completely still, waiting for something else to happen. As if from far away, he heard footsteps retreating and the sound of a door clicking shut. In the ensuing silence, he tried to prise his hands apart but it was no use. They were tied firmly together and he sat down properly, trying to think of a plan.

'Will, Arthur, Rai?'

He called their names out in his aloud, only to realise his voice had been muted. He tried again, speaking with his mind this time, even though he knew they wouldn't answer. Sighing into the silence, he began rocking back and forth, trying to clear his thoughts. In the stillness, he then heard a faint whispering and realised that it was coming from inside his mind.

'James?'

He cocked his head in an attempt to hear better. The voice came again, repeating his name until he realised with surprise who it belonged to.

'Aralia? Is that you?' Hardly daring to believe it, he waited for her answer.

'James? Can you hear me?'

'How're you doing this?' he asked in bewilderment. 'I didn't know you could talk with your mind.'

'Neither did I. I don't understand'

'I suppose what matters is that we can hear each other,' James returned.

Aralia cleared her throat but whether aloud or in his mind he didn't know. 'What's he doing here?' she asked. 'The man with the scar?'

'You mean Kedran,' James replied stiffly. 'If Arvora is linked to the Belladonna as the captain said, then it's inevitable that he's involved too.' Engaging his feet, he tried to stand but rolled onto his side instead. 'How can we escape if we can't move?' he continued, more to himself than to Aralia.

'Maybe we can move,' Aralia suggested, her voice sounding more confident. 'If we can find each other, we might be able to untie our wrists at least.'

James nodded and shuffled backwards a little. He followed Aralia's voice inside his mind, listening as it grew closer. Inching forward a fraction, he bumped into something solid and heard a groan.

'Sorry, I guess that's you,' he said apologetically. 'Here, let me find your hands.' He fumbled around on the floor until his fingers brushed against hers. Grateful that she couldn't see him blush, he felt for a rope about her wrists but found nothing there. 'There are no ropes,' he said in his mind. 'They've used magic.'

'No ropes?' Aralia's voice came back thin and anxious. 'Then we're stuck here.'

A tense silence settled between them. James lowered his head to his knees and tried to think. He felt something move against his face. It was rough and taut and felt like a piece of fabric. Struck by a new idea, he sank back into the depths of his mind.

'Rai, are you still there?' There was no reply and he tried again. 'Rai, the blindfolds are real. We can untie them.'

Still, she didn't answer. Determined not to be beaten, he wriggled his legs and managed to pull himself onto his knees. Facing away from where he believed Aralia to be, he leant back and his hands met with her hair. Shaking strands from between his fingers, he felt for a fabric knot. He found it wrapped in slippery tendrils but grabbed onto the end and pulled. It grew tighter but he tried again and the cloth fell away in his hands.

'It worked,' Aralia breathed in his ear. 'Here, let me help you.'

He felt her hands against his scalp, tugging at the knot. After several attempts, it came free and he opened his eyes. Everything around him was completely dark and he frowned.

'It's still dark,' he whispered. 'Can you see anything?'

A light flickered beside him and he turned towards it. It lit up Aralia's face and behind her, the curled up forms of Will and Arthur. Jumping to his feet, James hurried over to untie their blindfolds.

'You won't tell them, will you?' Aralia's voice sounded in his mind again as she bent to free her brother.

'Tell them what?'

'That I seem able to speak with my mind. It's hard work, but if I concentrate I seem able to do it. I didn't answer you before because I couldn't remember how.'

'Alright, I won't,' James promised and pulled Will's

blindfold free.

'Where are we?' Will immediately asked. 'What happened?' His eyes glittered wildly and he rubbed his hair until it stood on end.

'Calm down,' James reassured him. 'We found a way to untie the blindfolds and that broke the spell. As for where we are...'

He looked around, realising he didn't know. They appeared to be inside a square-shaped room that was painted entirely black. Even the floor was black and there was no sign of an exit anywhere.

'Clever,' Arthur said faintly, 'to put us in a blackout cube where we can't see or hear anything.'

'I think it's glass.' Aralia moved to press her hand against one of the walls. 'Feel it.'

James placed his hand on the nearest wall. It felt cold and smooth, just like a window might. Pulling his fingers away again, he looked intently at the black marks left on his skin.

'Why paint the glass?' he frowned. 'Why not just use magic?'

'It's not painted,' Will stated. 'Watch!'

He placed both hands against the wall, fingers splayed. Where his skin and the glass met, patches of black began fading away to reveal a clear panel beyond. A faint light shone through from the other side but the gap was too small to see through clearly.

'It responds to heat,' Arthur said incredulously.

Will nodded. 'If we take a wall each, we might be able to clear more.'

They each chose a wall and pressed their hands to the glass. Almost immediately, the black coating began to melt away. It faded away beneath their fingers and spread across the ceiling before making its way onto the floor.

'Keep your hands on the glass,' Will ordered.

James stared through the window in front of him. It was almost entirely dark on the other side, apart from a faint shimmer that wavered like a candle in the wind. At first, it looked like the light was moving from side to side but the harder he looked, the more convinced he became that it was in fact the darkness. It undulated to and fro, drawing away from the glass before returning.

'It's water,' he breathed. 'We're under the water.'

As he watched, the wavering light appeared to grow brighter. Small bubbles rose from the depths below, latching themselves onto the glass and remaining there. All around the cube, the water underwent a change. Its peaceful rhythm slowed before suddenly rushing forward with a great force. It raced towards the glass but dissipated before it had the chance to strike. James felt horribly small in its presence, as if he were a fish waiting for a predator to attack.

'Can you see that?' Will's voice drifted across the space, sounding almost fearful. 'Can you see?'

'See what?' Aralia returned. 'The boiling water? The darkness?'

'That shape, the shape in the water.'

James twisted around to look through Will's window. There was nothing there but swirling water and yet more glimmering darkness.

'I can't see anything,' he announced.

Turning back to his own window, he stared with fresh amazement. Something *was* moving in the water, a dark shape floating towards him. At first, it had no defining features but as it drew closer, he gasped. Resting amongst the swirling darkness was a familiar scene. A bedroom lay before him, scattered with an array of boyish paraphernalia. The bed in the corner was occupied by a young boy who was fast asleep. As James watched, the boy woke up and suddenly started screaming. He leapt from the bed and ran to the door, trying to tear it open. James felt a familiar tightness rising in his chest as he realised that the boy in the vision was himself.

Cast back into a memory from his childhood, he fought against the fear filling his mind. The scene gradually began to fade but was swiftly replaced by a new one. This time, he found himself inside the scene, rather than just observing it. He was lying in his bed at home, in a body that was far too small for him, dreaming a child's dream. A figure stood above him, a knife in its hand. He tried to close his eyes, knowing what was about to happen, only to realise he couldn't.

As the blade plunged towards him, the child in his memory screamed again. Looking up, he saw a pale face beneath the figure's hood. It was a face he'd seen many times before but hadn't known. Only now did he realise that it belonged to someone familiar. As the memory faded away, he realised that his whole body was shaking. The face of the knife-wielding figure swam before his eyes, haunting him anew. He hadn't suffered from this nightmare for years but the face was one he could never forget. It belonged to the Belladonna.

Chapter 20

'TAKE your hands away,' Arthur called. 'Take them off!'

Hearing the shout as if from a distance, James tried to pull his hands away from the glass. He knew that the dream wasn't real now, even if it had been many years ago. As his fingers slipped from the window, the vision faded away and the room went dark.

'It was an illusion,' Arthur continued, his voice lowering to a whisper. 'We imagined all of it.' A light glowed and his pale face appeared behind it.

'I was falling off a cliff,' Will said unsteadily. 'Literally falling.'

'I saw someone dying who I couldn't help,' Aralia added. 'At first I thought it was Yulan, but I didn't recognise the face.'

Arthur sank to the floor and let the light drift away from his hand. 'I was an old man,' he admitted. His voice bore a note of defiance, as if he was ashamed of what he had seen.

'Were they predictions of the future?' Will asked.

'They can't be.' James slid to the floor and looked down at his hands. 'I saw a nightmare from my childhood.'

No one said anything. The light flickered restlessly and Arthur drew it against his chest to preserve the glow.

'They're our fears,' Aralia whispered at last. 'This room is enchanted. It makes us project our darkest fears onto the glass and then they're reflected back at us.'

'Our fears?' James looked at her intently but she refused to meet his gaze. 'What are you afraid of?'

'I'm afraid of people dying,' she said slowly. 'I'm afraid that I won't be able to help them.'

'Heights,' Will stated as all eyes turned to him, 'but I suppose that's obvious.'

Arthur looked at the floor, his reluctance even more evident than his sister's. 'I'm afraid of growing old and weak,' he muttered. 'I don't know why, when it's inevitable. What about you James?' he quickly asked.

James said nothing for several moments as he searched for the right words. He knew his friends would be concerned if he told them the truth, but he also knew that it was only fair to do so.

'The dark,' he began quietly. 'I've always thought it was a fear of literal darkness, but it's not. She's been following me my whole life.'

'Who has?' Aralia asked.

'Her, the Belladonna. When I was younger, I used to have recurring nightmares of a dark figure standing over me. I never realised it was her. She's been there since the beginning.'

He saw Aralia glance sharply at Will and Arthur but no one said anything. Watching their faces, he knew what they must be thinking.

'If what you say is true, then we're in more danger than any of us thought,' Aralia whispered. 'You should be careful James. If she can enter your dreams, who knows what else she is capable of?'

'Finding the crystals before she does is the only way to stop her from growing stronger,' Will joined.

FRANCESCA TYER

They looked at each other anxiously but no one knew what to say. The waterstone was an elusive force that they knew next to nothing about. As the silence dragged on, James felt himself growing drowsy. The lull of the sea drew him into a false sense of security and he tried to empty his mind of thoughts.

'What if the crystal has a living host, like the firestone did?' Will's voice cut through the stillness.

Dragging himself from the borders of sleep, James opened his eyes. 'What?'

'The firestone was protected by the Chinjoka dragon,' Will continued excitedly. 'What if the sapphire also has a living host?'

'What kind of host?' Arthur asked, straightening himself up. 'A water animal?'

'Yes!' Will exclaimed. 'Exactly. There are many legends of animals connected to the element of water. The sea turtle is the most common example. It appears in lots of mythologies as a spirit protector of the water and sea. It also has close ties to the moon.' He paused for effect before continuing. 'What if the sapphire isn't simply a water stone, but a sea stone?'

'A seastone?' Aralia repeated. 'Of course. The blue sapphire in particular is connected with the sea.'

'How d'you know that?' James asked curiously.

'I read about it once,' she returned with a slight shrug. 'I can't remember why.'

'A sapphire seastone, an ancient sea turtle, an eternal gift,' Will listed. 'It all makes sense. We're getting closer to the truth and who knows what we'll find out once we reach Arvora.'

Silence fell again and Will, Arthur and Aralia drifted in and out of sleep. James watched them flick between dreaming and reality but no longer felt tired himself. He sat staring into the flickering darkness, his mind on the seastone. It made sense that

174

the crystal should come from the sea. If Arvora really did exist on the island of Opoc, perhaps the sapphire was hidden in the surrounding ocean. He hardly dared hope that it was there when he didn't yet know if they would make it to the island alive. A loud banging startled him from his thoughts and he stiffened. Beside him, Arthur stirred and opened his eyes.

'Wake up,' James hissed. 'All of you. Wake up!'

'What's happened?' Will sat up quickly and winced as his shoulders cracked.

'Can you feel it?' James asked.

Will groaned. 'Feel what?'

'The boat. It's stopped.'

Will stared at him, now fully awake. 'Does that mean…?'

James nodded. 'It has to. We must have reached Arvora.'

'We shouldn't have fallen asleep.' Aralia stood up and brushed the dust from her cloak. 'We need to find a way out of here.'

'The door,' Arthur said quietly.

'There isn't one,' Will snapped. 'Otherwise we might have thought of that before.'

'I know, calm down,' Arthur reassured. 'What happens if we put our hands on the walls again? The door might not be visible, but there must still be one.' He pressed his hands to the glass and waited expectantly for James, Will and Aralia to join him.

With each of them touching a wall again, the blackness began to melt away. Scanning the walls, James searched for any sign of a door, but there was none. The glass panels were joined smoothly together with no evidence of a door frame.

'Nothing,' Will sighed. 'Just nothing.'

'Well we got in here somehow,' Aralia returned sharply. 'There has to be a way.'

'Wait,' Arthur's deep tones filled the space. 'Look at the floor, in the corner over there.'

He pointed to the corner between Will and James. Faint markings were visible on the floor, so thin that James thought they must only be noticeable if deliberately looked for.

'An exit?' Will asked. 'How d'we get to it? The walls will turn black again if we let go.'

'We could try one by one,' Arthur suggested.

Taking his hands from the wall, he hurried across to the corner. The glass began to cloud over again, seeping towards the ceiling. Kneeling on the floor, Arthur put his palms over the faint markings. Nothing happened. The water continued to swirl beneath them as before. Pulling up his sleeve, he pressed his wrist against the glass. There was a spark of light and he hissed inwards as it struck his skin.

'Art, what're you doing?' Aralia whispered anxiously.

'Wait, I've got it,' he returned in an unusually animated voice. 'The water isn't really there. It's an illusion.'

'An anagroma.' Will's eyes widened and he moved to join Arthur. 'We each need to mark our symbols onto the glass in order to be let out.'

Arthur nodded. 'Exactly, but we'll have to move fast.' He stood up and hurried to replace his hands on the blackened window. 'We can do it one at a time.'

He signalled to James who broke away from the wall and knelt by the markings. Pressing his symbol to the glass, he waited for the spark of light. It burnt his skin as it struck but the pain was not unbearable. Once finished, he returned to the wall and Will took his place. With all four symbols printed onto the glass, they stood back and waited. At first, nothing happened. Then there was a flash of light and the room went dark.

'My light's gone,' Arthur muttered. 'Hold on.'

A new beam flickered into being and he held it above the corner of the room. Where the markings had been, there was now a square hole. The glass had melted away entirely, opening the floor to the dark water below.

'Everyone ready?' Will asked. He strode over to the corner and squatted beside the opening. 'It's our only chance,' he said and without waiting for a reply, dropped into the water and disappeared.

James, Arthur and Aralia stood staring after him. They crowded around the opening, trying to spot him, but the water was too dark. Kneeling, James settled himself at the edge of the hole. He looked up at Arthur and Aralia who nodded encouragingly despite their anxious expressions. Taking a deep breath, he closed his eyes and dropped. For a split second, he was submerged in freezing water. Then just as suddenly, the water disappeared and he found himself standing in a darkened passageway. Hearing a splash, he turned to find Arthur and Aralia had joined him. Both looked completely dry and patting his own clothes, he realised that he was too.

'A sensory anagroma,' Will stated, emerging from the shadows. 'It's more than just a visual illusion. You can experience sounds, smells, feelings and even tastes. It's clever.'

'We need to move,' James said urgently. 'I have an idea. Follow me.'

Nudging Will aside, he began walking down the passageway. It looked like all the others they'd been through, long and lined with many doors.

'James, where're we going?' Aralia asked, hurrying to catch up with him.

'Portholes,' he returned briefly. 'We're looking for portholes.'

The doors all led to empty cabins but none were like the one Oede had found. There were no portholes in sight and he began to wonder if they were too far below the surface. He could see a set of stairs at the end of the passage and hurried towards them with fresh urgency. Just as he was about to join the first step, he heard footsteps in the corridor above. Glancing at Will, Arthur and Aralia, he flung open the nearest cabin door and slipped inside. All four of them peered around the frame as the footsteps progressed to the stairs.

A blue cloaked woman appeared. Two figures trailed behind her, both dressed in brown. The group passed by the companions' hiding place, but none of them seemed to notice the open doorway. As soon as they'd gone past, James hurried back out into the passageway. One of the brown cloaked figures stopped mid-step and turned around. James froze as his eyes came to rest on the features of the Garian slave boy. He was looking straight past James to where Will, Arthur and Aralia stood staring. Aralia started towards him, her hand outstretched, but Arthur gently drew her back.

'We can't help him,' he whispered.

The boy looked away and carried on walking. James signalled for his friends to move too and they hurried back towards the steps. Only Aralia kept glancing back. On reaching the top of the steps, James flung open the nearest door. His eyes fell on a porthole in the far wall and he breathed a sigh of relief.

'In here,' he directed. 'There's one in here.'

The porthole was covered with a fine mesh but he pushed his fingers between the holes and tugged. The wire came away and he dropped it to the floor.

'Why are we here?' Aralia asked. 'What have portholes got to do with anything?'

James paused in his work. 'They're our way out,' he

explained. 'I did it before with Kaedon and Oede. That's how we got onto the ship.'

Grabbing onto the porthole rim, he heaved himself upwards and pushed himself through. He felt a cold breeze ruffling his hair and his head popped out on the other side. Holding onto the outside edge, he slid himself out headfirst and managed to lower his feet onto the ledge below.

'Be careful,' he whispered to Will who was just emerging behind him. 'This ledge is quite narrow.'

He shuffled away from the porthole to make space for his friends. They appeared one at a time and lined up on the ledge beside him. Looking at their surroundings for the first time, James felt his heart sink. He wasn't sure what he'd expected Arvora to be, but it certainly wasn't this. Empty sea stretched out before them, grey and still. There was no sign of land close by or even on the distant horizon. The ship had stopped moving but there was nothing to be seen for miles around.

'This can't be Arvora,' Aralia stated. 'It just can't be.'

'No,' Will agreed. 'We'll have to go back inside the ship. We can't stay out here.'

'We can't go back,' James objected firmly. 'When they find out we're missing, they'll hunt us down and kill us.'

Aralia leant her head against the ship's side. 'What about Dina? We can't just leave her here.'

Before James could answer, a bell began ringing somewhere deep within the ship. It wasn't the sharp tone of an alarm but rather the brassy note of a bell.

'For the prisoners?' Aralia asked.

'Or for us?' Will added.

Arthur edged away from the porthole and a nervous sigh escaped his lips. 'Do we really want to find out?'

'We'll have to jump,' James concluded in a strained voice.

'We jump and then we swim.'

Holding onto the side of the ship with one hand, he began to untie his shoes. Once removed, he laced them together and hung them around his neck. Will, Arthur and Aralia copied his movements before looking at him expectantly.

'Ready?' James asked. 'We jump on three.'

As the last word left his lips, he let go of the boat and jumped. He was only in the air for a couple of seconds before he struck the water and sank down into the freezing depths.

Chapter 21

RISING to the surface again, James gasped for air. The water was so cold that he could feel his limbs seizing up but he forced them to keep moving. Rubbing the salt from his eyes, he looked around for any sign of his friends. Three heads bobbed in the water nearby and he quickly swam to join them.

'We'll freeze if we don't keep moving,' Aralia warned through chattering teeth. 'We should go back to the boat.'

James looked behind him to where the ship lay. Its hulk was dark against the sky which was itself shadowed by the clouds of evening. Curious to see beyond the hull, he began swimming towards it. Propelling himself around the vast structure, he paused to stare at the scene before him. A wooden jetty floated on the waves in front of him. It rested freely on the water, attached neither to land or the ship. A faint light hovered around it, indicating the presence of magic. The wooden boards creaked on the tide, an eerie, echoing sound.

His eyes were drawn to a flash of movement close to the ship. A black cloaked figure emerged from an open hatch and moved to stand on the tiny platform attached to the side of the vessel. Although James couldn't see the face, he could tell the figure was a man from the way he stood. A cluster of brown cloaked individuals stepped from the hatch behind him. The man arranged them in single file before directing them towards a steep ladder that led down to the jetty. Left without a choice, the captives began to descend one by one.

'Where're they going?'

Aralia's voice sounded but James kept his eyes fixed on the line of people making their way down the side of the ship. He didn't dare look away, fearful that one of them might not make it if he did.

'I don't know where they're going,' he said quietly.

He shivered, but it wasn't just from the cold. Watching the captives made his insides twist with anger. They moved without spirit and fight, knowing that their fate was already sealed. He wanted to jump onto the jetty and yell at the man in black, but he knew his words would be meaningless. The laws were different in this world and for now, he had to accept it.

'Maybe they're not going to Arvora at all,' Will suggested. 'Maybe they're simply brought out here to die.'

The companions watched as the first captive reached the end of the jetty. They stopped as if to assess their next move and suddenly stepped off the edge. There was no splash as each one hit the water and disappeared beneath the waves. Others followed, arriving at the end of the jetty and stepping from the edge. A whole line of captives was now pouring onto the jetty. They rippled along its length like a great wave before letting the sea take them. When the last victim had jumped, an eerie silence descended. The companions looked at each other desperately, but no one knew what to say.

'Look out!'

Will's voice broke the silence and he started waving frantically. Looking towards the ship, James saw with horror that it had begun to move. Hovering just inches from the hull, he began to swim. The ship cut the water like a knife but he skirted away just in time. Aralia floated beside him but Will and Arthur were nowhere to be seen. He suddenly felt a hand on his arm and found himself being dragged beneath the water. Salt filled his mouth and he choked but the hand wouldn't let go.

He fought against the grip and eventually it slipped from his arm. Bursting above the surface, he gasped for air and immediately looked for the ship. To his surprise, it had completely disappeared. There was no white wake on the waves and the horizon lay quiet. Hearing a splash, he turned to find Will, Arthur and Aralia behind him. All three were staring with amazement at where the ship had been. Too cold to speak, James started swimming towards the jetty. Gripping onto the slippery wood, he hauled himself from the water and lay on his back shivering.

'We're going to die out here,' Will said as he pulled himself onto the jetty.

'We will if you just lie there waiting to,' Aralia snapped.

James raised his head. Aralia was standing at the end of the jetty, her face turned to the horizon. Her blonde hair had been darkened by salt and lay in strands along her scalp. She turned to look back at him and he let his head drop back onto the planks.

'You're right, we might just die here,' he said. Will snorted with tense laughter but fell silent as Aralia shot him a fierce glance.

'If any of you stood up to look for yourselves, you'd see that we're not stuck here,' she reproached.

It took a moment for her words to sink in. James was first to jump up and join her but Will and Arthur were quick to follow. Aralia pointed to the swirling waves but the boys simply shrugged.

'What're we looking at?' Will asked.

Aralia folded her arms and sighed. 'Our passage to Arvora. Can't you see the water shimmering?'

Letting his eyes lose focus, James looked at the water again. At first, there was nothing, but faint streaks of light then appeared in his peripheral vision. Every time he looked at the streaks directly, they disappeared. Looking beyond the light, his eyes came to rest on a more solid shape. It looked like the outline of a long rowing boat but when he blinked, it vanished.

'You saw it, didn't you?' Aralia turned to him, her eyes sparkling. 'There are boats lining the jetty but they're invisible from the water.'

'Boats?' Will asked. 'I see lights but no boats.'

'None of the prisoners drowned,' Aralia continued. 'They simply boarded the boats and became invisible too.'

Kneeling on the wooden planks, she lowered her foot over the side of the jetty. Just before it hit the water, it vanished. She smiled and raised her shoulders in a questioning shrug before sliding from the jetty and disappearing.

'Rai?' Arthur called. 'Are you alright?' Pushing past Will, he stepped off the jetty after her.

Will turned to James with a look of uncertainty. 'Go on, you next.'

James nodded and knelt at the edge of the jetty as Aralia had done. He lowered himself towards the water until his feet struck something solid. Letting go of the jetty, he felt himself wobble as the boat took his weight. Before he had time to adjust his balance, Will collided into him and they both stumbled backwards. They grabbed onto each other, trying to steady themselves and ended up falling onto the bench behind them.

The boat itself was long and narrow. It had six benches along its length but there were no oars. Arthur and Aralia had settled themselves in the bow and James and Will moved to join them. Almost as soon as they sat down the boat began to move. It drifted away at remarkable speed and the jetty was soon lost amongst the dancing waves. Feeling something against his ankle, James bent to look under his bench. The space beneath was filled with black cloth. Pinching a section between his fingers, he pulled and a ragged strand came free.

'What's that?' Will backed away as James dropped the rag on the bench between them.

'I think they might be blindfolds,' Aralia answered. 'They must be for the captives.'

'We don't need them then,' James concluded and put the cloth back under the bench.

He turned to look at their surroundings and noticed a white line on the horizon. It looked like a band of mist but it was too far away to be certain.

'We must be close to land,' Arthur suggested. 'You don't get mist like that out at sea.'

'A mask for Arvora,' Aralia said quietly.

James felt his heart beat a little faster. None of them had thought about what they would do if they made it to Arvora. Their original plan had been to discover more about it, not actually go there. Yet here they were, alone on a boat in the middle of the Eeron sea.

'I guess we'll find out,' James said.

As they drew closer to the mist, thin trails began creeping around the boat. These grew gradually thicker until they were surrounded by a sea of white. Nothing around them was still, the mist and the waves continually shifting and changing. The atmosphere was different too. It felt thick and oppressive, like that of a stormy day. It was impossible to see more than a few inches ahead of the boat. Somewhere far away, a rasping sound drifted across the water. It was like an echo, a faint sound that reverberated against the mist.

'Did anyone else hear that?' Arthur asked.

Before anyone could answer, a dark shape emerged from the mist ahead of them. At first, it was just a shadow, but as it drew closer it took on a human form. It hovered just above the water, the blackness of its body wavering in the misty air. Torn between states of solidity and translucency, the spectre floated towards the boat and slowly raised its head. Beneath the shadows of its hood, a pair of white eyes burnt. As these came to rest on the boat, the creature let out a horrifying shriek. It raised an arm and the sleeve of its cloak fell back. Shrinking back in his seat, James suddenly noticed that its left wrist bore the mark of Arvora.

'Let the water take you,' it whispered. 'It's peaceful here. Jump and let the water take you.'

A second voice joined it, whispering the same words over and over again. James stuffed his fingers in his ears but realised he could still hear them. He shuddered, suddenly wondering if the voices were inside his head. In an attempt to expel them, he started to hum, quietly at first but gradually getting louder.

Movement caught his eye and he turned to see Will standing in the base of the boat. He was staring straight at the ghostly figure who was beckoning to him. No longer aware of anything else, he leant towards the spectre and reached out a hand.

'Will, what're you doing?' Aralia called. 'Will, sit down. You don't need to do this.'

James shook his head, trying to block everything out. Aralia's voice was making him anxious and he felt the sudden urge to jump. He knew he was losing his mind but didn't care. The harder he tried to clear it, the foggier it became. He felt as if he was drowning in mist, gasping for air which didn't come.

The sea looked inviting and he leant greedily towards it. Part of him knew he shouldn't jump but the voices kept urging him to do it. He rose to his feet and stepped towards them, his eyes half closed. Something sharp struck his face and he hurriedly sat down again. The brain fog started to lift and he realised Aralia was glaring at him.

'Did you just slap me?' he asked.

'Yes, I had to.' She folded her arms across her chest. 'You were going to jump. All three of you,' she added, looking at Will and then Arthur. 'I'm sorry.'

'Thanks,' James mumbled. 'What was that thing?' He looked out over the water, relieved to see that the spectre had vanished.

'Who knows,' Will said quietly. 'Maybe the ghost of a captive.'

James turned his gaze on the bow of the boat where Arthur was standing. His hand hovered above his eyebrows as he scanned the distant horizon.

'Look,' he said suddenly. 'I think I see land.'

Amongst the swirling trails of mist, an uneven shape had emerged. Its solid form pierced the mist; a lonely island in a sea of white. Although the shore wasn't visible, they could see black cliffs looming over the water.

'Is that…?' Aralia's words trailed away as she stood up next to her brother.

James nodded. 'It must be.'

'We'll have to swim to the shore,' Will announced.

'Swim? Why?' James asked but he was already moving to collect his bag.

'The boat will take us to the same place as the captives,' Will explained. 'We don't want anyone to see us, right?' James nodded and he continued. 'We can wait until the last possible moment.'

The boat drew closer and closer to the mass of land. Before long, they could see the outline of a beach just above the water. Will waited until they were close enough to see the shale before giving the signal. He stood up on his bench and James, Arthur and Aralia copied him. On the count of three, they stepped from the starboard side and plunged into the water. It was much colder than it had been at the jetty. James felt it numbing his skin and seeping into his bones as he swam towards the surface. Breaking through the waves, he breathed in deeply before turning towards the shore.

The rolling waves made progress difficult. They kept pushing him backwards and the shore never seemed to get any closer. With each stroke, he looked out for any sign of his friends. Rising from beneath a wave, he spotted two blond heads just ahead of him. Reassured, he scanned the water again, this time in search of Will. He spotted him close to the shore but it looked like he had stopped swimming. He was lying on his back and the waves were washing over him. James squinted through the mist, feeling suddenly alarmed. The harder he looked at Will the more obvious it became that he wasn't moving at all.

Chapter 22

KEEPING his eyes on Will's unmoving form, James began swimming with all his strength. He pushed the waves aside with powerful strokes, trying to reach the shore. For a few minutes, he felt like he was progressing but when he looked up the beach was even further away than before. Exhausted from fighting against the current and the cold, he let his arms drift freely in the water. He let his head fall back against the waves and felt his eyes droop shut. Instead of sinking, he felt the water lift him up and propel him forward.

Suddenly, hands were on his shoulders, pulling him from the sea. His knees grazed against a rough surface as he was lowered to the ground. Opening his eyes, he saw Will standing above him, his clothes dripping onto the surrounding stones.

'Well, we didn't drown,' Will said cheerfully. 'That's something.'

James sat up and spat out a mouthful of seawater. He spotted Arthur and Aralia nearby, perched side by side on a large rock. Dragging himself to his feet, he moved over to join them.

'What happened?' he asked, directing his question at Will. 'I thought you'd stopped moving.'

'I was tired,' Will explained. 'I stopped swimming for a

second but then I realised something.' Peeling off his wet cloak, he dropped it next to his bag. 'The water is enchanted, making it impossible to swim ashore. If you swim, you drown. The only way to do it is to float.'

'It's a cruel kind of magic,' Aralia added through chattering teeth. 'It relies on the fact that most people who try to swim will drown.'

'The ghost was a drowned captive then,' James presumed with a shiver.

He tilted his head back to look at the steep cliff above. The rocks were smooth and appeared almost black against the oddly lit sky. A soft glow hung around the island, seeping through the ever changing mist. The white trails didn't encroach upon the land however but hovered by the shore.

'I can feel it in the air,' he whispered. 'It's everywhere.'

'Feel what?' Will perched himself beside Arthur and Aralia on their rock.

'I'm not quite sure how to describe it. It feels like I imagined.'

Arthur looked at him with narrowed eyes. 'By it, d'you mean Arvora?' He stood up and moved to stand at the base of the cliffs. 'We can't climb up here,' he continued before James had a chance to reply. 'There's no way.'

'We don't have any other choice, do we?' Will asked. 'The beach is blocked off by water on either side.'

'If you want to try climbing, be my guest,' Arthur replied evenly.

'If we don't climb, what will we do?' James walked to the water's edge and let the freezing waves lap over his toes.

'We swim,' Arthur said.

'Swim?' Aralia turned to her brother with an expression of disbelief. 'We can't do that either. We were lucky before but we might not be again.'

Arthur shrugged and went to stand beside James. 'If we don't swim, the tide will rise and we'll drown anyway. If we keep close to the shore, the enchantments shouldn't affect us.'

'I suppose the island can't be impenetrable the whole way around,' James remarked. He waded further into the water, letting it rise to his shins.

'So we're agreed,' Arthur concluded, ignoring the uncertain looks Will and Aralia cast him.

The water somehow didn't seem as cold this time but the current was stronger. James let it push his feet from the seabed and drive him away from the shore. He began to swim, following Arthur as he led the way alongside the cliffs. They followed the curve of the island, keeping well away from the rocks. The beach soon disappeared behind them, hidden behind a protruding crag. There was nothing between them and the cliffs but mist. James could feel it clinging to his hair and face, threatening to suffocate him. It was as if Arvora hung in an everlasting gloom that was neither day or night, twilight or dawn.

'There! look!' Will's voice echoed eerily in the silent atmosphere.

Holding still in the water, James looked to where he was pointing. Against the cliffs, a patch of rock stood out darker than the rest. It curved above the waves, breaking the even pattern of the rocks. It looked like a cave of some sort, resting at the base of the cliff with its small mouth drinking in the sea. He started swimming towards it and didn't stop again until he was close to the entrance. To the left of it, a rocky outcrop protruded into the water. On the right however, a steep bank ran from the sea and into the cave mouth.

'Come on, let's climb up the bank and have a look inside,'

Will suggested. He swam past James and sluggishly pulled himself ashore.

James, Arthur and Aralia pulled themselves up behind him. After quickly pulling on their shoes, they crouched on hands and knees and began to crawl up the bank. Although it was steep, tufts of wiry grass gave them something to grab onto. Suddenly, Aralia let out an exclamation and came to a halt. She bent close to the ground and began inspecting the rocky hollows.

'What is it?' James hissed. 'What're you looking for?'

'My ring,' she returned sharply. 'I've dropped it.'

James vaguely recalled seeing a silver band on her finger in the antique shop in Eriphas. 'It wasn't expensive, was it?'

'No but I liked it. It doesn't matter,' she continued resignedly. 'Let's keep moving.'

The slope began to level out as they crawled. While the larger swathe continued up to the top of the cliff, the smaller section dipped towards the cave mouth. Keen to reach the cover of darkness, the companions chose the second route. They were forced to move along the cliff edge, taking care to avoid the piles of loose shale. It didn't take them long to reach the opening and they slipped carefully inside. Once their eyes had adjusted to the murky light, they realised they were sitting on a precariously narrow ledge. It overlooked the cave itself which, despite the small entrance, was vast.

The cavern stretched so far up and back that it appeared endless. Glowing orbs were suspended along the walls at random intervals and these cast a dull light into the surrounding space. This light glinted on the sea which lay ten or so metres below. Resting just inside the cave entrance was the silhouette of a ship. The sails had been lowered but James was sure it was the same vessel they'd been on hours before.

Shadowy figures were moving to and fro from the ship. All were holding crates, ferrying them along a jetty before disappearing into the darkness.

'D'you think this is it? Are we really in Arvora?' Will whispered.

Sitting in the semi-darkness, James noticed how the air had changed again. It was no longer oppressive but hung lifelessly in the surrounding space. Every time he took a breath, he felt as if he couldn't get enough of it. He sensed a darkness here, soaking into every fibre of his being. It was a darkness far deeper than any he'd felt before and it made him shiver.

'We should keep moving,' Arthur encouraged. 'We won't find out where we are by sitting here.'

They began to move again, balancing precariously on the crumbling ledge. There were a few orbs near the entrance but as they turned a corner the light changed. Rows of burning torches lit the walls, creating a much brighter atmosphere. The flames revealed a myriad of pathways which lay between a network of tunnel entrances. A pulley system had been constructed alongside the paths and numerous crates were making their way along it. Hidden in the shadows, the companions sat watching with fresh intrigue.

'We should follow the crates,' Will suggested, 'see where they go.'

They crawled for several more metres before continuing on foot. The ridge they were on dipped downwards and joined a path that led between the tunnel entrances. The pulley ran into three of these and they followed the closest one. It was so narrow inside that there was only just enough room to squeeze through. The burning torches inside the entrance increased the temperature to an unbearable degree. Their clothes steamed in the unnatural warmth, creating a dense and sulphurous atmosphere.

The passage was short and they soon broke out into fresher air. They found themselves standing on a small platform that was suspended above three more passages. A metal railing ran along the outside edge and James leant cautiously over it. A circular pit lay below, filled with wooden crates. Several of these were open and he could see masses of white and black gemstones glittering inside.

'Crystals,' he whispered.

'What would they need crystals for?' Will moved to stand beside him and looked down into the pit below.

James shrugged. He could feel magic tingling in the air around them. It was a raw, untainted power, one that came from the earth itself. He recognised it as a power bound within crystalline forms, but a darker version of that which had emanated from the firestone.

'Let's keep going,' Arthur said. 'I have a feeling that this is just the beginning.'

He led the way into a second tunnel. This one was wider but equally short and opened onto another platform. From here, they were able to see the same pit and several others, all filled with stacks of crates. After a brief glance over the railing, they walked on again. The next passage was as narrow as the first. Instead of opening out however, it grew gradually tighter until they were forced to stop altogether.

There was only a slim gap left through which they could see an open space. It was barely wide enough to fit through but none of them wished to turn back. First to reach the gap, Arthur turned sideways and began to push himself through. James followed, holding his bag at his side and sliding between the narrow rock formations. Sharp stone pressed against his chest but he managed to squeeze himself through to the other side. Another platform appeared before him. It was larger than the others and instead of a metal railing, it was blocked off by a set of pulley rails.

'It's a dead end,' Arthur announced. 'There aren't any more passages.'

'Maybe this is it,' James said dejectedly. 'Maybe Arvora is just this.'

'I don't believe that,' Aralia stated as she emerged from the gap. 'As Art said before, this can only be the beginning. Right, Art?' She turned to him but he was no longer paying attention. He was leaning over the pulley rails, his face dark with concentration. 'Art,' she tried again. 'What're you doing?'

'I'm making a plan,' he returned thoughtfully. 'We said we should follow the crates. Well, these rails keep going up.'

'Does that help us?' Will asked. 'We can't follow them if there aren't any tunnels.'

'That's just it,' Arthur continued, testing a rail with his foot. 'Instead of finding our way through more tunnels, we could climb into the crates. I've estimated that the two at the base of the rails will arrive soon.'

Leaning over the edge, James saw two crates making their way upwards. Neither one had a lid and it was clear that they were empty. Both were larger than the ones they'd hidden inside in Eriphas, providing just enough room for two people in each. As they climbed towards the platform, Arthur put out an arm to stop them in their tracks. They came to a gentle halt but continued to nudge against him as he held them there.

'Climb in quickly,' he urged.

James and Will clambered into the second crate while Aralia and Arthur took the first. As soon as Arthur let go, they began to move. The additional weight slowed the pace and the crates wobbled precariously on the rails. A steep drop lay to their right, leading down to the crate filled pits. They had only progressed a few metres when Arthur uttered a sharp exclamation. He pointed to a platform ahead of them around which there were several closed doors. The rails passed alongside the platform and when the crates drew close enough, he jumped out.

James, Will and Aralia followed his lead and the empty crates disappeared behind them. Arthur pulled open the closest door and stood aside to let everyone through. The faint light coming from the caves revealed a small room on the other side. It was packed with old crates, all jammed together in wobbly rows. Another door was visible at the back of the room and they crossed over to it. A faint light shone through the cracks on the other side and they stopped to listen. Hearing nothing, James pulled the door open. Daylight flooded inwards and he put his hands protectively over his eyes.

As the spots faded from his vision, the scene before him came into focus. A thin mist moved towards him, reaching out with its trailing white limbs. It felt cold and damp, reassuring him that it was real and not just an illusion. The sky shone with a strange light and for a moment he wondered if he was looking out into No Man's Land. As he looked harder however, he realised he could see an outline of cliffs beyond the mist. Surprised, he cast his gaze downwards and gasped. The ground in front of him fell away in a sheer drop. Black cliffside lay beneath him, stretching down to the Eeron sea.

Chapter 23

THE sight of the sea so far below took James' breath away. He took a hasty step away from the doorway and let his friends peer through. They too stepped backwards and Will turned a little pale.

'That was close,' Aralia remarked. 'We'll have to go back and try another route.'

'Unless…' Arthur leant around the door frame but his sister pulled him back. 'There are metal rungs up the cliffside,' he continued. 'They go from the sea right to the top of the island.'

'There's no way I'm climbing up the cliff,' Will stated firmly. 'No way.'

'It's not far,' Arthur encouraged, 'and it looks pretty solid.'

'Pretty solid isn't solid,' Aralia objected. 'I'm with Will on this.'

Stepping into the doorway again, James looked out onto the cliffs. He spotted a metal rung to his right and reached out to grab it. The bar felt firm beneath his fingers. Reassured, he turned back to the room.

'I think we could do it,' he said slowly. 'It would save us some time.'

Will and Aralia looked at each other with equal uncertainty. 'Alright,' Will conceded at last. 'I'll do it, but if we die I'm blaming you.'

'What about you, Rai?' Arthur asked.

She shrugged in defeat. 'Alright.'

Still holding onto the metal rung, James swung his legs onto the bar just below it. Once secure, he began to climb, keeping his eyes fixed on the cliffside above. The rungs were cold and damp from the misty air and he held on tightly. He didn't dare glance down for fear of losing his nerve and simply kept climbing. Scanning the cliffside, his eyes came to rest on a dark hollow. It looked like a cave or tunnel entrance, buried deep within the dark rock. He was too far away to see inside it but climbed towards it with fresh vigour.

Drawing parallel with the opening, he peered inside. It was dark but looked more like a tunnel than a cave. There were no rails to grip onto but the ladder was just close enough for him to swing himself into the entrance. Landing safely on the earthy floor, he extended his hand to Will who was just behind him. Will clung stiffly to the ladder but took James' arm after some encouragement and pulled himself into the tunnel. Arthur and Aralia followed, both appearing relieved to be on solid ground again.

'Let's hope this doesn't have a dead end,' James muttered as they started down the tunnel.

The black rocks gave an illusion of darkness, despite the daylight seeping in behind them. They could only see a little way ahead to where the walls vanished among the shadows. The tunnel came to an abrupt end and they stopped. A small, circular room faced them. It was empty apart from a staircase that spiralled upwards from the centre of the room. There were no windows or doors in the walls which were painted a bright white.

'I guess we go up,' Will said.

Stepping onto the bottom tread, James looked up through the twisted centre. The staircase seemed to go on forever, winding towards an invisible end. He started to climb, taking the narrow steps one at a time. Will, Arthur and Aralia joined the stairway behind him, keeping up with his steady pace. The higher they climbed the narrower the steps became. This slowed their progress but they kept going, driven by urgency and stubborn determination.

Rounding a tight curve, James spotted a doorway just a few steps ahead. It was cut into the wall right alongside the steps which continued to wind upwards. Hurrying to reach the door, he turned the handle. There was a soft click and it swung smoothly open. Bright light flooded into his eyes and he winced before stepping through. As his eyes adjusted to the light, he realised he was standing on a balcony. Looking around, he saw that it was one of many which were suspended around the circumference of a vast room. The scale of it made him gasp and he hurried to look over the balcony railing.

'This is more like it,' Will whispered behind him.

A network of pipes ran between the balconies, extending right out into the middle of the room. The bronzish structure glittered in the light which shone from thousands of hovering orbs. Far below, on the ground floor, clusters of white robed people were standing around long tables. These were joined together by more pipes which carried silver pods between them. The pods were removed and reattached by the robed people. Some emptied and others refilled but they all worked in silence.

'It's so quiet,' Aralia breathed, breaking the awed stupor which had fallen over them. 'That's what's so strange here. It's completely silent.'

'You're right,' James agreed. 'We should be careful what we say.' His eyes came to rest on a door on the opposite side of the room. Even from here, the markings on its surface were unmistakable. 'Look,' he whispered. 'The circle and the diamond. If Dina, Oede and Kaedon are imprisoned here, we should try to find them.'

'You think they could be through that door?' Aralia asked.

James raised his hands in a questioning gesture. 'We have to start somewhere.'

'The balcony is a dead end,' Arthur said quietly. 'We'll have to go back the way we came if we want to get anywhere.'

'Either that, or we can carry on up the staircase,' James replied.

'Hey, wait!' Will was leaning over the edge of the balcony, both hands gripping onto the railing. 'I think I see something.' He tilted his head sideways and closed first one eye and then the other. 'It might be my imagination but look between this balcony and the next one. D'you see anything?'

Intrigued, James leant over the balcony edge. His eyes quickly focused on a shimmering light that ran alongside the wall. It looked like a border or even a walkway that passed between the balconies. Every time he blinked however, it temporarily disappeared.

'Is it a path?' he asked.

'It's like the boats,' Aralia breathed. 'It's pretty much invisible to anyone who isn't on it.'

'Only one way to find out for sure,' Arthur said with a wink.

Before anyone could stop him, he jumped over the balcony railing and lowered himself down on the other side. Will, James and Aralia watched anxiously as his legs swung free. He flashed them a quick grin before letting go. For a heart-wrenching moment, he dropped. Then his knees buckled as he hit a solid surface and he instantly disappeared.

'There's our answer,' Will said and quickly clambered over

the edge.

James followed, hopping over the railing and dropping down on the other side. His feet struck solid ground and he steadied himself before daring to open his eyes. As Aralia had predicted, the pathway was now visible to them. Though narrow and faintly translucent, it ran all the way around the circumference of the room.

'Here goes,' Arthur said and began to walk.

They were halfway between the balcony and the door when a swishing sound startled them. Turning to their right, they saw a large glass ball moving towards them along the bronze pipes. It was finely balanced at the epicentre of its own shape and glided along at a steady pace. Two figures stood inside it, one dressed in blue and the other in brown. They stood facing away from the companions, their postures rigid.

'Can they see us?' James whispered.

'They might be able to sense disturbances,' Will answered. 'Try not to move.'

The glass lift came to rest alongside the nearest balcony. Standing just inches from it, the companions held still and waited. One of the glass panels melted away and the figures stepped out together. Opening the door at the back of the balcony, they passed silently through. As soon as they had gone, Arthur pulled himself over the balcony railing and hurried over to the lift.

'I've never been in one,' he explained as he stepped into it. 'I bet it can take us anywhere we like.'

A thud sounded behind them and they all spun around. The balcony door was opening again but it was too late to return to the pathway. James, Will and Aralia jumped into the lift beside Arthur just as the blue cloaked figure stepped from the doorway. As the lift began to move, the figure looked up. His eyes fell on the companions and his unshaven face twisted into an ugly snarl. Striding to the edge of the balcony, he raised both hands and flung a beam of light towards the lift.

'Duck!' Will shouted.

They crouched down as the light streamed towards them. Just before it hit the glass, it burst and disintegrated into tiny sparks. Suddenly, the lift rolled onto its side and they were thrown against the windows. James closed his eyes, waiting for the glass to shatter. Instead, the lift began to slow down and he realised it had simply rolled onto a new line of pipes.

'We've got to do something,' Aralia gasped. 'The next one might hit us.' Regaining her balance, she looked anxiously towards the balcony.

'We can't really do much,' Will replied. 'We're stuck in a glass ball about thirty metres up!'

James let out a shaky breath and his gaze fell on a balcony just a few metres in front of the lift. The rails ran right alongside it, with just a small gap between them and the railing bannister. A wild idea flashed through his mind and he felt the hairs on the back of his neck stand to attention.

'The balcony,' he said urgently.

'The what?' Will looked to where he was pointing and his eyes widened. 'We won't make it.'

'It's our only chance,' James insisted. He pressed his hand to one of the glass panels and it swiftly melted away. 'Our only chance,' he repeated. 'Are you with me?'

A rush of air struck him and he breathed it in. The balcony was just a leap away and he knew there would only be a short window in which to jump. From the corner of his eye, he saw another beam of light racing towards the lift. He turned to look at his friends and Will shouted something which he couldn't hear. Summoning up fresh courage he stepped to the edge of the lift and jumped. The air caught him for a split second before he began to fall. Light flashed in the air behind him and he heard the sound of glass shattering.

Chapter 24

JAMES hit the balcony with a thud and immediately rolled himself over. To his relief, Will, Arthur and Aralia lay strewn across the balcony but the lift had disappeared. Brushing shards of glass from his cloak, he sat up and groaned.

'They know we're here,' Will mumbled. 'They'll come after us. We don't have long.'

Rising to his feet, James moved to lean over the balcony edge. The white robed people went about their work as before, seemingly undisturbed by the chaos above. His eyes came to rest on an odd structure that was just visible through a large gap in the wall to his left. It looked like a temple, made up of stone archways and bridges. All this was held up by a vast column that stood beneath the central point. Looking for a way to reach it, he remembered the invisible pathway and turned back to his friends.

'I know that look,' Will commented. 'What mad idea have you come up with now?'

'It's not mad,' James objected. 'Look, can you see those archways through the gap in the wall? I think we should head over there.' He swung his legs over the side of the balcony and waited.

'Lead the way,' Arthur stated.

The pathway was narrower than before and they had to walk slowly along it. Fortunately, the next balcony was close and they pulled themselves onto it. There was no door against the back wall but a stone walkway passed through the gap in the wall and joined a bridge on the other side. The companions walked along it in single file but stopped when they came to the base of the bridge. From up close, the temple was even more impressive. The domed roof was covered with intricate engravings that crept down onto the archways. There were seven of these, built in a circle on top of the vast column.

James kept his eyes fixed on the nearest archway as he walked over the bridge. He could see light glimmering on the other side and hurried towards it. Passing beneath the curved stone, he entered a circular room. The space was hemmed in by the archways through which the light seeped in. A single orb hovered in the centre of the room, casting a faint light over the airy interior.

'What is this place?' Aralia asked in awe.

The room was simple but beautiful. The spaces in between the arches were painted white and decorated with an array of symbols. Animals and flowers were interspersed with seemingly random triangles and squares. The floor was equally intriguing, made of coloured marble and laid in a spiral pattern to complement the shape of the room.

'Here, take a look at this,' Arthur whispered. He was kneeling in the centre of the room and peering through a circular window in the floor. It was fixed between three marble slabs and enclosed by a thick metal edge.

James knelt on the floor beside him and looked curiously through the glass. 'There are people down there,' he said with surprise.

The room below the glass was the same size as the space they were in. It had no doors or windows and was lit by several flickering orbs. It was occupied by five white cloaked figures and a sixth who was dressed in brown. This last individual was a woman and she had her arms wrapped around her body as if trying to keep warm. Although her face was hidden, a mass of dark hair flowed from beneath her hood. A tall mirror hovered in the air in front of the woman. She stood facing it and the white cloaked figures gathered around her.

As the companions watched, a grey-haired woman broke away from her companions. She took hold of the captive and started to remove her cloak. The brown fabric peeled away to reveal the skinny form of a young woman beneath. Dressed in nothing but a threadbare tunic, she began to shiver uncontrollably. A strand of hair fell across her cheek and she brushed it away with a trembling hand. Her bare wrist bore the familiar symbol of the Arvorian anchor and flower.

'What do they want with her?' Aralia whispered. 'She's frightened.'

In the room below, the grey-haired woman took a white cloak from a nearby chair and presented it to the captive. The young woman shrank back as it was draped around her shoulders but she stopped shivering. She was alone in front of the mirror for just a moment before a man moved towards her. He pulled open her palms and placed an object in each. When he stepped away, she held her hands up to the light. Both cupped a stone, one white and the other black.

'Crystals,' James breathed. 'Jet and quartz. They're the same ones Yulan spoke about.'

As he spoke, the captive suddenly looked up. Her piercing blue eyes met with his for a split second before she lowered her head again. The look on her face was one of such desperation that he felt his stomach twist.

'I can't watch,' Aralia said, a faint tremble in her voice. She looked away but immediately turned back.

'There's no way that we can help her,' Arthur commented, 'though I wish we could.'

Left alone in front of the mirror, the young woman stepped forward. The scene behind the shimmering glass began to change. Her own image disappeared and was replaced by white mist. She reached out towards it and her hand passed through the invisible glass. The cold air made her shiver but she tried to hold still. A bright flash suddenly burst from the mirror. It struck her in the chest and she stumbled backwards with the force. The light shot through her skin like bolts of lightning and she stared down at her body in terror. She stood this way for several seconds before crumpling to the floor. No one tried to help her and she shook for a while before her body grew still.

A deep silence descended, one that carried the weight of death. James, Will, Arthur and Aralia sat completely still, quietly refusing to look at one another. Unable to tear himself away, James continued to stare at the scene below. The girl's death bothered him somehow but for a greater reason than just the loss of her life. He knew the mist she'd tried to enter and had stood in its presence many times. It belonged to in-between places, like No Man's Land and the strange spaces he entered in his dreams. Sitting here, wrapped in the shadow of death, he started to understand what it all meant.

'James?'

Aralia's voice sounded close by and he looked up. He sensed her eyes on his face but refused to meet her gaze. Instead, he focused on a tear that had fallen onto the window.

'James, is this place what I think it is?' she asked, her voice barely audible.

He didn't answer at first, knowing that to say it out loud

would make it more real. Rising to his feet, he went to stand under one of the archways. His ideas about Arvora were just a guess but they frightened him more than anything else.

'I don't know how I didn't see it before,' he said quietly. 'This place… this is what it's all about. Jasper, the crystals, Arvad, everything.'

Walking over to join him, Arthur took his shoulder and gave it a gentle shake. 'It's alright, calm down,' he reassured.

James rubbed his temples and nodded. 'Arvora isn't just a place to keep wayward prisoners and slaves,' he said quietly. 'It's a science lab. This is where they experiment.'

'Experiment? Will asked sharply. 'What for?'

'D'you remember the slave town?' James turned around to face his friends. 'D'you remember what it was for?'

'To find your world,' Aralia whispered.

'The first time I came to this world, I passed through a place called No Man's Land,' James continued. 'There was a mirror there that I had to pass through to reach Arissel.'

'A mirror, like the one down there?' Arthur queried, pointing to the window.

James nodded. 'It gave me the ability to pass between worlds and across time itself. Those people in the room below were conducting an experiment to see if they could do the same.'

'The crystals,' Will began, 'is that what they're for?'

'I don't know but it's possible, isn't it? Jet and quartz must have some power that we don't know about. The Belladonna won't rest until she's found a way into my world.'

'If she's successful, she'll be the most powerful enchantress in history,' Arthur added. 'If Arvad's crystals get into her hands, it makes her job easier.'

Before he could continue, a low humming sounded beneath them. Hurrying to the window, they looked down to find that the figures were closer than before. They were standing on a small platform that was moving slowly towards the glass.

'Quick, to the bridge,' Will commanded.

They ran through the nearest archway and onto the bridge. Behind them, the white cloaked people stepped from the platform into the circular room. They carried the young woman's body between them as if she were no more than a sack of onions. Laying her down on the marble floor, they formed a tight circle around her. One of them raised a hand and a white beam struck the corpse in the chest. Flames burst into life around it, turning the woman to ashes where she lay. The companions paused to watch in horrified silence as the fire sank to glowing embers.

'I hope she finds peace now,' Aralia whispered.

'She won't be the last,' Will commented. 'We have to keep looking for the seastone. It's the only way we can help.'

Arthur wrapped an arm around his sister and drew her away. Will followed them but James lingered behind for a moment longer. As he stood watching, one of the figures turned. It was the same woman who had undressed and redressed the captive. Her gaze fell on the companions and her placid expression changed to one of puzzlement. She looked at them intently, as if trying to work out whether they belonged. Locked beneath her stare, James didn't dare move until he saw her raise her hand. A bolt of light shot from it and he ducked as it burst in a shower of sparks above him.

Chapter 25

'WHERE are we going?' Aralia called over her shoulder.

They had left the bridge behind and were running down a long pathway. Stone archways curved above it, casting striped shadows on the areas below. A single doorway stood at the end and they ran towards it with increasing urgency.

'We have to find Dina, Oede and Kaedon.' James slowed his pace and took a great gulp of air. 'We have to find out if the seastone is here.'

He stopped just behind Will who was first to reach the door at the end. A plaque was nailed beside the handle, blank apart from a tiny engraved circle. Will placed his fingers on the smooth metal and a light glowed. Lines began to appear on the surface, interspersed with words and numbers. As these engravings settled, it became obvious that they were looking at a detailed map.

'It's a floor plan of Arvora,' Will said.

James leant in to take a closer look. The carved circle had moved from its original spot and now hovered at the end of a corridor. He touched it and a code appeared beneath it, written in miniscule letters.

'Room codes,' Arthur explained. 'They make it easier to reach specific locations quickly.'

'Wait.' Aralia also leant in closer to the plaque and her eyes flickered over the diagrams. 'Look, this corridor is marked out for the captives.' She pointed to a line on the map beneath which the word 'Gota' was written. 'Gota means prison in Henlan.'

'I thought you didn't speak Henlan,' Will frowned.

Aralia glanced uneasily at her brother. 'The dryads used to use 'gota' in reference to our father. Some words aren't so easily forgotten.'

Will nodded uncomfortably and focused on the map. 'Two lefts and a right,' he directed. 'Let's hope we find Dina and the others there.'

They passed through the door and into another corridor. The air was colder here, caused by some wayward draught. Instead of doors, the walls were lined with metal gates. There were five on either side and each was lit by a single orb. They stopped in front of the first and peered through the thick bars. A dull haze swirled on the other side, touching the metal but not quite seeping through. It was from this that the cold air came. In the depths of the mist, a shadow moved. It let out a long, hollow moan and the companions hurriedly withdrew.

'What is that?' Aralia asked with wide eyed horror.

'I think… they might be… souls,' Will tried. 'You know, souls lost to experiments. They must keep them here for something.'

James walked along to the next gateway and looked inside. Another shadow hovered there, close to the bars but too faint to see clearly.

'Come on,' he said quietly. 'Let's not stay here.'

Opening the door at the end, they passed through into a new corridor. It had no doors but was lined with large alcoves, each containing a glass tube. These were fixed onto bronze runners which ran through the floor and ceiling.

'I think they're lifts,' Arthur said. He pulled open the door to one of the tubes and poked his head inside. 'It's like the one we were in before, only a different shape.'

'The diagram showed us two rights and a left,' Will pondered, 'but there aren't any doors in here!'

'Maybe we should try using the lift,' Arthur suggested. 'We might get there quicker.'

'How do we programme it to go where we want it to?' James asked. 'We can't just go anywhere.'

'I don't know,' Arthur shrugged, 'but what I do know is that we're running out of time.'

James stepped into the lift. Will and Aralia squeezed in behind him and the door swung shut. For a moment, nothing happened. Then the lift suddenly dropped. James felt his stomach lurch as it plunged downwards at a terrifying speed. Just as abruptly, the motion stopped. As James' eyes came into focus, he realised the lift had stopped halfway down the wall of the vast central room. Another lift was crossing the rails beneath them and he realised why they had stopped.

'James Fynch.'

A voice sounded in his mind, thin and urgent. It was familiar, even though he'd never heard it in his mind before. He looked down at the occupants in the lift below but the voice didn't belong to any of them.

'Dina?' He closed his eyes, trying to locate her. 'Where are you?'

'No time to explain,' she replied urgently. 'They know there are imposters here. Finish whatever you came here to do and then go.'

'We're coming to find you.'

'I know who you are, James. Trust me, you have to go. I have to stay here a little longer but I'll follow you. I promise.'

Before he could answer her, the floor lurched beneath him. The lift dropped, plunging into an impenetrable darkness. When it eventually stopped, he opened his eyes to find that it was still dark. Creating a light in his hand, he held it up in front of him. It came to rest on the anxious faces of Will, Arthur and Aralia.

'I think we're underground,' Will whispered. 'The air is warm.' He pushed open the lift door and stepped into the darkness beyond.

They appeared to be standing in a small cave. Black rock surrounded them on every side and there was only one tunnel leading out of it.

'I heard Dina, in my mind,' James began. 'She said that she's fine and we should go on without her.'

'You heard her?' Aralia spun around and her face was close to his. 'Are you sure?'

'Certain.' He stepped away from her and held his light up to the tunnel entrance. 'Come on, we should get out of here.'

He dived between the earthy walls, taking the light with him. The tunnel was flat and straight and they walked in silence for a long time. The air maintained its warmth, making the route stuffy but not unbearable. Having settled into a monotonous rhythm, James was caught out by a sudden dip in the path. He stumbled and grabbed onto the walls for support. Clumps of wet earth came away in his fingers and his light went out. Standing still in the darkness, he then felt water seeping through his shoes.

'Are you alright?' Arthur asked and the tunnel was illuminated again.

'It's wet over here.' James looked down at his feet which were completely submerged in the murky water. 'It's not too deep at the moment but that could change.'

'We can't exactly go back,' Will said. 'This is the only way out. If it gets too deep, we'll have to swim.'

James waded further into the water and Will, Aralia and Arthur splashed along behind him. Arthur sent the guiding light up to the roof and let it hover along above them. The water was cold but not unbearable and they waded through it at a steady pace. There were no more sudden dips in the path but the water gradually rose towards their thighs.

'It's getting deeper,' Aralia whispered. 'The tunnel must be on an angle.'

'We have to hurry up,' Arthur said urgently. 'The tunnel itself isn't the problem. It's the tide.'

'The tide?' James asked. 'We must be getting closer to the sea.'

Arthur nodded. 'Yes and if we don't hurry the tunnel will fill up completely.'

Moving quickly through the deepening water proved difficult. As it rose towards their chests they decided to try and swim. They managed a few strokes before giving up as the water was still too shallow. Half-walking, half-paddling, they continued along the tunnel with increasing urgency. No one noticed the exit until they had almost reached it. Light glimmered on the other side, not the natural light of day but that of burning torches. Relieved to have reached the end, James swam towards the light. He emerged into a shallow pool and pulled himself onto the earthy bank.

'We made it,' Will groaned as he wriggled from the water. 'I was worried for a moment.'

'There's a path leading out of the cave.' Arthur pointed to where the ground rose towards the cave mouth. 'We should get out while it's quiet.'

As he spoke, something changed in the air outside the cave. A shimmering light hovered there, only just visible against the sky. It had a filmy appearance, just like the skin of a soap bubble. As they watched, the skin expanded and began to drip down over the cave mouth.

'What is that?' Will asked incredulously.

Aralia jumped to her feet and brushed wet strands of hair from her face. 'It's a barrier,' she exclaimed. 'They're shutting down Arvora.'

James, Will and Arthur stood up hurriedly. They weren't far from the cave entrance but the path was steep. Led by Aralia, they started to run, fighting their fatigue with every step.

'We'll have to dive under it,' Arthur shouted as they approached the entrance. 'Do it now.'

The light had nearly reached the ground and taking Aralia's hand, Arthur dived beneath it. Will launched himself after them and skidded safely to the other side. James was about to follow when a soft whispering filled in his mind. He realised it was the sound of many voices and sensed that they were close. Ignoring the calls of his friends, he slowly turned around. Shadowy forms slithered from the shadows behind him. They moved quickly, soon joining forces at the base of the path. He watched them hurrying towards him but a shout from Will broke him from his trance and he turned back to the cave opening.

The shield was now too close to the ground to dive under. He looked desperately around him but both ends of the path were blocked. A prickling sensation spread across his palm and he looked down. Light glimmered there, a small but powerful mass. He wasn't sure why it was there as he hadn't created it on purpose. The light continued to grow with an immense force. He could feel it in his hand but felt strangely detached from it, as if he was observing someone else.

His fingers began to shake and raising his hand, he let go. The light shot from his palm and struck the cave wall. Instead of shattering, it rebounded and he ducked. It hit the shield and bounced off again, this time flying towards his shadowy pursuers. A counter light struck it and the two burst in mid-air. Trapped between the barrier and the whispering voices, he looked over the ledge which separated him from the sea below. The shimmering shield hadn't yet reached the water and in a moment of madness, he jumped. Someone screamed as he fell but the voice was deadened as he sank beneath the water. He began to swim, propelling himself through the cave mouth and out into open sea.

'James, are you alright?'

He looked up to see Aralia kneeling on the bank. Will and Arthur stood behind her and Will extended a hand to help him ashore.

'Come on,' Arthur urged, helping him to his feet. 'We have to keep going.'

James stumbled up the slope behind his friends, water pouring from his clothes. He put his hand to his chest, relieved to feel the regular ticking of the clock. This side of the island was different from the other. The steep cliffs had been replaced by grassy slopes that dropped gently down to the sea. They were halfway up the bank when Aralia suddenly stopped. She turned towards the sea and her expression turned to one of horror. Following her gaze, James froze. A body was lying face down on the bank, its legs trailing in the water. A few steps away, a small boat hovered, its bow caught in the wiry grass.

'Are they dead?' Will asked.

Aralia didn't look at him but began scrambling back down the bank. Arthur tried to stop her but she pushed him away and hurried to kneel by the water's edge. Placing her hands on the body, she carefully rolled it over. A strangled sound escaped her lips and she let go. Kneeling beside her, James found himself staring again at the face of the Garian slave boy. Reaching across Aralia, he grabbed the boy's wrist and felt for a pulse. A faint flutter flickered beneath his fingertips and he let go with a sigh of relief.

'He's alive,' he said quietly.

Aralia whipped off her cloak and bunched it up under the boy's head. She then reached into her bag and drew out a glass bottle. James recognised it as the same one she'd used for Yulan. Holding it to the boy's mouth, she shook two drops inside. His throat moved to swallow the liquid but he didn't open his eyes.

'Rai, come on,' Arthur hissed. 'We don't have much time. We can carry him if we have to, but we can't stay here.'

Glancing back over the cliffs, James saw that several shadowy figures had appeared at the top, accompanied by huge dog-like creatures.

Aralia turned on her brother, eyes blazing. 'If I don't help him now, he won't make it. He helped us escape and now it's our turn to help him.' She bent over the boy again and wiped a stray hair from his face.

Hovering at the edge of the bank, Will bent down to grab the tangled boat. Holding onto the bow, he gave a few short tugs and it came free.

'Put the boy in the boat,' he commanded.

'I'm not leaving him,' Aralia snapped.

'You don't have to.' Will drew the boat alongside the boy. 'We're all getting in.'

Aralia stared at him defiantly but eventually nodded. Will took the boy's shoulders and James his legs while Aralia and Arthur secured the boat. He let out a soft moan as he was lowered into the base and Aralia jumped in after him. Light flashed in the sky behind them and they turned. Their pursuers were gaining on them but were not quite close enough to strike. Light whizzed past them again and the boys joined Aralia in the boat.

Looking over his shoulder, James noticed one man had detached himself from the rest. As he drew closer, he noticed that he held a glittering object in his left hand. Although he couldn't see the man's face, he felt darkness pressing against his chest and somehow knew that it was Kedran. Standing in the boat, he watched as the bright object left Kedran's hand and flashed towards him. He tried to duck but it struck him in the shoulder and his skin screamed with pain. The sensation filled his mind and his body, stinging, aching, tearing. Clutching his shoulder, he stumbled where he stood and everything went dark.

Chapter 26

'JAMES, stay with us.'

Aralia's voice sounded somewhere above him, gentle but firm. A hand was on his right shoulder which burnt with blinding pain. He couldn't remember what had caused it and it made him feel dizzy. It felt like the hand was digging into his flesh and pulling him apart from within.

'Help me.'

He heard Aralia's voice again, sounding more desperate this time. Someone touched his neck and cold fingers felt for his heartbeat. He wanted to roll away from them but he didn't have the strength. The hands pinned him down and Aralia continued to speak, trying to bring him back.

'He's dying,' she whispered, though not to him this time. 'I don't know what to do.'

'Give him the liquid again,' Arthur's voice suggested.

A bottle was pushed to his lips and he squeezed them shut. Fingers prised them apart again and liquid trickled down his throat. He coughed, rejecting some of the liquid and letting it form a pool on his chin. As he lay recovering, he heard another voice beside him but didn't know to whom it belonged.

'Woman, end of island,' it whispered. 'Will help you.'

He tried to use his own tongue but his mind was fading.

The voices around him dimmed and he lost consciousness again. In the depths of some empty dream, he felt the rocking motion beneath him stop. The next thing he knew was that his shoes were being removed and he flinched as his arm burnt with fresh pain. Opening his eyes, he saw a strange woman was bending over him. Her hair was grey and her face wrinkled, but her eyes sparkled with life.

'Who are you?' he croaked.

He waited for her to answer but she moved away. His eyes followed her and when she turned to him again, he saw that her blue cloak was marked with the symbol of Arvora. He opened his mouth to question her further when three anxious faces bobbed into his line of vision.

'You're awake,' Aralia smiled and she patted his uninjured arm and he was grateful she didn't try to hug him.

'You gave us quite a scare,' Will added with a relieved grin.

James nodded towards the woman and pain shot through his arm. 'Who is she?' he whispered. 'She's wearing the Arvorian crest.'

'She brought us in from the sea.' Will sat down next to him on what appeared to be a makeshift bed and his expression grew serious. 'We can trust her.'

Sweeping back across the room, the woman brushed Will, Arthur and Aralia out of her way. She held a cup to James's lips and he took a hesitant sip. The liquid inside was warm and sweet and he swallowed it gratefully. Looking past the woman, he saw that they were in a large room. The walls were lined with shelves of bottles and bunches of herbs hung from the beamed ceiling. A mixture of spicy and sweet scents filled the air, making his stomach rumble. He noticed a perch in the corner on which a tiny, blue-feathered bird sat watching him with keen yellow eyes.

A fresh stabbing pain made him turn back to the woman. She was pulling fabric from his shoulder and he tried to see the wound beneath. The movement was too much and he pinched his leg to try and ease his agony. A trickle of blood snaked its way down his arm and the woman wiped it away. The sight of it made him feel sick and his hunger dissipated.

'Still,' the woman commanded in a gentle accent.

She peeled more fabric away, cutting some of it with scissors. Taking up a cloth, she washed the wound in warm water until it was clean. She then opened a bottle and poured a little liquid over it. This time he cried out, the stinging sensation too much to bear. It was only momentary however and the pain began to subside.

'How long have we been here?' he asked through gritted teeth.

'Not long,' Arthur answered briefly.

The woman straightened up and looked at James closely. 'Are you hungry?'

He shrugged but then nodded as his stomach rumbled again. The woman moved away but quickly returned with a tray of steaming soup bowls. The content smelled of meat and onions and was accompanied by dark bread that tasted of herbs and malt.

'Who are you exactly?' James took a bite of his bread and watched her closely as he chewed.

She smiled and started binding his arm with a strip of gauze. 'My name is Eir. It means healing and mercy.'

'What're you doing here, on Opoc?' Will asked bluntly. 'Are you Arvorian? Do you work for… them?'

Eir kept her eyes fixed on her work. 'I live here and I work here. I work for them but I am not one of them.' She tucked the end of the gauze into the wrapping and turned to Aralia.

'You saved his life.'

Aralia sat down on a chair beside James' bed and frowned. 'How did you know it was me?'

'You are a healer.'

'A healer?' Aralia's eyes widened. 'What makes you say that?'

Eir stepped over to her and gently picked up her left arm. She drew back the sleeve and lightly traced the branch-like on Aralia's wrist. 'This mark, the mark of your family, tells me you are a healer.' She let go and didn't elucidate any further.

Aralia covered her wrist again and followed Eir as she moved across the room. 'You're a healer yourself,' she commented softly.

'I learnt how to heal long ago in the temple where I lived with my sisters. They taught me all I know.'

'Religious sisters?' James asked curiously. He recalled the temple they'd stumbled across in their search for the firestone, tucked at the edge of the Hidden City.

Eir dropped his bloodied cloak into a basin and began to wash it. 'You have been there,' she said after a long pause. 'Of course.'

'Been where?' Will frowned as he pulled off his wet shoes and tucked them next to the bed.

'To my home temple, to the Temple of Electra.'

Eir bent to collect a stray rag from the floor and a necklace swung from beneath her robes. The silver chain bore a white crystal, carved in the shape of a young woman.

'Your wear the statue of Electra,' James noted.

She straightened up and cupped the pendant in her palm. 'I wear it always. It reminds me of my home.' Dropping it beneath her robe again, she turned to James. 'We must not tire you. You must rest and I will attend to your companion.'

Her words triggered a memory in James' mind. He recalled

a voice speaking next to him in the boat and a body in the grass by the water.

'Is he alright, the boy?'

Eir didn't seem to hear. She ushered Will, Arthur and Aralia through a door at the back of the room and closed it behind her. Finding himself alone, James pulled a blanket over his legs and lay down. The pain in his shoulder was present but no longer unbearable. It ached dully, like a new bruise or scar. He thought he lay awake for a while, turning over his thoughts, but at some point must have fallen asleep.

When he awoke again, the room was dark and he was still alone.

He was tired and his arm throbbed but he carefully pushed himself upright. Inching forward on the bed, he slid his feet to the floor and, after several attempts, managed to stand up. Igniting a small light, he tiptoed away from the bed. The glow was weak but it gave off just enough light for him to see his surroundings. A sharp glint caught his eye and he blinked. It was coming from an object on the kitchen table that was partially wrapped in a dark cloth. Pinching the fabric between his fingers, he pulled it away. A knife lay beneath the folds, its golden hilt fixed to a bluish crystal blade. Feeling the urge to touch it, he picked it up and ran his fingers along the blunt edge. As soon as it touched his skin, a creeping chill passed through him. It wasn't just a shiver, but the feeling that someone had reached inside his chest and squeezed his heart.

'The opal knife.'

Eir's voice made him jump and he turned to find her standing behind him. She held out her hand for the knife and he reluctantly passed it to her.

'It gave me this wound, didn't it?' James asked, pointing to his bandaged shoulder.

Placing the knife back among its fabric folds, Eir nodded. 'I've never seen one like it,' she said quietly. 'Only three were ever made. They were designed to kill anyone who was pierced by the crystal blade. Whoever threw this knife must have wanted your life desperately.'

James frowned and his eyes flickered to the bundle of cloth on the table. He started when Eir touched his arm and pulled back his sleeve to reveal his star spattered symbol.

'Why didn't the knife kill me?' he asked.

'You are not immortal and like all others, your life will one day end,' Eir began. 'But your light is greater than the darkness carried in an object such as that. Some are born with light, others with darkness and one day it will be up to you to decide which path you truly wish to take.'

James looked at her steadily. Her words sounded strange, almost as if she were talking about someone else. Eir gestured to the table, inviting him to sit, and he obliged. Settling himself in the closest chair, he drew his light to hover above the table.

'I've been wanting to ask you something,' he mumbled. Eir inclined her head and he continued with more confidence. 'Do you know anything about Arvad the Wanderer and The Lost Years?'

Eir sat down opposite him and her eyes glittered beneath the light. 'Perhaps you should wake your friends.'

She gestured to the closed door through which Will, Arthur and Aralia had disappeared just hours before. James crossed over to it and knocked. No one answered and he pushed the door open. His gaze fell on a crowded room lined with tall shelves. His friends were lying on the carpeted floor, wrapped in blankets. They woke up as the soft light from the main room shone in their eyes. He didn't say anything but beckoned for them to follow him back to the kitchen table. Taking a seat, they all turned to look at Eir who stared past them into a distance they couldn't see.

'Your friend has asked me about The Lost Years,' she began. 'These were a time of great darkness, much like the years which are upon us now. A man named Jasper, who had taught himself dark magic, began building himself an empire. It was unlike any ever seen before on this earth. He chose this island as his base and grew his forces.'

She paused at the sound of a disturbance in the corner of the room. The little blue bird, which James had completely forgotten about, flew to perch on her shoulder. She tickled it under the chin and it flapped its wings in protest.

'He's a blue jay,' she said with a smile. 'His name is Banshee. Now, where was I?' She nudged Banshee away from her ear before continuing. 'After a time, when Jasper had conquered this world, he began searching for another.' Her eyes flickered over to James. 'Since time began, the wise had known of another world. These elite few were divided into those who wished to find it and those who sought to protect it.'

'Does Arvad come into this?' Will asked, rubbing the sleep from his eyes.

Eir nodded and touched the crystal pendant at her neck. 'Long ago, in the temple, my sisters and I spoke of Arvad. Here too, I hear whispers of his name. Those who exist in the highest circles of magic know that his story is not merely a legend.'

'Why did you leave?' Aralia queried, resting her elbows on the table. 'Why didn't you stay with your sisters?'

'I was brought here many years ago. I refused to go blind for my faith, unlike my sisters. I adored Electra, but I could not stay without sacrificing my sight to prove my faith. They sent me away and I lost my way for a while. It took time, but I have returned to my faith and once again serve my sister Electra.'

Banshee let out a horrifying shriek and Eir lifted him from her shoulder. He flew down onto the table and settled himself against James' hand.

'How long did The Lost Years last?' he asked, tentatively stroking the bird.

'A whole century. They refer in part to a time lost to Jasper's darkness.'

'What about the other part?' Will pressed.

'The other part concerns Arvad,' Eir replied. 'There was a time in which Arvad disappeared and all trace of him was lost. They were not called The Lost Years then. Only in years since have they acquired that name. People started believing that Arvad was a myth and true knowledge of him was lost from that moment on.'

James pulled his hand away from Banshee who had started nibbling at his fingers. 'Does anyone know what happened to him? We know that his brother, Ira, took his name at some point after his disappearance.'

'Some versions of the legend say he died, lost in the wilderness. Others say he never existed at all. The story I know is that he left the world entirely.'

James looked at her with narrowed eyes, trying to make sense of her words. A realisation began to dawn on him, one that he didn't quite believe. A chill ran through him and he involuntarily shivered.

'He went to another world, didn't he?' he whispered. 'He went to my world.'

Chapter 27

NO one spoke for a long time. The silence hung heavily in the air, daring someone to break it. After a while, Eir quietly got up and filled a kettle on the stove. Once the water had boiled, she distributed it between five mugs and placed them on the table. The companions took one each and looked at one another over the curling steam.

'What does it mean?' James asked at last. He took a sip of his tea but it burnt his tongue. 'Is there no ending to Arvad's story?'

Eir sat down again and picked up the remaining mug. 'No tale is ever complete. Stories go on forever and it is only we who end them. Arvad's tale was never written down as a finished story. There were only ever parts and predictions.'

'Then surely the crystals of his legend can't be found?'

'I think you know that can't be true,' Eir reproved. 'There may not be a penned document, but the power of the spoken word can't be forgotten.'

Will set down his mug with a thud. 'What d'you mean?'

'There are four people in this world who know the tale. In part at least. Each of them knows a quarter that is passed down by those who kept the secret before them. When the four parts are put together, it forms the whole. These quarters are the greatest secret ever kept by mankind. To know them all would be to truly understand the light and the darkness.'

'Who are these people?' Arthur asked curiously. 'Do you know their names?'

Eir shook her head. 'Not even the bearers themselves know who holds the other parts. All four are oracles or prophets, known as Lekkaro in the old language.'

'Haven't these prophets been sought out?' Aralia finished her tea and fixed her eyes on the dregs in the base of her mug. 'Has the code of secrecy never been broken?'

'These quarters aren't just simple secrets that can be shared with anyone who asks,' Eir explained. 'They are wrapped in ancient magic, a magic that comes from the earth itself. The tales and their bearers belong neither to the light nor the dark. They are of the spirit.'

She fell silent and got up to refill the kettle. Someone moaned in an adjacent room and Eir wiped her hands dry on a towel. She crossed the room to a door hidden behind a wooden post and gently opened it. Aralia hurried to join her but Eir put out a hand to stop her. She passed inside the room but re-emerged moments later with a soft smile on her lips.

'He asked for you,' she announced. She didn't say a name, but her eyes turned to Aralia.

Aralia slid through the open door and James, Will and Arthur crept curiously after her. They entered a small and sparsely furnished room. A bed stood against the back wall, draped in blankets. The slave boy lay among the folds, his eyes wide in the faint light coming from the doorway. He smiled weakly as Aralia entered and held out his hand for her to grasp.

'How are you?' she asked gently.

'Alive.'

'What happened to you?'

The boy coughed and raised himself onto both elbows. 'Slave who fail sent to drown. I did not drown.'

'Slaves who fail?' Arthur asked from the doorway. 'What does that mean?'

'Slave are too awake,' the boy replied. He kept his eyes on Aralia's face and held out his free hand. 'I have something for you,' he whispered. 'I think it yours.' He uncurled his fingers to reveal a ring on his palm, the silver band set with a yellow gemstone.

Aralia stared at it in amazement before taking it from him. 'I thought I'd lost it,' she murmured. 'Where did you find it? How did you know it was mine?'

'I find it on cliff, down by sea. Pick it up and think it yours. I see it before, on the ship. I remember you.'

Eir appeared in the doorway, her face stern. 'You are talking too much,' she reproached. 'You must leave now and let him rest.' She ushered the companions out of the room and they returned to the kitchen table. Aralia twisted the ring on her finger and it glinted in the light. James saw her glance at Eir, as if wanting to ask her a question, but no words came. As if sensing her uncertainty, Eir spoke for her.

'The ring is pretty. The boy must care for you.'

'I bought it in an antique shop,' Aralia said hurriedly. 'It was cheap.'

'It is silver,' Eir returned. She held out her hand and Aralia passed the ring to her. 'The gem is a sapphire.'

'A sapphire?' James sat up straighter and fixed his eyes on the ring. 'I thought sapphires were blue?'

'Many are and such yellow sapphires are rare. Only a rich man could afford to have such an item made.'

'So it's an engagement ring?' Aralia leant on the table and Eir passed the ring back to her.

'Like all rings, it is a symbol of eternity.' The companions stared at her in amazement and a flicker of curiosity passed across her features. 'If you wish to learn more about this ring, I know someone who may help you. His name is Tasi. He lives in a little fishing village called Muir in the region of Davo, just across the sea. It has been many years since I saw him last, but he will remember my name.' She stood up and smiled. 'You will be safe with him. I have a boat that will take you there. It is the only vessel I have and I must warn you that it is not the most seaworthy. If there is a storm, your lives may be put in danger.'

'Thank you,' James acknowledged. 'It's a risk worth taking.'

'Yes, thank you,' Aralia echoed. 'You've been kind to us and we've already outstayed our welcome.' She glanced at James, Will and Arthur with bright-eyed wonderment and slipped the ring back onto her finger.

'If I thought it was safe, I would let you stay longer,' Eir replied, 'but they are searching for you. The Arvorian Hounds have been calling since nightfall. You should go before dawn.' She shuffled away from the table and opened a cupboard above the stove. 'I will fetch food and water for you and take you down to the sea. The last clouds of night will hide you and you should be well away by morning.'

The companions dispersed to gather their belongings. Once ready, they gathered in the front room where Eir handed them some provisions. Before they could thank her, she disappeared through a doorway at the back of the room and called for them to follow.

'What will happen to the boy?' Arthur asked as they entered the room behind her. 'Will he live?'

'The boy may stay with me until he is well,' Eir returned. 'He is a slave, bound by magic and must remain in Arvora.'

She pushed aside a curtain at the back of the room to reveal a door on the other side. It opened onto a veranda that overlooked a vast swathe of sea. A wooden jetty was attached to it and this ran all the way down to the misty water. A boat bobbed at the end of it but there were no mooring ropes tied to the bow. Eir led the way onto the jetty, followed by Will, Arthur and James. Noticing that Aralia lingered in the doorway, James paused to wait for her. She walked towards him but stopped again and cast her eyes towards the house.

'You like him, don't you?' James asked.

In the faint light coming through the open door, Aralia blushed. 'How do you know?'

James shrugged, feeling suddenly embarrassed. 'You don't seem to want to leave him here.'

'We don't really know each other,' she replied, her cheeks darkening, 'but we both know what it's like to not belong. If I go in and say goodbye, will you wait for me?'

Before James had time to answer, a figure appeared in the doorway. The slave boy was standing there, bowed with fatigue but smiling. He ignored James and looked straight at Aralia who greeted him with sparkling eyes.

'You go then?' he asked.

'Yes.'

The boy's smile widened. 'I say thank you, for saving life. I remember you, long time.'

Aralia took his hand and gently shook it. 'My name is Aralia.'

'I have no name to tell you,' the boy returned and his smile vanished.

'May I choose one for you?'

The boy looked at Aralia with such hope that it made James pity him even more. He began to walk away, but could still see

231

the pair from the corner of his eye.

'Lirim,' Aralia said after a thoughtful pause. 'It's a dryad name meaning freedom. Do you like it?'

The boy nodded and seemed to stand a little straighter. He didn't say anything but let go of Aralia's hand, giving her permission to leave. In one quick movement, she leant forward and kissed him. Lirim looked surprised and James glanced awkwardly away. Low calls from Will and Arthur urged him to walk more quickly. Aralia soon caught up with him and they walked in silence down to the waiting boat. Eir greeted them and looked out over the sea where dawn was just breaking.

'The way is dangerous, but not impossible,' she stated. 'The boat will take you south to Muir, in Davo.'

'Muir?' James' eyes flickered across to Will. 'Your dad wrote that name in his journal. He went there.'

'Why would someone want to travel there?' Aralia asked. 'Is there something special there?' She turned to Eir who smiled faintly.

'Why does anyone travel anywhere?' Reaching into her pocket, Eir drew out a cloth bag. The strings were already untied and she dipped a hand inside before speaking again.

'I have a gift for each of you,' she announced. 'They came from my home, in the temple and I wish to give them to you. Alone, power is great, but with companionship, it is even greater. I hope you remember that.' She drew a glass vial from the bag and handed it to Aralia. 'For the healer,' she said gently. 'This bottle contains an elixir that will heal when needed most.'

Before Aralia could thank her, she pulled out a sheathed dagger and presented it to Arthur. 'For the eldest,' she proclaimed, 'and the warrior. This dagger came from the eastern region of Tu-Larr.'

'Thanks!' Arthur murmured.

Eir then turned to Will. 'For the wise.' She placed a thin book in his open hands before gesturing to the boat. 'It is time,' she commanded.

James stared at her but she didn't turn to him. He threw his bag in the boat and was about to climb in after it when he felt a tap on his arm.

'You didn't think I'd forgotten you?' Eir asked. 'They said there was one who could cross between worlds, who could find the crystals of legend. It seems that one is here.' She moved to stand in front of him and he lowered his eyes beneath her gaze. 'You, James, are a leader.'

'Me?' he asked. 'A leader?'

She nodded and tapped the place where his symbol lay. 'Have you not wondered about this? Seven brothers, seven sisters, seven stars within a circle. You may not know it or feel it yet, but you are most definitely a leader.' She thrust a small crystal ball into his hand and folded his fingers over it. 'Quartz,' she explained. 'When the time comes, you will know what it is for.'

Taking the object in his palm, James thanked her and climbed into the waiting boat. The vessel drew away from the jetty and Eir raised a hand in farewell.

'Dawn shines on the horizon,' she said in a low voice. 'Go well.' As the boat drifted out to sea, James heard her voice deep within his mind. 'Farewell, wanderer. I hope, for all our sakes, that you find what you are looking for.'

The boat picked up speed and the Arvorian mist closed around it. Eir, her house and the island of Opoc were lost from sight as the waves bore the vessel out to sea and towards more southern shores.

Chapter 28

THE waves were calm and the boat drifted smoothly out to sea. Silence presided for a long time, disturbed only occasionally by the swish of the water from the boat's wake. The Arvorian mist still clung to the air and showed no sign of easing. It tried to push the dawn away, creating a strange half-light above the sea.

Sitting in the bow, James looked out over the water and toyed with the gift Eir had given him. It felt light in his palm despite being made from solid crystal. Its perfectly circular form reminded him of a full moon, only without the shadowy craters. Dropping the ball in his lap, he glanced at Aralia who was perched opposite him in the stern. She smiled at him but he didn't notice as his eyes came to rest on the silver band around her finger.

'None of us have dared to ask the question,' she said softly, 'but we're all thinking it.'

'What question?' Will asked curiously.

Aralia pulled the slim band from her finger and held it up to the misty light. 'The question that asks whether this ring could be Arvad's eternal gift?'

'It almost seems like too much of a coincidence,' Will replied haltingly. 'Why would Arvad's gift be lying in an antique shop that we just happened to go to? And why, of all things, would you pick it up?'

'Most people don't know that Arvad's gifts still exist,' James said quietly. 'Many believe they were a myth in the first place. Anyone could have brought the ring to the antique shop without knowing what it was. We don't even know whether it's authentic, so why would anyone else?'

Arthur leant forward in his seat, his face serious. 'It's not that much of a coincidence. Eriphas is linked to the sapphire and to water through its name and alchemical emblem. If you think about it, the antique shop was a logical place for the gift to be.'

He stopped speaking but no one else picked up his line of reasoning. Aralia began fiddling with the ring and James picked up his quartz sphere again. As the boat continued towards the south, the Arvorian mists started to lift. Water stretched for miles around them, turned grey by the pre-dawn sky. The horizon was tinged by a faint light but morning still seemed far away.

Lulled by the movement of the boat, James drifted into an uneasy sleep. He dreamt he was drowning in a river and then standing on a clifftop with a dark figure in front of him. The figure held a glittering knife, the same one that had haunted his nightmares as a child. Looking at it closely for the first time, he realised that the blade was made from a bluish crystal. A burning pain shot through his arm and he jerked awake. Salty spray hit his face and he frowned, sensing that the movement of the sea had changed. Straightening his back, he looked over the side of the boat.

'There's a storm coming,' Will said in his ear.

The water was no longer calm. Large waves slapped against the boat, whipped up by a northerly wind. Black clouds hung low in the sky, sweeping great shadows over the turbulent water. Shifting his feet, James realised that they were soaked through. Water had pooled in the bottom of the boat, caused by the powerful waves.

'A storm is the last thing we need,' he muttered.

'A storm?' Aralia sat up sharply and looked towards the horizon.

'The sea has changed,' Will replied calmly. 'It's heading straight for us.'

The boat lurched beneath them and James grabbed onto the side. 'How long d'you think we have?'

A gust of wind caught the bow and tossed it onto a rising wave. The impact flung all four of them into the base of the boat where they cowered and looked at one another anxiously.

'I think that's your answer,' Arthur said. 'It's here.'

As his words died away the clouds opened and it began to rain. It wasn't the gentle rain of a summer's day but a type only experienced at sea. It came down in great sheets, causing chaos where it met the rising waves. The spray formed a thin mist that soaked through their clothes and settled in the base of the boat. Waves splashed over the bow, adding volume to the pooling flood.

'We'll have to bail out the water,' Arthur shouted over the noise of the rain. Taking his water gourd from his bag, he gulped down the contents before refilling it with seawater.

'We won't be able to keep up with it,' Will called back but set to work anyway.

A powerful wave struck the boat and the companions were flung against the starboard side. They dropped their gourds and clung on to the gunwale, their apprehension replaced by terror.

'The waves will tear the boat to pieces,' Will said and his knuckles turned white with the force of his grip.

'The boat is guided by magic,' Aralia returned desperately.

'Maybe it'll get us through this storm alive.'

Sitting in the base of the boat, James became aware of a new sound. It was like a rush of wind, only it came in short bursts. Looking up through the pouring rain, he caught sight of a winged silhouette hovering beneath the clouds and gasped.

'The Shadows. They've sent the Shadows.'

The dragon-like form swooped across the sky and James stared up at it with a mixture of fear and awe. Its vast wings carried it above the sea at great speed. As he continued to watch, it paused in the air before diving towards the water.

'Get down,' Arthur yelled.

They ducked as the Shadow plunged downwards. Just before it hit the waves, it opened its wings in an attempt to slow its pace. Unable to hold its own weight, it struck the water and instantly sank beneath the surface. Seconds later, it emerged again, slashing at the waves with its long claws. Element and beast fought one another for a time before the Shadow launched itself into the sky again.

'It's looking for us,' Aralia gasped. 'There must be some kind of trace left by the boat.'

'We have to do something,' James said urgently. An idea was forming in his mind. He knew it was completely mad but he couldn't think of anything else. 'We have to flip the boat!'

'*What?*' Will turned to him with wide eyes. 'D'you want to drown?'

'Of course not, but I don't fancy being torn to shreds by a dragon either.'

Will looked at Arthur and Aralia for support but both of them shrugged. High above, the Shadow dived again and they ducked as it landed close to the boat. It hit the water a second time and the impact created a shock wave that threatened to tip the boat.

'We're going to go over anyway,' James shouted. 'Hold on.'

The bow caught the tip of a subsequent wave and the vessel flipped. James felt the salt sting his eyes as he hit the water. The tide pulled his hands away from the gunwale and he found himself adrift. He tried to latch on again but his bag and clothes were weighing him down. Beating the waves back with all his strength, he dived beneath the water and propelled himself forward. His hand brushed against the side of the boat and he pulled himself beneath it before coming up for air.

'Who's there?' Aralia's voice sounded muffled in the cramped space.

'James,' he spluttered. 'Are Will and Arthur here?'

'I am,' Will confirmed.

'Me too,' Arthur joined.

A thud sounded above them and something solid hit the boat. There was a horrible splintering and Aralia screamed as the wood caved in above their heads. The weight of the boat pushed them beneath the water and held them captive. Unhooking his sleeve from a splintered plank, James tried to find a way out. The boat continued to sink, pushing them further beneath the surface. His hand came to rest on a metal loop and he knew he was close to the bow. Holding onto the loop, he pulled himself out from under the boat and swam upwards for air.

He immediately looked for any sign of the Shadow but it was nowhere to be seen. The horizon was lighter than before and he felt hopeful that the storm was easing. A head emerged on the other side of the smashed up boat, followed by another. Will and Arthur turned towards him, spitting out mouthfuls of water and gasping for air. He looked for Aralia and she appeared beside him, her loose hair crisscrossed over her eyes. She brushed it away and promptly vomited into the water.

James recoiled and she looked at him with watery eyes.

'Rai, are you alright?' Arthur was by her side in an instant and threaded his arm around her shoulders.

She nodded weakly. 'I'm fine. It's the salt.'

'It's so cold,' Will said with a shiver. 'We can't stay in the water. We'll catch hypothermia.' He tried to pull himself on top of the crushed planks but slid off again.

'The boat is still moving,' Arthur remarked. 'Well, what's left of it. If we can hold on for long enough, I think it will still take us to Davo.'

'How far away is that?' Aralia asked through chattering teeth. 'We could still be days away and we won't make it.' Her eyes started to close but Arthur shook her awake.

'Don't go to sleep. Whatever you do, don't go to sleep.'

James let his head drop onto his arms. He could feel his body being dragged through the water. Holding on tightly to the shattered planks, he tried not to close his eyes. It was impossible to feel anything but the cold and the aching desire to sleep. From the depths of his mind, he then heard Will speaking.

'Look, land! I can see the shore.'

He raised his head and pain shot through his shoulder. A grey clump of land had appeared on the horizon and he felt a spark of hope. His eyes drooped over and over again but he forced them to remain open. He held on to the boat with shaking hands for what felt like an age. It was only when he felt rough shale scraping beneath his body that he finally let go.

Chapter 29

LYING on the shale with water lapping around him, James opened his eyes. He saw that he was lying on a small beach and somewhere quite close there were people. Hearing a shout, he tried to raise his head but realised he was too cold to move. Someone jabbed him in the ribs and tried to roll him over. He groaned as he was turned onto his back and unceremoniously dragged from the water. Looking up, he saw a boy standing over him. He was dressed in a fur cape and hood and stared down at James with fierce eyes.

'Papya,' he suddenly yelled in a guttural voice. 'Papya!'

Another figure appeared in James' eyeline. It was a man this time and he too was dressed in fur. Kneeling on the shale, he peered at James and felt for his pulse. His breath was sour and his clothes reeked of fish and the sea.

'Valken em isha?' he asked.

James looked at him blankly. The man shrugged and straightening up, wandered down to the water. Pushing himself up onto his elbows, James looked around for his friends. Their bedraggled forms lay strewn along the shoreline and he watched as the man bent to check their pulses too. Feeling a tap on his arm, he looked up and the boy gestured for him to stand. He managed to drag himself upright but his legs were weak and he stumbled forward.

'Lunga,' the boy uttered and held out a steadying arm.

James nodded in thanks and tiredly followed the boy as he started up the beach. Looking over his shoulder, he was relieved to see that Will, Arthur and Aralia were moving too. Turning his back to the sea again, he noticed that the upper edge was framed by dunes. Beyond these, he could just make out a row of square houses. The walls, which must once have been white, now looked weathered and yellow. He started to wonder if the houses belonged to a village but was too cold to finish this thought.

The boy led the way across the dunes and in amongst the houses. He stopped outside a blue painted door and pushed it open. James stood shivering on the doorstep, waiting to be invited inside. A plump, blonde haired woman appeared in the doorway and pulled him into the warmth. She had a kind smile and smelled of cooked fish and mixed herbs.

'Valken em isha?'

James recognised the question as the same one the man had asked but he didn't know what it meant. He shrugged apologetically and desperately tried to keep his eyes open. The woman pushed him into a chair next to the kitchen table and wrapped a thick blanket around his shoulders. He winced as it brushed against his wound. The freezing water had numbed the pain for a while but he could now feel it again. He sat still while the woman removed the blanket again and bent to inspect Eir's bandaging. She made an exclamatory sound and wrapped him up again before hurrying to bring Will, Arthur and Aralia in from the doorway.

Sitting quietly in the corner, James felt a fresh wave of fatigue crash over him. He leant his elbows on the kitchen table and took in his surroundings through semi-delirious eyes. The room he was in seemed to be both a kitchen and a living room. It was simply furnished and the walls were decorated with shells, presumably taken from the beach. Strings of dried fish and herbs hung from the ceiling, making the room smell of gardens and the sea. James breathed the scent deep into his lungs and closed his tired eyes.

'Triave, ital.'

He opened his eyes again to find the rough faced boy beside him. The boy placed a glass of water on the table and gestured to it. James thanked him and picking it up, took a tentative sip. His hand was still numb from the cold however and it slipped from his hand and smashed on the floor. He bent to pick up the pieces but the boy pushed him away. Too tired to feel embarrassed, James lowered his head to the table and sank into a deep state of drowsiness.

Someone wrapped another blanket around him and tried to shake him awake. He thought that he had opened his eyes but everything around him was dark. Warm liquid trickled between his lips and he swallowed. It tasted of cinnamon and was surprisingly pleasant. He accepted a second sip, feeling the warmth spread through his body. The scent of onion soup and freshly buttered toast roused him further. The combined smells reminded him of his grandmother's cooking and comforted by this memory, he opened his eyes.

'Weid ga.' The blonde haired woman set a plate of food in front of him and indicated that he should eat.

He took a bite of toast before realising that his friends were also sitting at the table. Will was slumped in his chair with his chin on his chest while Arthur and Aralia were huddled close together under one blanket. The woman tapped Aralia on the shoulder and handed her a towel. She pointed to a door at the back of the room and standing up on uncertain legs, Aralia walked over to it. She cast a quick glance at Arthur before disappearing into the room beyond.

Some time passed before she appeared again. She came out of the back room dressed in trousers and a jumper that were far too big for her. Her hair fell in a neat plait over her shoulders and was no longer crusted with salt. She smiled briefly at the boys before the woman intercepted her and led her into another adjoining room. In her absence, the boy stepped from the shadows in the corner of the kitchen and beckoned for James to follow him. He pointed to the doorway through which Aralia had first disappeared and handed him a towel too.

On entering the room, James' eyes fell on a bathtub standing in the centre. It was full of clean, steaming water and he felt the urge to jump in. After making sure the door was firmly closed, he peeled off his clothes and slipped into the tub. Warmth seeped into his skin as he submerged his body. He dunked his head in too and clumps of salt came away from his hair. Taking a bar of soap from the side of the tub, he quickly washed himself before clambering out. The woman had left a pile of clothes on a nearby chair and after drying himself, he slipped on an oversized jumper and pair of trousers.

'Arka,' the woman greeted him as he re-entered the main room. He smiled at her and she gestured for him to follow her.

She led him into a small bedroom where Aralia lay snuggled on a mattress in the corner. A bunk bed stood against the opposite wall but the room was otherwise empty.

'Imraya,' the woman said and folded her hands in a gesture of sleep.

James thanked her and clambered up to the top bunk bed. It felt odd to be warm and dry but he was glad to have stopped shivering. He lay down and pulled a blanket over himself. A few minutes later, he saw Will enter the room. His friend took the bottom bunk, leaving the mattress in the corner to Arthur and Aralia. He lay awake for a while, staring up at the ceiling while he waited for Arthur to appear. The absence of the clock against his chest made him feel nervous, but he was too tired to get up and retrieve it from his cloak in the main room.

He didn't remember falling asleep but woke up feeling stiff and sore. Sitting up, he disentangled himself from a pile of blankets and looked around the room. It was dark but he could just make out the sleeping shapes of Arthur and Aralia on the main mattress. A faint snoring coming from the bottom bunk told him Will was also asleep. Taking care not to cause too much disturbance, he climbed down the bunk bed ladder and crept over to the door. Peering through the open crack, he looked out into the central room.

Light streamed in through the cracks in the roof, suggesting it was daytime. The fire beneath the stove was lit but the room was empty. Opening the door a little wider, he slipped out into it. The sound of padding feet made him turn. Aralia emerged from the bedroom behind him, a blanket still draped around her shoulders. She smiled and accompanied him across the room. They had almost reached the table when the front door burst open. A man appeared and James recognised him as the same one who had helped them on the beach. He was dressed in tall boots and thick overalls and stank of raw fish. He stopped short when he saw James and Aralia and twisted his leathery face into a half smile.

'Arka,' he barked.

'Arka,' James returned, though he didn't know what it meant.

'Isma Ilal,' the man continued and pointed to himself.

'I'm afraid we don't know your language,' James replied quietly. 'I'm sorry.'

Aralia nudged him in the ribs. 'He's telling us his name,' she whispered. 'Isma Aralia Silene,' she said more loudly. 'This is James Fynch,' she added, prodding him again.

The man nodded in greeting. 'Ilal,' he repeated.

The front door opened again and the rough faced boy appeared. He also stopped when he saw James and Aralia and turned to look at the man.

'Papya, Mama kirnst,' he mumbled.

Ilal nodded and bent to pull up the boy's sleeve. 'Isme Erin,' he explained. The symbol on the boy's wrist was plain, a circle shot through with a single line. 'Hilal' Ilal said, pointing to the mark. 'Ilal e Erin Hilal.'

He coughed and gestured for James and Aralia to join him at the table. Will and Arthur emerged sleepily from the bedroom. They came to join the others at the table and looked at Ilal through bleary eyes. After introductions were made, Ilal got up to put a kettle on the stove. A door at the back of the room stood open, offering a view of the sea. A boat rested by the water and the blonde haired woman stood beside it. A young girl hovered at her side. She looked much younger than Erin but less rough around the edges.

'Isema Helena,' Ilal introduced as the two began walking towards the house. 'Wife,' he managed and looked at Aralia for approval. She nodded and he grinned with genuine pleasure. 'Ena,' he continued, pointing to the child. 'Girl.'

'Daughter,' Aralia hurriedly corrected and Ilal nodded.

Helena and Ena each brought two baskets of fish into the house. The stench was overpowering and James couldn't help covering his nose. Ena started laughing, pointing at James and pinching her nose. James grinned but didn't know how else to react. Helena called for her daughter to stop before turning to deftly gut a fish by the doorstep. She tossed this and several other fillets into a pan and the smell of frying oil overtook that of raw fish. Laying eight plates on the table, she placed a slice of bread onto each and flaked the fish on top. The fish was rich with butter and herbs and was consumed quickly.

First to finish, Ilal pushed his plate aside and took a slip of paper from his pocket. 'Fiorwa iwes, Ederal,' he growled. 'Tria lise.'

He pushed the paper across the table and James took it. The front edge bore a single mark; a circle surrounding a tight swirl. Before any questions could be asked, Ilal rose from the table and beckoned for the companions to follow him. He waited by the front door while they disappeared into the back rooms to change into their old clothes and collect their things. Back in the main room, they thanked Helena. She tutted at her husband for whisking them away so quickly but made no move to stop him as he hurried outside. James, Will, Arthur and Aralia hurried after him as he made his way between the houses.

Stopping outside a round, grey hut, Ilal rapped on the door three times. It opened immediately and he stood aside to wave the companions through. Ducking through the low doorway, they found themselves standing in a dimly lit room. The circular space contained no furniture but was heaped with piles of cushions. Sitting on a threadbare mat in the centre of the room was an old man. His eyes were closed in meditation but he opened them as the companions entered.

'Welcome, strangers.' His voice was deep and tinged with the same guttural tones that Ilal possessed. 'I hear of your coming,' he continued gently. 'Please, I must ask you to sit.' He gestured to the cushions surrounding him and smiled.

'You speak English?' James asked with surprise. He sat down on a fat orange pillow and looked at the man expectantly.

'If the language we're speaking is called English, then yes, I suppose I do.' The man didn't return his look and turned to peer impatiently through a doorway at the back of the room.

A younger man emerged from the shadows, carrying a single cup on a tray. His superior took the cup and drank the contents in one gulp before turning his attention back to his guests.

'Why don't you tell me why you have come to this village?' he suggested. 'I always seek to meet strangers who journey here.' He returned his empty cup to the tray and waved the young man away.

'Our boat got caught in a storm,' James replied truthfully. 'We were washed up on the beach where a man called Ilal Halil and his son found us.' He looked around the room to find that Ilal wasn't there.

'Ah, Ilal Halil,' the old man crackled. 'His family have lived in this village for generations.'

'You know him well?' Aralia asked.

'I know everyone here.'

Will cleared his throat. 'Who are you exactly? Are you the elder of this village?'

The man bowed his head. 'If you must call me that. My name is Tasi, of the Tisae family.' His eyes flickered to his wrist but he didn't expose his symbol.

'Tasi?' James looked at the elder in amazement. 'Tasi?' He glanced at Aralia and she leant forward on her knees.

'We've come a long way to find you,' she began. 'We were sent to this village by a woman named Eir.'

Tasi looked up sharply. 'Eir? I've only ever met one person with that name. We met many years ago when I sought refuge at the Temple of Electra. She was called Sister Eira then.' He paused and a frown spread across his features. 'If she sent you to find me, I must ask why?'

'She thought you could tell us more about this.' Aralia

twisted the ring from her finger and held it out to him.

Tasi looked at it for a long time before taking it between his fingers. He held it up to the dim light and the yellow sapphire glittered faintly. His frown deepened but he didn't say a word. Cupping the ring in his palm, he rose unsteadily to his feet and disappeared through the doorway at the back of the room. The companions watched him go before turning to each other with puzzled expressions.

'D'we follow him?' Will asked.

James jumped up and hurried over to the doorway. It was dark on the other side but he could just make out Tasi's form moving along a narrow corridor.

'Let's follow,' he whispered.

There was only one door at the end of the passage and Tasi headed towards it. The companions followed him, still unsure as to whether the old man wished them to. When he reached the end of the passage, he opened the door and slipped through. He left it ajar behind him and the companions hurried to join him on the other side. They found themselves standing in another circular room. There were no windows here and the walls were lined with curved bookshelves. A fire burnt in the centre of the floor, eating its way through a pile of logs. The flames were warm but didn't seem to give off any smoke.

'Take off your shoes.'

Although Tasi had his back to the door, he seemed to sense the presence of his guests. They obeyed him and pulled off their shoes before lining them up by the door. Sinking his feet into the carpeted floor, James looked around at the room. He noticed a soft light glowing on a table against the far wall and moved curiously towards it. As he drew closer, he realised it was coming from a crystal orb. The sphere was sitting in the centre of a mirror, poised on a single point of balance. Rather than reflecting the light from above, the mirror was filled with swirling smoke.

'You are looking at a Lunasphere,' Tasi uttered. He stood inspecting Aralia's ring beneath a small light but still didn't turn around.

'A Lunasphere?' James asked. 'What's that?'

'Like the moon, it waxes and wanes,' Tasi replied. 'It symbolises the rhythms of time and the conflict between darkness and light.' He suddenly turned around and gestured to the cushions arranged around the fireplace. 'If you'll all sit down, I will tell you more.'

Will, Arthur and Aralia took a seat around the glowing fire. James however hung back, his eyes still resting on the crystalline sphere. As he looked into its depths, a sharp pain suddenly shot up his arm. He flinched and tried to steady himself as thousands of coloured spots danced before his eyes.

Chapter 30

JAMES shivered and stepped away from the orb. He heard Aralia speaking his name and slowly turned around. Blinking the spots from his eyes, he looked directly at Tasi.

'What happened?' he asked. 'I felt a pain in my arm and my vision went blurry.'

Tasi placed Aralia's ring on a nearby shelf and a look of bewilderment passed over his features. 'I think you'd better sit down,' he suggested.

James nodded and lowered himself onto a cushion by the fire. He waited patiently as Tasi collected his long green robe about him and sat down on the other side of the flames.

'Lunaspheres aren't uncommon,' he tentatively began. 'They draw on vibrations in the atmosphere and these are then used to trace weather systems. Like the moon, they are used for navigating the world. The orb I possess is however different.

'When I was young, I lived in the region of Parimon, on the west coast of this continent. One day, when I was in my early twenties, a man came to my house and asked if I would go with him on a journey. I was young and curious, so I agreed. He took me to Garia, to the Hidden City, where I met Sister Eira.'

'How old was she then?' Will interrupted.

'Oh, no more than eighteen,' Tasi replied. 'The adventure

wasn't quite what I'd hoped, until the man brought out the Lunasphere. He told me that it was designed to envision the future between the forces of light and dark. When the darkness grows stronger, the light wanes, but when it is weak, well, you imagine. It serves to predict possible conflicts between the greater powers.'

'Conflicts?' Aralia leant forward and her eyes flashed in the firelight.

Tasi nodded briefly and his eyes strayed across to James. 'Now, the part that concerns you. While in the temple, my travelling companion split the crystal and gave a part of it to Eira. He said that the darkness was growing and a time would come when it would overshadow the light. When that time came, he made Eira promise that she should return her part of the crystal to me.'

Watching the old man through the flames, James suddenly realised what he was trying to say. He opened his mouth to speak but no words came. Lowering his eyes to the floor, he tried again.

'She gave her part to me,' he whispered.

The fire crackled and Tasi stirred it with a poker. 'It would seem so,' he said quietly. 'You felt the power of the orb because you carry the other part.'

'Wait, what?' Will asked incredulously. 'Are you saying that Eir gave us all a gift just so she could return the orb to you?'

James shot Will a silencing look before turning back to Tasi. 'If Eir thought it was time to return her part, then does that mean the darkness is already winning?'

Tasi shook his head. 'It simply means that the dark forces are more powerful than ever before. It is up to all of us who believe in something better to stop the light from waning altogether.'

'Who was this man, the one who gave Eir the orb?' James held his hands out to the fire and let the flames warm them.

'He never told me his name. He brought me here, to Muir, and asked if I would stay here to protect the orb. I had no family at the time and little money, so I agreed. He left and I never saw him again.'

Tasi rose stiffly to his feet and took Aralia's ring from where he'd left it on the shelf. He held it above the firelight and the sapphire glittered alluringly.

'Eira must have trusted you a great deal,' he continued heavily. 'She must have wanted you to learn about the orbs and their predictions. It has been known for a long time that there would be a war between the forces. Difficult times lie ahead and we must all be careful.'

'What can you tell us about the ring?' Arthur prompted. 'Is the gem really a sapphire?'

'It is a yellow sapphire, but unlike any I have ever seen. The depth of its colour is most likely caused by traces of iron.' He paused and looked at each of the companions in turn. 'My father was a jeweller and as soon as I turned thirteen, I became his apprentice. He used to tell me stories about precious gemstones and there is one I always remember. It was about a yellow sapphire.'

'Was it a true story?' Aralia asked curiously.

Tasi looked at her intently. 'I hadn't thought so, until now.' He let his words hang in the air for a moment before continuing. 'The story told of a young man who fell in love with a woman of a higher station than himself. In order to prove himself to her, he named a lake in her honour. She was pleased with him but her father was not. So the young man had men come and mine the lake for sapphires. He found a beautiful yellow stone and forged it into a ring.'

James stared at the silver circlet in Tasi's hand. 'Who was this man?

'He too was a jeweller, or so my father always said. His name was Ira.'

'Ira?' Will looked up sharply from the fire. 'As in one of the seven legendary brothers?'

'The very same.' Tasi's eyes narrowed. 'Perhaps you already know the name of his betrothed?'

'Celaeno,' Aralia whispered. 'You think this ring belonged to her?'

'The sapphire in her ring was the only one of its kind ever found. Few people know of the lake from which it came and even fewer have found it. Those who do are never heard of again. Some say it lies within the ocean itself. They call it the lake in the sea.'

'Like a lagoon?' Will asked.

'I do not know exactly,' Tasi replied but his eyes strayed to the floor.

'Did your father's story ever reveal what part of the world the lake was in?' Arthur queried.

'It is rumoured to be right here, in Davo.'

James breathed in sharply. 'D'you believe that to be true?'

'Perhaps it rests to the north, but it is impossible to truly know without first finding it.'

'Why d'you say that?' Will questioned. 'The bit about the north I mean.'

Tasi turned the ring over in his fingers so that the back of it was facing them. 'Look at the gem setting.'

Focusing on the silver setting behind the sapphire, James gaped. The thin metal was shaped to form a perfectly symmetrical reverse triangle.

'The alchemical symbol for water,' he breathed.

Tasi nodded. 'I see you have done some research already. In many cultures, water is associated with the cardinal direction, north.'

'Of course,' Will said so quietly that his voice was almost lost.

Kneeling on the floor again, Tasi passed the ring back to Aralia. 'I sense you have a great journey ahead of you,' he said. 'Will you share some food with me before you go?'

James shook his head reluctantly. 'I'm sorry, but we should go. Thank you for sharing your knowledge with us.'

'We're sort of racing against time,' Will added as he rose to his feet.

'Are we all not in that race?' Tasi didn't stand up this time but he gestured to the doorway. 'If it is your wish to go, I'll oblige you. The village path will take you north along the cliffs. You will then come to two pathways and from there you must choose the way for yourselves.'

Aralia bent down to grasp his hand. 'Thank you, for letting us stay in your village. Would you be able to thank Ilal for us too? We can't speak his language.'

Tasi smiled and the skin around his eyes crinkled. 'I will make sure he gets your message. I wish you the best of luck on your journey. If you do ever pass this way again, then you must come and eat with me.'

'We will,' Aralia promised.

The young man who'd brought Tasi his tea appeared in the doorway. He led the companions back down the passage and waited while they collected their things. Reaching into his bag, James pulled out the orb Eir had given him and laid it by the fire.

'Please see that Tasi gets this,' he said and the young man nodded.

The companions left Tasi's home and stood once again on the grassy path outside. They turned immediately right, heading towards the edge of the village. The path soon left the houses behind and wound its way up to the chalky cliffs beyond. These were not steep but the path itself was slippery with loose stones. The further away from the village they walked, the fainter the smell of fish became. James gratefully breathed in the cold air and stretched out his arms to let the breeze sift through his clothes. Halfway up the path, they paused to admire the view. A great sweep of ocean spread out before them, reminding them just how far they'd come.

The landscape changed around them as they continued to climb. The path sometimes curved closer to the sea and occasionally disappeared altogether. When this happened, they were forced to make their way cross country through the grass which was decorated with dew. Morning turned to afternoon as they walked. After a long climb, they stopped at the top of the cliffs to eat and rest but no one was able to sleep. As soon as the sun began to dip on the horizon, they ate a little food again before continuing their journey.

'Are we still heading north?' James asked, hovering at Will's shoulder.

Will stopped and pulled out his map. The paper was water damaged but the ink fortunately hadn't bled. He spread it on the ground and knelt to inspect it more closely.

'Here,' he pointed to a fine line close to the coast of Davo. 'I think we're around here somewhere. Look, the path carries on north but it then splits as Tasi said.'

Aralia knelt on the grass beside him. 'Which way do we go?'

'We follow the moon.'

'We what?' James asked.

'The moon,' Will repeated, his voice rising with excitement.

255

'Weren't you listening to Tasi? The moon can be used for earthly navigation. It influences time, light and of course the tide.'

'What about the stars?' Arthur asked. 'Navigation usually involves the stars.'

'You're right,' Will acknowledged, 'but there aren't any stars tonight. There is however a moon.' He pointed upwards to where a slim sickle moon had appeared from between the clouds.

'There's more to it than that though, isn't there,' James said, sensing that Will had more to say.

Will nodded. 'D'you remember, when we were on the ship, I said that turtles are associated with the moon in ancient mythology?' He looked between James, Arthur and Aralia and sighed impatiently. 'The turtle, the water, the north. They all relate to the moon. It is the moon alone that can guide us to the lake.'

'I suppose that makes sense,' Aralia said quietly and turned to look at Will. 'All of our clues relate to the moon.' She turned to look at Will. 'Do you know how to do it? To navigate using the moon I mean.'

'I think so.' Will pulled a pencil from his bag and flipped the map around so that the blank side faced him. 'The moon reflects the sun's light,' he began. 'This means that it either faces east or west. Look.' Leaning over the map, he drew a sickle moon with a line shot through it.

'The east-west line,' Arthur commented.

'Exactly.' Will drew a dot next to the line before speaking again. 'If this angle is east-west, then we can assume that a perpendicular line would be a north-south one. Because we are in the northern half of the world, the point where the line meets the horizon is south. If we know where south is, we can easily work out north.'

'That's brilliant,' James complimented. 'I never knew that.'

'It's only a rough guideline, but it should tell us enough,' Will replied modestly. 'When the path divides, we should start heading downhill to the base of these cliffs.' He pointed to a ragged line on the map before rolling it up and tucking it into his pocket.

'We'll follow your lead, Will,' Aralia said and rose to her feet alongside him.

The path wound its way along the edge of the cliffs for a long time. Twilight had already begun to descend by the time they came to the divide Tasi had spoken of. One continued along the cliffs while the other led in the opposite direction towards a dark line of trees. Looking up at the moon, Will crossed onto the second one and James, Arthur and Aralia hurried to follow. The trees were thin at first but gradually thickened out to form a dense barrier.

The forest went on for miles, stretching endlessly around them. Trapped beneath the dark trees, it was impossible to tell whether it was day or night. James started to wish that they'd taken the coastal path, even though it headed south. Ducking to avoid a low hanging branch, he felt a sudden rush of warmth strike him in the chest. His first thought was that the heat of the sun had been trapped between the dense trees, but he then remembered it hadn't really shone all day. He realised that this warmth was different to that of sunlight, seeping deep into his skin and filling his ears with a soft ringing.

'Can anyone else feel that?' he asked.

'Feel what?' Arthur stopped and turned his face to the needled canopy above.

'The air has changed. It's warmer somehow.'

'I can't feel anything.' Will stretched out his arms and spun around in a circle. 'Everything's so still and quiet.'

'Maybe you're just tired, James,' Aralia suggested.

He looked at her sharply, surprised that she of all people didn't believe him. He shook his head and continued down the path, leaving his friends behind him. The branches seemed to whisper to him in a language he couldn't understand. The sound made him nervous and he quickened his pace, trying to find his way out of the forest. With each step, the ringing in his ears grew louder. He put his hands to his head and tried to block it out, but it wouldn't stop. He began to run, pushing his way through the trees until suddenly, he found himself at the edge of the forest. A grassy cliffside stretched out before him and beyond it the twilight sea.

'This doesn't look like the map.' Will appeared at his side and stopped to look at the view. 'We should be at the base of these cliffs, not above them.'

'The feeling I had, it's gone,' James murmured, more to himself than to anyone else.

The ringing in his ears had ceased and all he could hear was the distant swish of waves. Walking right to the edge of the cliff, he stopped and sat down on the damp grass. Will and Arthur joined him but Aralia remained standing. She peered over the precipice and closed one eye, as if trying to measure the distance between herself and the sea.

'Careful,' Arthur called teasingly. 'You don't like heights.'

She smiled obligingly but appeared somewhat distracted. Squatting in the long grass, she tilted her head and held up her thumb and forefinger to the sky. A smile broke across her features and she hurried over to where the boys were sitting.

'You're right,' she said breathlessly, 'I do hate heights, but this isn't a cliff.'

'It isn't?' Arthur looked at her in disbelief and scrambled to his feet.

'No,' she confirmed. 'Come and look.'

Arthur, James and Will joined her at the edge of the cliff. She waved an excited hand towards the horizon where the sea merged with the gathering dusk.

'What're we looking for exactly?' James knelt in the grass and turned his head to the side as Aralia had done.

'Watch.' Aralia took her weight off one leg and extended it over the precipice. She held her balance perfectly and her foot simply disappeared.

'It's an illusion isn't it?' Will said with surprise. 'Another anagroma?'

James looked at the horizon and let his vision go blurry. The scene before him wavered and he watched it with growing anticipation. Beyond the cliffs, sea and sky, a stony beach stretched towards a calm stretch of water.

'I can see it,' he whispered. 'I see a lake.'

Aralia's smile widened. 'The most powerful magic works to hide the truth from the observer.'

The companions turned to each other, fresh hope in their eyes. Linking arms, they stepped over the edge of the cliff and onto the stony shore of the lake in the sea.

Chapter 31

THE lake was so vast that it looked as if it might still belong to the sea. Its grey-blue surface met with the horizon, stretching to touch the bleak sky. Where the two merged, a thin mist hovered, blurring the line of distinction between them.

'The lake in the sea,' James murmured. 'That's what Tasi called it.'

'What a wedding gift,' Will said with awe.

The beach they were on was bordered by tall cliffs that cast no shadow onto the stones below. If it hadn't been for this, it would have been impossible to tell that they were an illusion. The steep crags descended on a downward gradient, becoming low ridges a little further around the lake. To the right of the beach, the forest wound its way around the curves of the vast body of rippling water and disappeared into the mist. The scene was breathtakingly beautiful, wild around the edges but somehow peaceful.

'If you listen, you can even hear it,' Aralia whispered. 'The sea I mean.'

Tilting his head to the side, James listened. A gentle swishing sound could be heard, filling the surrounding air like the murmur of many voices.

'Is it really a lake or is it really the sea?' he wondered aloud.

'Surely if we're looking for the seastone, it has to be the sea.'

'Or a lagoon,' Will suggested.

Aralia took a step towards the water. 'I don't think it's specifically one or the other,' she said quietly. 'That's part of the illusion. On one side of the cliffs, it looks like the sea, but from the other side, it looks more like a lake. It has elements of both.'

James nodded, for the moment satisfied. He wandered down to the water's edge, his feet crunching on the stones. The lake looked temptingly cool after their journey and walking to the edge, he splashed a handful of water over his face. Will jumped past him and landed on a flat stone that protruded from the lake. It was one of five that created a precarious path into the lake.

'Come on,' Will called from the second stone. 'You get a better view from here.'

Tempted by this prospect, James stepped onto the first stone. He paused on the third to observe his surroundings. Everything was silent. Even the water lay still; a panel of misted glass. The air itself felt thin and lifeless, as if he was standing on top of a mountain. Turning ninety degrees to his left, his gaze fell on a section of cliff directly ahead of him. Between the rocks and shadowy hollows he spotted the cascading form of a waterfall. Even in the gathering twilight, it was an impressive sight.

'Here, come and look at this.' He waved to Will who had come to a halt on the final stone.

'I'm sure that wasn't there before,' Will said breathlessly. He stepped onto the same stone as James and it wobbled dangerously beneath them.

'Maybe you just didn't see it,' James suggested. 'Incredible, isn't it? We should walk across the lower cliffs and take a closer look.' He began jumping back across the stones and Will hurried after him.

Back on the beach, they rejoined Arthur and Aralia who were still standing beneath the cliffs. Although it couldn't be seen from the beach, he could just make out the outcrop of rock that it was hidden behind.

'We should find somewhere to sleep,' Arthur suggested in a low voice. 'It's getting dark and if there's a tide, this beach will be covered.'

'Will and I saw a waterfall hidden just behind that outcrop,' James said, pointing across the lake. 'If we climb up to it, we should be able to avoid any rising water.'

With this plan agreed, James led the way across the beach. Will, Arthur and Aralia hurried after him, stumbling over the uneven stones. When they reached the base of the lower cliffs, they all stopped to assess their next move. A small path led from the beach to the top of the cliffs but it had eroded in places and looked dangerous. The only other option was to clamber over the boulders that formed an uneven border between the water and the cliffs.

Both routes came with a risk but the companions deemed the second option as marginally safer. With James still leading the way, they began to scale the enormous boulders. Progress was slow as they had to keep winding their way around the many crevices that threatened to swallow them.

Almost all the light had gone from the sky by the time they drew close to the waterfall. They could hear and feel it before they could see it, the air filled with spray and the sound of rushing water. The rocks became slippery and they had to tread extra carefully to avoid falling.

Clambering over a sharp ridge, James suddenly found himself in the presence of the cascade. A thin slab of rock was all that divided him from the tumbling white water. Stepping onto the slab, he tentatively leant forward and peered over the edge of the cliff. To his surprise, the water beneath the cascade was completely calm. Where the white water met the lake, there was nothing but a faint haze.

'We can camp in this hollow for a while,' Arthur said from somewhere behind him. 'It might be loud but at least it's dry. Plus, we can't get any further around the lake. The waterfall cuts us off.'

James moved away from the edge and re-joined his friends. They were gathered around a shallow hollow that rested within the cliffside. There was just enough room for everyone to squeeze inside and sit back comfortably. Settling on the cold ground, James opened his bag and pulled out some food. Shards of glass from his smashed phone fell from the paper wrappings and he brushed them away. Most of the supplies had been ruined by seawater anyway, but he managed to pick out a few strips of dried meat that still looked edible. The outside was crusted with salt and he managed to brush some of it off before taking a cautious bite.

'It's cold up here,' Aralia shivered, nibbling on a piece of dried fruit.

'We could try lighting a small fire,' Arthur suggested. 'We're the only ones here, so it wouldn't matter.'

He crawled out of the hollow and started gathering up some loose stones. Laying them in a circle, he filled the centre with scraps of moss and lichen from the surrounding rocks. Holding out his hand, he created a small flame in his palm and cast it into the fire. The scraps immediately caught alight and burnt fiercely for a moment before sinking into a glowing pile of ash.

'We'll need wood to keep it alight,' Will remarked.

Silence fell between them as they sat watching the dying fire.

After a while, even the glowing embers went out. The air filled with a bitter smoke that smelled of salt and ash. Feeling restless, James got up and wandered to the edge of the cliff. From here he could see over the lake and across the vast sweep of forest beyond. The view was impressive but it reminded him of the journey that still lay ahead of them.

'I wonder if the seastone is here?' Aralia said, as if reading his thoughts. 'We've traced the ring to this lake, but that doesn't mean we'll find the seastone.'

James shrugged and wandered closer to the waterfall. 'I thought I'd be able to feel it if it was here, but all I feel is cold and hungry.'

Aralia extracted herself from the hollow and moved to stand beside him. 'We'll find it,' she said gently. 'We're so close now.'

She tilted her head to the sky where the sickle moon was just emerging from behind a heavy cloud. Its faint light touched the lake just below the cascade, making the water look like pale silver. Staring at the point where the two met, Aralia suddenly gasped.

'What is it?' James asked urgently. 'Is something wrong?'

Shaking her head, Aralia knelt on the rocks and traced an invisible line across the sky. Her eyes grew bright and she turned to look at him with silent awe.

'Come on, what's wrong?' he pressed.

'Look,' she whispered. 'Look at where the light hits the water.'

'It falls where the waterfall touches the lake,' Will answered, moving to stand beside her. 'Where the waterfall *should* hit the lake,' he corrected himself and stared down at the vanishing torrent with surprise.

'That's right,' Aralia confirmed. 'Now imagine the north-south line going down into the water. Then picture another

264

following the form of the waterfall. The two would form an almost perfect *V* shape.'

'And if we drew a third line between the moon and the waterfall, we'd have a rough triangle.' Arthur also emerged from the hollow in the cliffside and moved to kneel beside his sister. 'The symbol for water,' he stated and traced an invisible triangle against the sky.

James glanced up at the sky. 'The symbol for water,' he repeated. 'What does it mean?'

Aralia looked at her brother for support but it was Will who spoke. 'It means we have to enter the lake.'

'Enter it?' James looked at his friend in surprise.

'We have to enter it at the point where the waterfall and the lake meet,' Arthur explained. 'We'll have to climb behind the cascade.' He looked towards the waterfall and pointed to the space behind it. 'See that ledge? We should be able to jump onto it. We can leave our bags here.'

Looking to where Arthur pointed, James identified the ledge just behind the cascade. The water didn't spill onto it, but curved above it in a gentle arc. In the gathering darkness, the spray rising off the rushing torrent almost seemed to glow.

'It seems mad, but alright,' James said quietly. 'What's the worst that could happen?' As soon as he asked this question, he wished he could take it back.

'Alight,' Will added, although he didn't sound convinced.

Arthur stripped off his cloak and aligned himself with the ledge behind the waterfall. James, Will and Aralia gathered behind him, waiting with breathless anticipation for him to jump. Keeping his eyes fixed on the cascade, he ran towards it and leapt from the side of the cliff. His body broke the flow of the water which instantly swallowed him. He vanished behind the foaming torrents which continued to fall as if they'd never been disturbed.

James watched with growing anticipation as Will jumped next, followed by Aralia. Both broke the water as Arthur had done and disappeared on the other side. He was about to follow them, when a black dot appeared in his peripheral vision. He turned sharply to his right and looked across the lake to where the dark cliffs rose above the beach. High above him and only just visible against the night sky, was a Shadow. He stared at it, for a moment paralysed, before breaking from his trance and jumping from the side of the cliff.

The freezing water struck his face like a slap. It filled his eyes, his ears and his clothes and tried to drag him down towards the lake. Reaching in front of him, he managed to grab onto the stone ledge and haul himself onto it. Wiping water from his eyes, he saw that Aralia, Arthur and Will were sitting just ahead of him. They had tucked themselves beneath an overhanging section of the cliff, just out of the water's reach. Taking care not to let the torrent catch him, James slid over the ledge to join them.

'It's beautiful,' Aralia said, her voice echoing beneath the cascade. Its glistening arc tumbled above them but the space beneath was oddly silent.

'The Shadows,' James cut in breathlessly. 'There is a Shadow on the cliffs.'

'Already?' Will asked, a note of fear in his voice.

'They're not on the beach. They haven't broken past the anagroma.'

'Yet,' Will replied darkly.

James nodded slowly and looked up at the waterfall. Aralia was right, it was beautiful. From up close, he could see that the water really was glowing, but so faintly that the light almost wasn't there. As he stared up at it, he became aware of a new

266

sensation. It was a faint tingling, much like that which he'd experienced in the forest above the cliffs. He sat up straighter, cocking his head to listen more carefully.

'D'you feel that?' he asked.

No one answered. They too were watching the water where the light was slowly brightening. It grew to fill the surrounding space, making the air tremble like a living force. The sensation was strange, warm, yet restless at the same time.

'What is it?' Aralia asked. 'What's happening?'

A sound now accompanied the gathering light and James strained to listen. It was a faint whispering, like leaves in the wind on a summer day. Listening more closely however, he realised it was the sound of many voices clamouring to be heard. Suddenly, the light around them contracted into a tight ball. This hovered for a moment above the ledge before dropping over the edge of the waterfall. The voices fell silent and everything went dark, apart from a tiny spark of light that glimmered on Aralia's hand.

'The ring,' she whispered, 'it's glowing.'

James swallowed and felt a shiver run down his spine. 'I think it's guiding us.' He looked intently at the spark of light, letting it burn his eyes.

'We'd better follow it then,' Will said, his voice sounding thin and distant.

'Ready?' James asked. He created a light in his palm and sent it to hover in the space above them.

'As ready as I'll ever be to jump off the edge of a waterfall,' Will muttered.

James walked over to where the water struck the side of the stone ledge. Spray hit his face but he didn't reach up to wipe it away. Will, Arthur and Aralia lined up beside him, their eyes sparkling with raw fear. The light above them touched the water and fizzled out. In the semi-darkness, all that could be heard was the sound of heavy breathing.

'Is everyone ready?' James asked again. Someone slipped a hand around his arm and held on tightly.

'Ready,' Aralia whispered beside him.

'Then here goes.' Sucking clean air into his lungs, James leant forward, letting the water take him.

Chapter 32

THE fall lasted for a matter of seconds. In that moment however, it felt like a lifetime. Tossed amongst the foaming spray, James couldn't help wondering what it would be like to be crushed on the rocks below. The strength of the cascade tore at his limbs, carrying him like a rag doll down towards the lake.

The impact took him by surprise. He struck the water with such force that he gasped out in pain. Winded, he sank beneath the surface and everything went still. Somewhere, as if far away, he heard the whispering voices again but still couldn't hear what they were saying. Opening his eyes, he saw that the surrounding water was strangely translucent. Even though the world above lay dark, the lake depths shone with a faint light. He could see right down to the sandy bed where fish lurked in the shadows of the rocks.

Spinning himself around, he searched the water for Will, Arthur and Aralia. They were scattered around him, staring at their surroundings with awe. He began swimming towards them, but Will suddenly darted away and Arthur and Aralia followed. Peering through the wavering depths, James saw that they were heading towards an opening in the rocks. These belonged to the dark cliffs which surrounded this side of the lake. As James swam closer to the opening, he saw that it was crusted with white crystals. These glittered in the strange half-light and refracted in the water.

Despite his desperation for air, James followed his friends through the entrance and into the darkness beyond. It was impossible to see anything and he hovered in the water, waiting for something to happen. Unable to hold his breath any longer, he opened his mouth and let the salty water fill it. He choked and coloured spots swam before his eyes. Taking an involuntary breath, he suddenly found his lungs expanding. Even though his mouth was full of water, his chest expanded and the spots on his retinas faded away.

'We can breathe,' he gasped, but his words came out in gurgled slurs.

Holding out his hand, he created a small light and spun around in search of his friends. Will appeared at his shoulder, his eyes wild and bright and he raised his shoulders in a gentle shrug.

'Where now?' he mouthed.

James held up his hand so that the light shone on their surroundings. They appeared to be in a narrow tunnel, the end of which he could only just see. He pointed towards it and started to swim. Hearing a muffled splash, he looked over his shoulder. Will had also started swimming and Arthur and Aralia followed in his wake. The tunnel was quite short and they quickly reached the end of it. Breaking from the opening, they paused to stare in astoundment at the scene in front of them.

In the vast expanse of translucent water, there rose an ancient citadel. Composed of toppling towers and hollow houses, it appeared bleak yet somehow imposing. Nearly all of the buildings on this side of the city were ruins, with walls and roofs crumbling into the lake bed below. Windows and doorways gaped empty, making the houses look forlorn. The entire citadel was a metropolis of fragmented stone and rusted metal, all wrapped in great swathes of seaweed. It was a haunted place, filled with forgotten memories and ancient ghosts.

Breaking from his trance, James began swimming towards the city. His eyes were drawn to a tower that rose above the other buildings. Curious to take a closer look, he propelled himself towards it. Pulling a curtain of seaweed from one of the hollow windows, he peered tentatively inside. His gaze fell on the remnants of a small room. The broken visage of a statue lay on the floor, its eyes looking upwards to the sky. It looked like it might once have been a woman, but it was hard to tell. A fish darted from her open mouth and eyed him warily before dancing on. James turned away from the scene. He felt like a ghost here, passing through a place where he didn't really belong.

A flash of white caught his eye and he looked back through the window. The room was still empty and silent and he shook his head to himself. He was on the verge of swimming away when the white flash came again. It was closer this time but as soon as he looked for it, it was gone. Suddenly, a pale face appeared just inches from his own. He jumped and pushed himself away from the window, heart pounding. For a moment, he didn't dare turn around, but when he did, there was nothing there.

'I won't hurt you.'

He jumped again and spun around. Hovering in the water in front of him was the translucent form of a little girl. She was watching him intently, her head cocked to one side. He stared back at her with growing horror but she just smiled.

'I just want to help you. I haven't seen anyone here for a long time.'

271

James was sure the voice belonged to the girl, but her lips weren't moving. He wondered if she too could speak with her mind, even though she was just a ghost. Unnerved by this thought, he put his hands over his ears but the girl laughed and stuck out her tongue. She was dressed in a white nightgown and carried a large conch shell in her left hand. Seeing James glance at the shell, she tucked it behind her back and suddenly disappeared. He looked for her, but couldn't see her anywhere.

'Right behind you.'

He whirled around just as the girl passed straight through him. A shiver ran up his spine and he stared at her with deepening distress.

'Who are you?' he asked in his mind. '*What* are you?'

The girl continued to contemplate him seriously. 'I'm Leila. Who are you?'

'I'm James,' he replied calmly, trying to hold himself level with her.

'You're very much alive, aren't you?' she said, her big eyes watching him closely.

'I hope I am.'

She giggled. 'I'm dead you see. I died here years ago, when the city first went under.'

James looked at her curiously, his fear suddenly dissipating. 'Went under?'

'Yes, when Jasper ruled. His power was so great that he cursed a whole city to drown beneath the water. We all drowned too, every one of us.'

'We?' James asked nervously.

'The people. They're all around us now, if you just look.'

James glanced tentatively at the surrounding buildings. As his eyes focused on the depths of the city, he became aware of misty shapes rising from the houses. There were hundreds of them, all whispering together as they rose from amongst the ruins. He shuddered and he heard Leila laugh again, a soft, tinkling sound deep within his mind.

'They won't hurt you,' she murmured. 'They're just curious. You see, we haven't seen anyone since *he* came. We're all interested to know who you are.'

'Who's he? Jasper?'

Leila spun a circle around him before settling on the tower windowsill. 'No, not Jasper. I mean the wanderer, or so he called himself. He came not long after the city sank. We liked him. He promised us that one day the curse would be lifted and the people of Urru would be free.'

She offered James a sweet smile and he frowned, trying to clear his head. If the girl was speaking the truth, and if he'd understood her correctly, then Arvad himself had been here. He could hardly believe it. The seastone had to be here, somewhere in the depths of this lake. Rousing himself from his thoughts, he suddenly became aware of his friends waving at him. He waved back but a chill on his arm made him turn. He looked down to find Leila holding onto his wrist, her expression deadly serious.

'They can't see me,' she said softly. 'They don't bear the same light as you do. They can't hear the voices of the Urrukara in the same way you do.'

'What light?' James said.

'The light of a pure spirit. He had the same light. The wanderer.'

James let out a sharp breath and the water bubbled around his mouth. Leila laughed and dived forward to catch one, but he propelled himself away from her grasping fingers.

'This person you call the wanderer, where did he go?' he asked. 'Can you show me?'

Leila wrinkled her nose. 'What will you give me in return?' James shrugged and her face grew petulant. 'What about the ring, the one on your friend's finger?'

'No, I'm sorry. We need that.' He delved into his pockets and his fingers brushed against something smooth. Retrieving the object, he saw that it was a pebble he'd picked up on the beach. 'Will this do?' He held it out to Leila. She smiled broadly, taking the stone and placing it inside her shell.

'Alright, I'll take you,' she agreed. 'Follow me.'

James turned to look for Will, Arthur and Aralia. They were already swimming towards him and he waved for them to follow. Leila led him downwards, past the citadel and into the shadowy places of the lake. The light in the water subsided, leaving it still and dark. It soon became impossible to see anything and James created an orb to light the way. Leila immediately froze under its glare and her eyes grew wide and frightened.

'Put it out,' she whispered. 'It burns.'

'How can I see you if it's dark?' James asked.

Leila reached for his arm and he felt her cold fingertips gripping it. She began tugging at him but he resisted, worried that Will, Arthur and Aralia would be left behind. As if understanding his concern, Leila held out her own palm and a pale light appeared there.

'Follow this. They will see it too.'

James nodded and let his own light fade away. They began swimming again, diving even deeper into the lake. At last, Leila stopped and turned to face James with a serious expression.

'Here the wanderer came, to the darkest part of the lake. He disappeared into the depths, but we didn't dare follow. He told us never to go there or we'd face a fate worse than the one we already had. We've obeyed him ever since.' She paused and let go of James' arm. 'I go no further, but if you return, call my name and I will come.'

Before James could answer, she vanished. The water went dark and he felt a chill pass through him. Closing his eyes, he focused on his palm, encouraging the light to return. It flickered into being and it illuminated the worried faces of his friends. Unable to speak to them, he turned to look at the surrounding darkness. As his eyes adjusted, he became aware of a shadowy opening just a few steps away. It looked much like the first tunnel they'd been through, its mouth crusted with tiny water crystals. Beckoning to Will, Arthur and Aralia, he swam towards the entrance and dived through.

This time, he felt the atmosphere changing around him. The water disappeared completely and he found himself breathing in real air. His feet dropped to the rocky floor and he uncurled himself to stand upright. Looking around, he saw that he was in another tunnel. The craggy walls stood close on either side, although the roof towered high above. In the soft light coming from his hand, the whole space sparkled with thousands of water crystals. He gazed up at them in awe, knowing that he was never likely to see anything like it again.

'Where are we?' Will's voice echoed in the surrounding space. 'What's going on?'

James released his light into the air and turned to face his friends. 'There was a girl, in the ruins. I heard her voice.'

'A girl?' Arthur asked tensely. 'Down here?'

'She wasn't really here; she was a ghost. She told me that the citadel was cursed hundreds of years ago, by Jasper. She also said that no one has come down here for a long time, not since…'

'Since what?' Will interrupted curiously.

'Since the wanderer.'

'Arvad?' Aralia breathed.

James nodded. 'If she was telling the truth. She led us here because this is where he allegedly came.'

'The legend says Arvad asked for the crystals to be hidden within the elements,' Arthur frowned. 'That's why he gave each element a gift. He didn't bring the seastone himself, so why would he come here?'

Silence hovered between them. James knew that Arthur was right. According to the legend, even Arvad didn't know where the crystals were hidden. Sighing, he wandered further into the cave. It was quiet here, in this place where there seemed to be both darkness and light.

'A neutral place,' he muttered to himself. 'A twilight zone.'

A faint flash of light startled him. It came not from his hand or those of his friends, but from the end of the cave. It was hardly there, a soft greenish glow that looked as if it were being reflected through water.

'What is that?' Aralia took a step towards it, her eyes shining in the reflection.

Side by side, the companions walked towards the light. It grew fainter as they approached and suddenly disappeared. Several long seconds passed before it returned with new strength. A new scene appeared before them and they stopped in their tracks. The tunnel they were in opened out into a large cavern. A circle of stone figures stood in the centre and it was from this that the light was emanating.

Most of the statues were all holding hands, forming an unbroken ring. On the far side, one figure stood taller than all the rest. It was a statue of a young woman, draped in a stone dress and cape. She was the only figure who didn't touch the surrounding statues. One hand was extended in front of her, gripping a stone box. The other was raised above her, palm to the cavern roof. As the companions stood staring, the light in the centre of the circle grew brighter until it eclipsed the darkness entirely.

Chapter 33

THE light was now so bright that the companions had to shield their faces from it. It had a warmth to it that radiated through the cave to where they stood. This tingled on their skin, crisp like winter sunshine.

'Celaeno,' James said at last. 'The statue is of her. I can feel it here,' he added, dropping his voice to a whisper.

'The seastone?' Aralia asked.

'Not the seastone specifically but a powerful force. I can't quite explain it.'

Twisting the ring from her finger, Aralia handed it to James. 'I think it's time that you had it,' she offered.

He took it from her and slipped it carefully into his pocket. The light in the cavern had begun to fade and he reached out a hand towards it. His arm felt suddenly cold and he whipped it back, only to find it was soaking wet.

'The cave is full of water,' he announced in surprise. 'It must be a test. There's water but we can't see it.'

'We'll have to swim out to the circle,' Arthur said. 'I guess that's where we need to take the ring.'

'This must be it,' James whispered. 'We're finally here.'

Taking a deep breath, he slid from the tunnel and into the cavern beyond. It was strange to feel water seeping through his clothes but not be able to see it. The sensation made him feel as if he were flying. He beat his arms and propelled himself towards the stone circle. Trying to take a breath, he sucked water into his throat and choked. Realising that it was unlike the other caves, he swam back to the tunnel and pulled himself out of the water, gasping for air. He sat there for just a moment before diving back in.

He swam back towards the circle, passing Will, Arthur and Aralia along the way. They looked at him, cheeks inflated with air, before racing back to the tunnel entrance. Left alone in the water, James eyed the stone circle nervously. The linked arms of the statues formed a ring of low archways and he swam up to the closest one. A glint of blue caught his eye, floating in between the statues. He turned towards it, but just as suddenly it was gone. Shaking his head to himself, he ducked beneath the archway and tried to propel himself through to the other side. A powerful rush of water suddenly hit him in the chest. It expelled him from the circle and drove him back towards the tunnel.

Surprised, but no longer nervous, he started to swim around the perimeter of the circle. Passing behind the figure of Celaeno, he paused and let his feet drift against the sandy floor. Looking closely at her flowing robe, he realised that it bore an engraving on the back between her shoulder blades. Floating up towards it, he realised that it was of a turtle. Its shell was intricately designed with a sickle moon on its back and its legs bore a floral patterning. Tracing the shapes with one finger, he tried to memorise every line and groove. He wished he could stay longer but his desperation for air drove him back to the tunnel.

'I found something,' he spluttered, joining Aralia and Will who were standing at the entrance. 'Celaeno's robe is marked with an engraving of a turtle.'

'They all bear an engraving,' Aralia said, her voice filled with excitement. 'Look around the circle. All of the figures are women.'

James looked between the statues, noticing how all had long hair and flowing robes. He turned back to Aralia, a realisation dawning on him.

'The seven sisters,' he whispered. 'They're all here.'

Aralia nodded. 'Yes, and each of them bear a symbol. Perhaps if we find out what each of them are, it will help us figure out our next move.'

Diving into the water again, James headed straight for Celaeno's statue. He once again traced the turtle on her back before swimming to observe the figure beside her. This statue was marked with a triangle, the lines of which pointed downwards towards the cave floor. Curiosity further aroused, he continued around the circle. There were three more triangles and a circle but he ran out of breath before seeing the rest. Tracing the patterns in his mind, he returned to the tunnel. Kneeling on the hard ground, he picked up a sharp stone and began scratching the symbols into the rock.

'They're hyrogans.'

Hearing Aralia behind him, he turned to look over his shoulder. 'They're what?'

She came to kneel beside him and ran her eyes over his rough drawings. 'Hyrogans. They belong to an ancient language, spoken long ago by Emerans in the southern continent. Each of the symbols is used to represent something else.'

'D'you know what any of them mean?'

'We all know some already,' Arthur's deep voice joined. Pulling himself from the water, he came over to join them.

'The turtle and the upside down triangle,' James said.

Arthur nodded. 'The other triangles represent the remaining elements. 'Earth, fire and water.'

Hearing a splash, they all turned to watch Will emerge from the cave. He shook the water from his hair and his eyes immediately fell on the crude drawings.

'How many d'you have?' he asked.

'Two left,' James replied, tapping the sharp stone against his forehead. 'One is a circle but I don't know the last.'

Aralia took the stone from him and began tracing a sideways figure of eight. 'The lemniscate, or infinity symbol,' she explained and sat back on her heels to observe their work. 'The question is, what do they all mean when they're put together?'

Silence fell. They all sat looking at the symbols for a long time. The stillness was eventually broken by Aralia who stood up and went to stand at the edge of the tunnel.

'What if we write out the words?' she suggested. 'If we could see the names of these symbols, we might be able to make more sense of them.'

'It's worth a try,' James said quietly. Picking up the sharp stone, he started to write out the names of the four elements, but Aralia stopped him.

'They should be written in the old language,' she said. 'Here.' She took the stone from him again and kneeling beside the drawings, began writing out their names.

'Wait,' Will held out a hand to stop her. 'We have to think about this carefully. The circle, the turtle and the infinity symbol could represent multiple things.'

'Such as?' Arthur asked.

'For example, the turtle could represent the moon and the north. The circle could be for the ring, eternity, or again the moon.'

'Or the spirit,' Aralia added.

'The turtle had a moon on its back.' James pointed to the turtle he'd drawn which bore a sickle moon on its back. 'I think the meaning of that is clear.'

'Alright,' Will agreed. 'So what about the circle?'

'The infinity symbol must represent eternity,' Arthur suggested. 'The circle must be for the spirit. It would make sense, given that the other elements are present.'

Aralia began writing the remaining words beneath the pictures. 'I've written them in the old language, because that is how Arvad might have known them,' she explained. 'Mone, pfyr, earth, ayr, water, speyrit and eternyte.'

'What d'we do with them now?' Will knelt beside her and stared at the letters, as if hoping they would reveal some secret.

'Watch.' Aralia created a light in her hand and it drifted over the letters. They began to shift and change, eventually settling in a new formation. 'The old language is powerful and can be used to create and break enchantments,' she explained. 'Look.'

James ran his eyes over the words that had taken shape on the rocky floor. 'What do they say?' he asked.

'Ere a safpyr, rit ym te wyrth, pyt orne eterne. The first part translates to, 'Here a sapphire.''

'The last word clearly means eternity,' Will joined. 'Rit could mean written. Written in words?'

'Here a sapphire, written in words, for all eternity.' Aralia looked down at the words with fresh excitement but nothing happened.

'It must be some sort of riddle, like the one we had to answer for the firestone,' James said.

Will nodded. 'Yeah, but we haven't quite got it right. Maybe rit means something else.'

'You're right,' Aralia whispered, kneeling on the ground

again. 'It could mean brought, or maybe hidden. Here a sapphire, hidden...' she paused to assess the next words. 'Brought by the...'

'I've got it,' Will suddenly announced and his voice echoed along the tunnel. 'Wryth, earth, wanderer. Think about it. Wanderer means earth, or traveller of the earth. Here a sapphire, created by the wanderer, to hide for eternity.'

Silence hung heavily in the air around them. The words began to fade against the rocks and the light Aralia had cast over them dimmed. For a moment, everything was still and then a light began to glow in the centre of the stone circle. It seeped out into the cave, reflecting off the invisible water and dancing on the walls. It emanated straight from Celaeno's hand and under its spell the statues dropped their arms and the circle was broken.

'Go,' Aralia whispered to James. 'Take the ring into the circle. We'll follow.'

He looked at her and then at Will and Arthur before jumping into the water. It tingled around him with an electric energy, spurring him on towards the statues. This time, when he tried to enter the circle, he wasn't pushed away. He swam to the centre and let his feet sink to the cave floor before looking up at Celaeno. Will, Arthur and Aralia swam to join him and stood in a semi-circle behind him. As soon as they were inside the circle, the light faded away. The statues took hands again, trapping the companions in their midst.

Taking the ring from his pocket, James held it up to Celaeno. He could feel his whole body trembling, whether with the power of its ancient magic or with nerves he didn't know. His eyes were drawn to the statue's left hand which pointed towards the sky. He noticed that her ring finger bore the imprint of a circular mark. Heart racing, he reached up and tried to slip the silver band onto it. Before he even managed to touch the stone hand however, a gentle wave pushed him back down to the cave floor.

A nudge at his elbow made him turn. Aralia held out her hand to him and he placed the ring in her palm. He watched with growing anticipation as she floated up to Celaeno's hand and slipped the ring onto her finger. A moment of suspended calm descended before the water began to ripple around the stone circle. It rushed forward with a gentle force and receded just as suddenly. Breathing inwards, James realised that it had disappeared.

'You bring the gift of Arvad the Wanderer.' A voice spoke, making him jump. It came from the air itself; a whisper that echoed all around the stone circle. 'Just a boy,' it murmured. 'So young and so pure.'

'Who are you?' James turned a full circle but no one else was there. 'Are you one of the quartet keepers?'

'You bring the gift of Arvad the Wanderer,' the voice repeated.

Behind Celaeno's statue, a white shape flickered. As it drew closer, it took on the form of a young woman. She was tall and elegant but so translucent that she almost wasn't there.

'Celaeno,' Will breathed.

'Celaeno?' the woman said. 'I am not she. You speak my sister's name.' She drifted a little closer, but her eyes watched them warily. 'I am Teygete.'

'Teygete? Like the waterfall?' James asked.

She nodded and slid gracefully between two of the statues. Watching her, James thought he saw flashes of blue light in the water behind her, but when he looked closer, they disappeared.

'Sea sapphires.' Teygete's voice drifted across the circle. 'They are creatures of the sea, invisible unless light shines on them.' She reappeared beside Celaeno's statue, her eyes darting between the companions. 'I sense among you another of my sisters,' she continued quietly.

'Another ghost?' Will queried.

'People call us that, but I prefer spirit,' she replied and her voice slithered gracefully through the air. 'I don't speak of my generation,' she continued. 'I speak of yours. The girl who brought the ring, she is my sister.'

'Me?' Aralia stared at Teygete with bewilderment. 'I don't have any sisters.'

Teygete cocked her head to the side, as if analysing her. 'Perhaps not by blood, but by spirit. Did you not know? You, child, are of a new generation. You are one of seven sisters.'

'Me?' Aralia said again.

'Did you not wonder why only you could gift the ring? It is because you are of our nature. Time will repeat itself and the sisterhood will be bound again.'

James frowned. 'A sisterhood. Who else is part of it?'

Teygete slipped behind a statue and exhaled. 'You spoke before of quartet keepers. Just four among the sisterhood are the bearers of that secret. I cannot tell you who, for I do not know. The riddles are yours to answer, not mine.'

'We've met one of them already,' Aralia whispered. 'Nuria.'

'Nuria?' Arthur turned sharply to his sister. 'The Chinjoka dragon keeper?'

Before Aralia could answer, Teygete spoke again. 'You have come here, to this sacred place and brought an ancient gift. You do not need to be shown the way. It is in your hearts already. A second darkness has been lifted, here in the cursed citadel of Urru Thath. The light will shine again.'

As she spoke, the statue of Celaeno lowered her arms, bringing the stone box in her right hand closer to the ground.

James nodded to Aralia who stepped forward and gently took it into her hands.

'Is the seastone inside the box?' James asked, but Teygete had disappeared.

'It's in your heart James,' the soft voice came back to him. 'Look for it with your heart.'

A sudden rumble sounded and the water surrounding the circle started to tremble. James, Will, Arthur and Aralia clustered together in the middle of the stone circle, feeling the ground shake beneath their feet. The rumbling grew louder and before their eyes, the statues started to disintegrate. One by one, the great stone figures collapsed and fell to dust. Last to fall was Celaeno. Her proud spine crumbled and as she fell, the ring on her finger became dust like its bearer.

With the circle broken, water rushed inside. It was no longer invisible but fierce and ugly. There was no time to look inside the box and desperate to get out, the companions swam back towards the tunnel. They had almost reached it when a blinding flash of light shot through the cavern. The water rippled with electricity and James could feel it burning on his skin. Fighting against the growing chaos, he reached the tunnel and pulled himself inside. Arthur pulled him to his feet before hurrying to drag Will and Aralia from the water.

'Run,' Will gasped, shaking water from his hair.

Great waves hit the edge of the tunnel, spilling inside and catching at their heels as they ran. They didn't stop until they reached the other side of the tunnel. Facing the black water, they each ignited a light before diving in. James called out to Leila in his mind, but she didn't answer. Closing his eyes, he imagined the citadel and his limbs started to remember the way back. When at last they saw Urru rising before them, it was a different scene to that which they had left. Powerful ripples chased each other through the citadel and stones began to fall.

As the tide grew stronger, the buildings began to crumble as the statues had done. Piece by piece they toppled to the lake bed and turned to a fine dust. The sight was mesmerising and heartbreaking but the companions had to turn away for fear of being drowned. Casting one last look at the collapsing city, James noticed Leila watching him from amongst the clouds of dust. She didn't come any closer, but raised a hand in farewell.

As he hovered in the water, a great sigh rose around him. He realised, with a faint shiver, that it was the sound of hundreds of tired souls as they passed on. In this moment, he understood that the whole citadel had been guardian of the seastone, bound to eternity not only by Jasper but by Arvad and the elements. With the return of the ring, the curse had been lifted. The lake, like the dragon who had guarded the firestone, was now free.

Chapter 34

EVERY time James tried to push towards the surface of the lake, he was forced downwards again. He felt like he was right under the waterfall, struggling beneath its tumbling cascade. With every passing moment, his desire to breathe grew harder to control. He could feel his lungs expanding and began to fear that they would burst. The feeling was by now familiar, but this didn't make it any easier to bear.

His shoulder was throbbing again and he briefly let his arms rest by his sides. Taking this opportunity, the water tugged at his limbs and pushed him down into the pressurised darkness. In the same moment, a surge of water rushed upwards from below. It caught him in its midst and bore him towards the surface. Cold air suddenly slapped against his face and he gasped. He was thrust against something hard, rock perhaps, and grappled at it with slippery fingers. After three attempts, he managed to drag himself from the water and lay on his back, panting.

'Will? Arthur? Rai?' he called. 'You there?'

Three voices drifted back to him and he breathed a sigh of relief. Opening his eyes, he saw that the sky above was pitch dark. The moon was no longer visible and there weren't any stars either. His own light had gone out during his struggle below the surface but pushing himself onto his elbows, he created another. It glistened on the surrounding rocks which were wet in the wake of the receding tide. Holding up his hand, he scanned the lakeside for his friends. His eyes fell first on Aralia and the stone box clutched in her hands.

'You still have it,' he breathed.

'Somehow,' she returned and pushed it across the rocks towards him. 'It's heavy.'

James reached out to take it, feeling the rough stone beneath his fingers. The surface was engraved with seven symbols, the same ones which had marked the statues. Curling his fingers under the rim of the lid, he gave it a gentle tug. He could feel the stone resisting him and tried again, but the lid stayed firmly shut.

'Here, let me try.' Arthur took the box and tapped it gently on the ground but it still wouldn't open.

'We should try to find our way back to the waterfall,' Will suggested. 'I have a knife in my bag that we could use to prise it open.'

'Alright,' James consented, 'let's try to find our way back.'

He stood up, clothes dripping on the rocky shore, and turned to look behind him. Low cliffs stretched away from the water's edge but there was no sign of the waterfall anywhere.

'We must be further along the cliffs,' Arthur remarked. 'If we climb to the top and then turn left, we should be heading in the right direction.'

Squeezing water from their clothes, they began their ascent. The tide hadn't touched the higher sections of cliff, making the rocks easier to grip onto. They climbed quickly, driven by the desire to open the box and see if the seastone was really there. Scrambling over the last ridge, they paused to catch their breaths. It was too dark to see the lake below, but as they stood there, the moon slipped out from behind a cloud. It illuminated the water which glowed with a thin white mist. A shadow passed across the unbroken surface and they all looked up. High above them, hovering close to the moon, was the silhouette of a dragon.

'The Shadows,' Aralia gasped. 'They've found the lake.'

'Keep low,' Arthur commanded. 'Extinguish your lights.'

James however was no longer listening. He'd seen something out on the lake, a dark mass poised on the water like a low hanging cloud. It was hardly visible amidst the swirling mist, but he couldn't tear his eyes away from it. A voice began murmuring deep within his mind and he let it in, knowing it belonged to the girl.

'You must cross the water,' she whispered. 'You must go now.'

'Cross it?' he asked. 'How?'

'Ask for an answer and it will come.'

Before he had a chance to press her further, she was gone. He turned to his friends, his eyes shining in the light from his hand.

'We cross the water,' he whispered.

'We what?' Will looked at him with an expression of disbelief. 'We *what*?' he repeated.

'We cross it. The girl in my mind said that's what I have to do.'

'When?' Will asked.

'Just now. I'm not sure what she meant, but I have to get back down to the water.' Without waiting for a further reply, he began clambering back down the rocks towards the lake.

He didn't stop until he reached the water's edge. Looking out across the dark lake, he searched for the dark mass hovering on its surface. He tried to memorise the shape, but it kept changing due to the swirling mist. Closing his eyes, he imagined himself walking towards it. He saw a pathway stretching across the water and at the end of it, the shore of an island.

'James, look.'

He opened his eyes to see Aralia pointing across the lake. Something was moving towards them through the mist and as it drew closer, he realised it was a boat.

'Our way across,' he whispered. 'Of course.'

The boat slid gracefully towards them across the water and came to rest against the rocks. James stepped carefully into it and held it still while Will, Arthur and Aralia climbed in behind him. There was only one bench which Will and Aralia squashed onto while James and Arthur sat in the base. As soon as they were seated, the boat began moving again, bearing them across the lake towards the shadowy island. It didn't look as far away as it had done from the cliffs. As the boat drew closer to it, the shadows melted away and the rocky edges came into sight. In the surrounding mist, it looked as if it didn't even touch the water.

A jetty stretched from the island and into the lake. The boat moored itself against it and held still, as if waiting for the companions to disembark. James stepped out of it first and bent down to take the stone box from Arthur. He turned to look down the jetty. At the end of it, a stone archway led onto the island. It reminded James of the place where the firestone had been set free and he felt his heart beat faster. He took a step towards the arch before turning back to his friends. They were standing on the jetty behind him but none of them moved to join him.

'Aren't you coming?' he asked.

Aralia gently shook her head. 'We'll be right behind you,

but it's you that should take the box onto the island.'

'I can't do it alone,' he protested. 'We're a team.'

'You won't be alone,' a soft voice said in his mind. 'I'll be with you.'

Reluctantly, he turned away from Will, Arthur and Aralia and walked towards the archway. He paused at the end of the jetty to look through it but the other side was hidden in mist. Clutching the box tightly to his chest, he stepped through. The mist cleared away instantly and he found himself looking across a stretch of rocky ground. In the centre of this, a ring of seven stones stood protectively around a table. Walking around the circumference, he saw that each of the stones was engraved with a familiar hyrogan symbol.

Stepping tentatively into the circle, he set the box on the table in the centre. A hollow basin had been cut into the middle but the surface was otherwise smooth. He ran his fingers around the edge of the basin, waiting for something to happen. Part of him hoped that the lid of the box would just pop open, but the minutes ticked by and nothing transpired. Turning away from the table, he called for the girl in his mind to come but she didn't answer. A soft light glowed against one of the stones and surprised, he turned around. His gaze fell on a shimmering beam that was coming from the basin. Leaning towards it, he saw that it was now filled with glistening water.

Heart racing, he picked up the box and carefully lowered it into the basin. It sank straight to the bottom and water closed over the lid. As he watched, the stone casing started to melt. The process was slow, like the softening of metal. A low whispering began around him, slithering between the stones and echoing across the island. A stream of light suddenly burst from the basin. It sent the water out with it, showering the table with silvery droplets. This light gradually expanded, spreading beyond the stone circle and out onto the rocks beyond.

Far away, in the depths of his mind, James felt the anger of the darkness. It made him shudder but he pushed the thought away, determined to focus on the light alone. Keeping his eyes on the basin, he saw that it was once again filled with water. This was no longer clear however but deep and blue. At first, he thought the basin was empty but as he looked more closely, he saw that something lay in the depths. It was from this that the blue colour was emanating and he closed his eyes, suddenly fearing it to be an illusion.

'Open your eyes,' a voice whispered in his mind. 'Pick it up. It is yours to hold.'

James jumped as a hand touched his shoulder, but he didn't dare turn around. 'How're you here?' he asked the girl. 'You're only ever inside my mind.'

'I'm not really here,' she answered. 'You just think I am. Pick up the crystal.'

Slowly, fearfully, James opened his eyes. Leaning over the rim of the basin, he let his eyes fall on the object at the bottom. Trying not to tremble, he dared to slip his hand into the water. His fingers brushed against smooth stone and the sensation sent a shock through his body. The crystal felt warm against his skin, even though the water was cold. He wrapped his hand around it and carefully drew it out into the open air.

'The seastone,' he whispered. 'The sapphire.'

It was smaller than the firestone and less refined. Deep blue swirls filled its depths, rippling like waves. At its heart, a fleck of yellow glimmered. Looking at it, James realised that it bore within it the gift of the yellow sapphire. He held the crystal to his chest, feeling it tremble with an invisible power. As he stood there, he sensed the presence behind him fading away.

'Will you tell me your name before you go?' he asked the

girl. 'I know so little about you.'

There was a long pause before she answered. 'Don't you know it yet?'

'You've never told me.'

She removed her hand from his shoulder before replying. 'My name is Sylvia.'

'Sylvia?'

'For the moon, for womanhood, for the seven sisters.'

James frowned. 'For the seven sisters? Are you one of them? The other girl I heard in my mind, Tala, is she one of the seven too?'

Although he couldn't see the girl, he sensed that she inclined her head. Before he could question her further, he became aware of a darkness beyond the mist at the edge of the island. Another voice called out in his mind, pushing Sylvia's away. He recognised it as Aralia's and let it in, only to realise that Sylvia had vanished.

'James, we have to leave,' Aralia called. 'The Shadows… there are so many…'

Her voice also faded away and needing no further encouragement, James began to run. Bursting onto the jetty, he saw his friends still standing at the end of it. When they noticed him, they hurried back to the boat and jumped in. A deep rumbling resonated in the air and James looked fearfully over his shoulder. To his horror, he saw that the wooden planks were starting to crumble. He picked up his pace, not stopping until he'd reached the boat.

'Do you have it?' Will shouted above the noise of snapping wood. 'D'you have the seastone?'

James nodded and looked up at the sky. There was no longer just a single Shadow but dozens of them swooping across the clouds. He could feel the rush of wings above him and hurriedly stepped down into the boat. Somewhere near, he could feel a great darkness, and he knew the Belladonna was close.

'She knows I have it,' he gasped. 'She'll find us.'

The boat rocked beneath them as it slid gracefully away from the crumbling jetty. Looking back at the island, James saw that it had vanished into the mist. His fingers closed around the crystal in his pocket and he shivered.

As soon as the boat touched the mainland, the companions leapt from it and ran towards the shadow of the cliffs. Driven by fear, they began clambering upwards, heading towards the top. Only when they broke over the final ridge did they turn to look at one another.

'Keep close to the rocks,' Will ordered, 'and listen out for the waterfall.'

They began to run, taking care to remain in the shadows. While the sky above was still dark, the sickle moon was oddly bright. After what felt like a long time, they skidded to a halt. Beyond the sound of wings came the sound of tumbling water.

'The waterfall,' James hissed. 'We must be close.'

Guided by the sound of the cascade, he led the way across the clifftops. It wasn't long before he felt cool spray on his face and the waterfall came into sight. It shone white in the soft moonlight, but the wavering glow beneath it had vanished. Making sure the crystal was safe in his pocket, James began climbing down the rocks to where they'd left their bags.

'What's our plan?' Aralia whispered behind him. 'Where do we go now?'

'To the beach,' James answered automatically. 'We have to find our way back to Muir.'

'To Muir?' Will frowned. 'Why?'

'We have nowhere else to go,' James replied simply. 'I have to take the crystal away from here.'

Will glanced at Arthur and Aralia before turning back to James. 'Can we see it then? The crystal?'

James took it carefully from his pocket and held it out in his palm. His friends leant in to take a look, eyes filled with awe, but none of them tried to touch it. He slipped it away again and turned towards the beach.

'We should go along the top of the cliffs this time,' Arthur suggested. 'It'll be quicker.'

Following his lead, they all climbed back up to the top of the cliffs. The beach wasn't visible from here but they knew the general direction. They didn't run this time, but crept slowly along the clifftop, keeping to the shadow of the rocks where they could. Dipping beneath a small overhang, James suddenly collided with something solid. He jumped backwards and knocked into Will who hissed with frustration. A bright light blazed in front of them and they both froze.

'James Fynch, you have to stop creeping up on me!' A face appeared behind the light, framed by a halo of red hair.

'Dina!' Will exclaimed loudly. 'What're you doing here? How are you here?'

Dina's eyes flashed. 'Keep your voice down. We're not exactly in a position to scream from the clifftops. I'm here to help you,' she continued in gentler tones. 'You seem to have a lot of people after you.'

'How did you get out of Arvora?' Will asked in a lower voice.

'Even Arvora can be broken out of if you're not meant to be there.' Another voice sounded and Kaedon stepped from the shadows. His beard had grown longer but his sharp features were still recognisable.

'Come on,' Dina whispered. 'You should come with us.'

Light burst in the sky above them and they ducked. Dina's light went out and James, Will, Arthur and Aralia were left to follow her silhouette. Kaedon moved behind them, keeping his head turned to the sky. After walking just a few metres, they stopped and Dina spoke again.

'Thuir, fiar,' she hissed.

'Fiar.' A female voice came back to her, sounding broken and ragged.

Two more silhouettes emerged from the shadows. The shorter of the two touched Dina's arm and the other turned to face the companions.

'Greetings.' Oede's calm voice came through the darkness. Seconds later, his face was illuminated as Dina moved to stand beside him.

'Thuir, fiar.' A woman stepped from behind Dina and the companions stared. She too had red hair and deep green eyes that sparkled in the dim light.

'This is my sister,' Dina introduced.

For a moment, James didn't know what to say. He caught eyes with Dina's sister who gently shook her head. 'How did you get her out of Arvora?' he eventually asked.

'A story for another time,' Kaedon muttered. 'We need to get moving.'

'Listen up.' Dina turned her gaze onto James. 'Oede will take all of you and my sister to Muir. Kaedon and I will follow. It's important that we move quickly and quietly.'

'How do you know of Muir?' Aralia asked with surprise.

Her question was cut short by a flash of light which seemed to brighten the entire sky. Everyone ducked as the beam struck the rocks just below where they stood. There was a splintering sound and shards of stone scattered everywhere. Looking up, James saw that Dina's sister hadn't moved. She stood close to the edge of the cliffs, her head turned up to the sky. A second burst of light plunged towards the earth but she saw it too late.

The beam struck her directly in the chest and burst into sparks across her skin.

Dina let out a horrified scream. It was a terrible sound, worse than any James had ever heard. It made his skin tingle and his hands began to shake. Hearing a muffled sob beside him, he reached out to take Aralia's hand. She squeezed it tightly and he could feel that she too was shaking. Dina's sister stood facing them, but her lips made no sound. Light raced through her skin like lightning and her frame slowly crumbled to the ground. It was horrifying to watch, but James somehow couldn't tear his eyes away. Splayed on the grass, her body shuddered once before lying still.

Chapter 35

THE air rang with Dina's howls of grief. She tried to kneel beside her sister but Kaedon held her back, whispering to her in his own tongue. James felt a pang in his chest and gripped Aralia's hand more tightly. She however let go and delving into her bag, brought out the bottle Eir had given her. She took a step towards Dina's sister but Arthur stopped her.

'It can heal, but it can't bring back the dead,' he whispered.

'You should go.' Kaedon turned to look at the companions and his expression was pained. 'Please, go. Oede will take you now to Muir.'

'We can't leave you,' James insisted, 'not after this.'

'You must go,' Kaedon said, his voice suddenly harsh. 'We will follow.'

James opened his mouth to object again but Will took his arm and drew him away. 'Leave it,' he whispered. 'We have to take the seastone to safety.'

Oede beckoned to them and they responded. He led them away from the edge of the cliff, away from the body of Dina's sister. Shadows swooped in the air above them but none dived towards the cliffs. Oede took them down the cliff path that they had previously chosen not to take. It was narrow and eroded in places but they made it safely down to the beach. It was quiet down here and Oede glided across the stones without a sound. James, Will, Arthur and Aralia tried to follow suit, but it was impossible to stop the pebbles from crunching under their own feet.

At the far end of the beach, Oede stopped. The craggy cliffs towered above, casting no shadow as before. He waved the companions past him one at a time and they stepped through the illusory cliffs to the grassy ground beyond. The forest looked even darker than before, hidden in deep shadow. The trees whispered in a faint wind but James no longer wondered what they were trying to say. He followed Oede closely as he dived between the needled branches and into the darkness beyond.

They hadn't walked for long when Oede held up a hand for them to stop. Squinting ahead, James saw two white ferastia standing patiently by a nearby tree. Neither were tethered to the trunk and bent to nuzzle Oede as he approached them. He stroked each of them under the chin before turning to face the companions.

'James, Will, you go on one,' he commanded. 'Arthur, Aralia, you're with me.'

James stroked one of the beasts before hauling himself up onto its back. He was just settling himself in the soft space behind its neck when he heard a twig snap somewhere in the surrounding trees. He froze, but he let his eyes wander amongst the shadows. A shape was moving there and as it came closer, it took on the form of a woman. She was dressed in a dark robe but her long black hair spilled from beneath her hood.

'Is that…?' Will's hands slipped from the ferastia's mane and he moved to stand behind it.

James stared at the woman with recognition, suddenly feeling sick. As he watched, she woman raised her hand and light burst from her fingertips. The ferastia bucked in fear but didn't run. The light struck the surrounding trees, shattering their lower branches.

'Why are you here?' James whispered, his voice barely audible.

From behind the woman, another figure emerged. Looking at the dark space beneath the hood, James saw it was Kedran. His white scar burnt in his face and his eyes glittered dangerously. As he came closer, the figure of the Belladonna wavered and James quickly realised his mistake.

'You conjured her!' He looked at Kedran with a mixture of hatred and pity. 'Why?'

Kedran laughed and rubbed his hands together. 'Let's not talk of unimportant things. I know you have it, so hand it over.'

James curled his fingers around the crystal in his pocket. 'If she wants it, why doesn't she come and get it herself?' he retorted.

'Why raise an army and then come to fetch it herself?' Kedran sneered.

'One day, she'll have to face me,' James returned. 'She can't keep hiding forever.'

'People are afraid of what they don't know.' Kedran bared his teeth and came another step closer. 'They hear of a dark force and they cower. That is how it should be. One day you will meet her and she will face you with her army. You'll start to wish that you'd never begun this quest. You'll never forgive yourself for letting people die for you.'

'He's winding you up,' Will warned in James' ear. 'Don't let him.'

'People don't die for me,' James hissed, his anger mounting. 'They die to stop the darkness from spreading.'

'Isn't that the same thing?' Kedran goaded.

Before James knew what he was doing, he raised a hand and light burst from his fingertips. It was so bright that it illuminated the surrounding forest and exposed many shadowy figures lurking behind the trees. They shrank away from the light and slithered away into a darker place. Shaking the beam from his hand, James watched as it shot towards Kedran and burst at his feet. He stumbled backwards but none of his army came forth from the trees to defend him.

'Ride,' Oede suddenly shouted. 'Ride and don't stop.'

Will flung himself onto the ferastia behind James and kicked it in the sides. It let out a sharp whinny and suddenly lunged forward. Slipping on its back, James held tightly onto its mane with one hand, leaving the other free to defend himself. Light whirled in the air around them, a kaleidoscope of colours. It could almost have been beautiful if it hadn't burnt with the bitter scent of battle.

The ferastia rode hard, whining as the light chased after them. They were surrounded on all sides by Shadows who glided through the trees as if they were floating. Even without their serpentine steeds, they were frightening. James observed them stalking through the forest with growing fear, knowing that there were too many to fight without an army of their own. He clung on to his ferastia, hurling bolts of light into the air behind him. The Shadows shrank away from every beam yet somehow seemed to be coming closer.

At long last, the animals reached the edge of the forest. Dark clouds still filled the sky but the horizon was lightening. Too tired to fight anymore, James slumped over the ferastia's back. He watched the ground speeding by below the ferastia's hooves until he felt dizzy. Raising his head again, he glanced over his shoulder. The Shadows hovered at the edge of the forest but didn't follow. There was no sign of Kedran anywhere and he heaved a sigh of relief. Letting his shoulders relax, he realised that he was shaking.

'You alright?' Will asked but James was too tired to answer.

It was dawn by the time the village came into sight. The ferastia, tired from their long journey, loped unevenly towards the houses. As they entered the village, people came out of their houses to point and stare. Fear lay in all of their eyes and none of them offered to help Oede and the companions from their steeds. The animals eventually came to a halt outside Tasi's hut. As before, the door opened of its own accord and dismounting the ferastia, James, Will, Arthur and Aralia stumbled inside.

The young man they'd met before greeted them with wide eyes. He waved them past before hurrying outside to attend to the ferastia. Entering the main room, James' eyes fell on the fire glowing in the centre. Beside it, sat Tasi, his legs crossed together in meditation. His eyes were closed but he raised a hand and gestured for them to sit. James tumbled onto a plump purple cushion and tried to stop his body from trembling. From the corner of his eye, he saw Oede enter the room and hover stiffly in the doorway.

'Greetings, elder,' he said. 'Greetings messenger.'

James frowned. He only knew one person with the name messenger. Refocusing his eyes, he became aware of another presence in the room. Turning his head, he saw a man standing on the opposite side of the room to Oede. He raised his head as James stared at him and his gingery stubble glowed in the firelight.

'Albert?' James managed to whisper.

'James Fynch,' Albert's kindly voice returned. 'I find you once again at the end of an adventure.'

'Where have you been?' Will demanded a little too harshly.

'I'm glad to see you all alive,' Albert replied, ignoring the snappish comment.

'We are, but not everyone survived,' Aralia imparted and lowered her eyes to the floor.

'Ah,' Albert said, as if reading her mind. 'The prisoner.'

Oede came in from the doorway and stood beside the fire. 'Her name was Daphne, Sir,' he cut in, his tone firm but respectful.

Albert nodded and moved to join him in the circle of firelight. James noticed then that his body was faint, as if it was not really there.

'We found it,' James said quietly. 'We found the seastone.' Reaching into his pocket, he cupped the crystal in his palm and drew it out into the light.

Oede stared at the crystal and even Tasi opened his eyes a fraction to observe its glittering form. Only Albert didn't move a muscle. He stood contemplating a candle which stood in an alcove next to him and caught a drop of wax on his finger. When he eventually turned around, he didn't look to the waiting group, he didn't look at the crystal but started muttering to himself.

'Darkness comes and darkness grows. Time is precious and we don't have long before the Belladonna touches us all. She spreads like a poison, ever greater by the day. In this darkness, in this race, no one is invincible. But we must all remember that where there are shadows, there must always be light.' He looked at James, his eyes calm and cool despite the firelight.

'Her army grows larger,' Oede stated. 'There are Shadows, and not just them. A network of seamen, scientists and Laithe also grows. It won't be long before she takes ordinary people into her forces.'

Albert frowned and his fingers curled into his palms. 'Laithe? You mean spirits of the dead?' Oede nodded and the lines on Albert's forehead deepened. 'It is worse than I imagined. You have done well.'

'You know each other?' Will asked, looking between Albert and Oede. 'Is that why you're here?' He aimed this question at Albert who turned to him with a smile.

'The darkness stirred.' He turned to the candle again and passed his fingers through the flame. 'It passes over us like a shadow, touching not only this world but others.'

Albert didn't turn around, but James knew these words were aimed at him. He wanted to ask hundreds of questions, but before he could say anything, Albert spoke again.

'In the next few hours, a woman will arrive at this house. Her name is Isla. She is my sister, the eleventh messenger of the Zodiac, and you must give the crystal to her.'

'How will we know it's really her?' Arthur asked sharply.

'You will know,' Albert replied evasively. 'I must leave you now, for my strength wanes. I will see you all again and soon, I promise that.' He glanced at James again and his body began to waver.

'Wait,' James said suddenly. Everyone in the room turned to look at him but he kept his own eyes fixed on Albert. 'The barrier is thinning,' he said, hoping Albert would understand what he meant. 'They're using crystals to break it down. Jet and quartz. I'm not quite sure how.'

For a moment, Albert's body became still again. 'Of course,' he murmured, his voice oddly calm. 'One crystal expels negative energy while the other takes that power to a state of perfection.' He smiled and his form wavered. 'Quartz helps to regulate time itself. You should be wary of the timepieces in your pockets, James.'

James opened his mouth to speak again, but Albert swiftly faded away, leaving nothing but a drip of wax on the floor in his wake.

As soon as he had gone, Tasi rose to his feet and bowed over the fire. 'I did not know I had such great guests in my house,' he uttered, casting a curious look at James. 'I will leave you now, to sleep and eat before your journey home.' He bowed again and left the room, taking Oede with him.

'How could we possibly sleep?' Aralia said into the ensuing silence. 'I can't stop thinking about Dina and Kaedon.'

'It's been a strange adventure,' Will said through a yawn. 'I might not have found out any more about my dad, but I'm glad his work led us towards the seastone.'

'I'm sorry you didn't find the end to your dad's journey,' James consoled. 'Thank you for sharing his journals with us. We couldn't have found the seastone without them.' Reaching into his pocket, he drew out the gold clock and stared intently at its numberless face. 'What d'you think Albert meant?' he asked quietly. 'Why do I need to be wary of this clock?'

Will sat up on his elbows, his eyes barely open. 'They use quartz in some clocks,' he said simply.

'Albert mentioned timepieces,' Aralia whispered. 'He can't just have been talking about the clock.'

James stared at her, fresh realisation dawning on him. Unzipping his bag, he reached inside and brought out the broken remains of his phone.

'This,' he breathed. 'My phone also has a clock.' He swallowed and his heart skipped a beat. 'The callers. It's them. The dark. They were using the quartz to track my phone and now they're using it to try and reach my world.'

'Even if you're right,' Arthur said through a yawn, 'the device is destroyed and we have the seastone. We're one step closer to beating the darkness.'

James nodded. 'You're right, we have the seastone,' he said

quietly and slipped the phone and clock into his bag. Tired but sleepless, the companions lay on the cushions and watched the fire turn to embers.

Time passed neither slowly nor quickly, it simply was. They were startled by the sound of someone entering the room. None of them knew how much time had passed and sat up sharply. Tasi was standing in the doorway and he beckoned for them to follow him. Trailing in his wake, they passed down the hallway and into the room at the end. Entering behind Will, James' eyes immediately fell on two familiar figures standing on the far side of the room. Both looked tired but thankfully unharmed.

'Kaedon, Dina,' he said with relief.

Dina stepped forward and shook each of them by the hand. The rims of her eyes were red but she showed no other signs of her grief.

A flicker of white disturbed James' vision and he turned his eyes to the door. Another person had entered the room, a woman dressed in flowing white robes. As his gaze fell upon her face, she nodded to him in greeting.

'James Fynch,' she said softly. 'I have wanted to meet you for a long time.'

'You're Isla, aren't you?' he said.

She didn't answer him but drew a wooden box from beneath her cloak. Unhooking the clasp, she opened the lid to reveal the inside. It was lined with a hollow cushion that bore four impressions. James immediately recognised it as the same box in which he'd laid the firestone. Holding the sapphire in both hands, he stepped towards the box and laid it gently inside.

'Thank you,' Isla said softly. 'You have all done well and the crystal now goes to rest beside the firestone.'

'Are we allowed to know where it goes?' Will asked, wrinkling his nose as if he already knew the answer.

Isla shook her head. 'I'm afraid I can't tell you where they go.' She smiled and James wondered if she even knew herself. 'I must go now,' she continued, 'as must you. The ships are waiting.'

'Ships?' Arthur said through a yawn.

'To carry you home.'

Isla bowed to Tasi and moved towards the door. James also turned to Tasi and shook his hand firmly. The old man looked surprised but returned the shake before leading the way out of the room. At the front door, he turned to shake hands with all of them again. The companions thanked him many times over before he waved them out into the street. As they turned away, James heard him speaking again, but this time in his mind.

'All my life I have protected the Lunasphere and only now do I understand its purpose. The light will come again and it is you who will carry it.' He raised a hand in farewell and disappeared into his house.

James waved back before hurrying after his friends. As the weary group walked down to the beach, people waved to them from their houses. Their manner was friendly now, as if they had somehow changed their minds about the strangers. Spotting Ilal and his family outside their home, James, Will, Arthur and Aralia hurried over to shake their hands. As they parted ways again, the Hilal family continued to smile and wave until the companions lost sight of them over the dunes.

Down on the beach, a pair of boats lay resting on the shale. Two men stood beside them, both dressed in long grey robes. One of them offered his arm to Isla and she took it before turning to face the companions. Her eyes were bright in the morning air and she smiled at them each in turn.

'I bear a great gift of light to its home,' she said gently. 'We may meet again one day, but for now I must say farewell.'

She stepped into one of the boats and raised a hand. One of the grey clad boatman jumped in after her and the vessel slipped into the water. The group on the shore watched as it slipped away over the waves and disappeared around the headland.

'We did it,' Aralia said with a weak smile.

James nodded and turned to where Oede, Dina and Kaedon stood by the water's edge. He crossed over to them and all three turned around.

'I'm sorry,' he said, looking directly at Dina.

'I know,' she said quietly and James was glad she didn't expect him to say more.

'She was never really free, but now she can be,' Kaedon added, taking Dina's hand.

'What will you do now?' Will asked.

Dina wrinkled her nose and smiled. 'Well, you see, it wasn't just chance that led you to meeting me in Eriphas.'

'It wasn't?' James said.

'I was asked to follow you, to keep track of your movements,' Dina explained.

'Asked? Who by?' James demanded, even though he already had a hunch.

'Albert of course.' Dina's face grew serious and the fire in her eyes dimmed. 'Your power grows stronger, James, and Albert wants someone to train you and teach you. He has asked me to fill that role. The world is a dangerous place and you need to be prepared for anything that comes your way.'

'So you're coming with us then, back to Arissel?' Arthur asked, glancing at the boat waiting on the shale.

Dina nodded. 'I'm afraid so.'

'We could have worse company, I suppose,' Will said with a grin.

Led by Dina, they all walked down to the boat and climbed

aboard. Up on the dunes, clusters of villagers gathered, all waiting to wave the travellers farewell.

'Where will you go next, James?' Aralia asked as she settled herself in the boat. 'Will you go back home, to your world?'

James thought for a moment, even though he already knew the answer. 'I wasn't planning on going back this time. Arissel feels like more of a home to me somehow. Plus, it looks like I've got work to do,' he added, grinning at Dina.

He turned to face the front of the boat and the vast expanse of sea beyond. The sky was light and Arissel was out there somewhere, waiting for their return. They were safe, for now, and this adventure was complete. Reaching up to his breast pocket, he let his hand rest on the gold clock. Its regular ticking accompanied the boat as it drifted away from the shore and out into open seas.

* * *

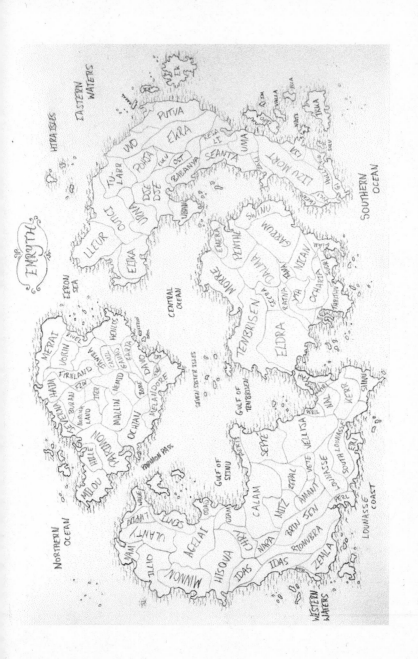